Hired to chase a runaway bride, Lew Archer un-
covers a trail of murder that leads half-way across
America and twenty years into the past – with a
suitably unsavoury cast of characters in attendance.

A policeman drowning his conscience with
whisky . . .

A Senator's daughter paying out blood money . . .

A beautiful blonde with a bent for blackmail . . .

A double-dealer with a dubious alibi.

And on its long dark journey into the present,
the case becomes even more murderous – as Archer
discovers to his client's cost.

ROSS MACDONALD

The Chill

FONTANA / Collins

First published 1963
First issued in Fontana Books 1966
Second Impression May 1974

First published in Great Britain 1964
Printed in Great Britain
Collins Clear-Type Press London and Glasgow

To R. W. Lid

The people and institutions in this novel are all
imaginary, and do not refer to any actual
people or institutions.

R.M.

ACKNOWLEDGEMENTS
The author and publishers wish to thank Mrs.
Yeats and Macmillan & Company Ltd. for
permission to quote from the poem *Among
School Children* by W. B. Yeats.

CHAPTER ONE

The heavy red-figured drapes over the courtroom windows were incompletely closed against the sun. Yellow daylight leaked in and dimmed the electric bulbs in the high ceiling. It picked out random details in the room: the glass water cooler standing against the panelled wall opposite the jury box, the court reporter's carmine-tipped fingers playing over her stenotype machine, Mrs Perrine's experienced eyes watching me across the defence table.

It was nearly noon on the second and last day of her trial. I was the final witness for the defence. Her attorney had finished questioning me. The deputy DA waived cross-examination, and several of the jurors looked at him with puzzled frowns. The judge said I could go.

From my place on the witness stand I'd noticed the young man sitting in the front row of spectators. He wasn't one of the regular trial-watchers, housewives and pensioners filling an empty morning with other people's troubles. This one had troubles of his own. His brooding blue gaze stayed on my face, and I had the uncomfortable feeling that he might be willing to share his troubles with me.

He rose from his seat as I stepped down and intercepted me at the door. 'Mr Archer, may I talk to you?'

'All right.'

The bailiff opened the door and gestured urgently. 'Outside, gentlemen. Court is still in session.'

We moved out into the corridor. The young man scowled at the automatically closing door. 'I don't like being pushed around.'

'I'd hardly describe that as being pushed around. What's eating you, friend?'

I shouldn't have asked him. I should have walked briskly out to my car and driven back to Los Angeles. But he had that clean, crew-cut All-American look, and that blur of pain in his eyes.

'I just got thrown out of the Sheriff's office. It came on top of a couple of other brush-offs from the local authorities, and I'm not used to that kind of treatment.'

'They don't mean it personally.'

'You've had a lot of detective experience, haven't you? I

gathered that from what you said on the witness stand. Incidentally, you did a wonderful job for Mrs Perrine. I'm sure the jury will acquit her.'

'We'll see. Never bet on a jury.' I distrusted his compliment, which probably meant he wanted something more substantial from me. The trial in which I had just testified marked the end of a long uninteresting case, and I was planning a fishing trip to La Paz. 'Is that all you wanted to say to me?'

'I have a lot to say, if you'll only listen. I mean, I've got this problem about my wife. She left me.'

'I don't ordinarily do divorce work, if that's what you have in mind.'

'Divorce?' Without making a sound, he went through the motions of laughing hollowly, once. 'I was only married one day – less than one day. Everybody including my father keeps telling me I should get an annulment. But I don't want an annulment or a divorce. I want her back.'

'Where is your wife now?'

'I don't know.' He lit a cigarette with unsteady hands. 'Dolly left in the middle of our honeymoon week-end, the day after we were married. She may have met with foul play.'

'Or she may have decided she didn't want to be married, or not to you. It happens all the time.'

'That's what the police keep saying: it happens all the time. As if that's any comfort! Anyway, I know that wasn't the case. Dolly loved me, and I loved – I love her.'

He said this very intensely, with the entire force of his nature behind the words. I didn't know his nature but there was sensitivity and feeling there, more feeling than he could handle easily.

'You haven't told me your name.'

'I'm sorry. My name is Kincaid. Alex Kincaid.'

'What do you do for a living?'

'I haven't been doing much lately, since Dolly – since this thing happened. Theoretically I work for the Channel Oil Corporation. My father is in charge of their Long Beach office. You may have heard of him. Frederick Kincaid?'

I hadn't. The bailiff opened the door of the courtroom, and held it open. Court had adjourned for lunch, and the jurors filed out past him. Their movements were solemn, part of the ritual of the trial. Alex Kincaid watched them as if they were going out to sit in judgment on him.

'We can't talk here,' he said. 'Let me buy you lunch.'

'I'll have lunch with you. Dutch.' I didn't want to owe him anything, at least till I'd heard his story.

There was a restaurant across the street. Its main room was filled with smoke and the roar of conversation. The red-chequered tables were all occupied, mainly with courthouse people, lawyers and sheriff's men and probation officers. Though Pacific Point was fifty miles south of my normal beat, I recognized ten or a dozen of them.

Alex and I went into the bar and found a couple of stools in a dim corner. He ordered a double scotch on the rocks. I went along with it. He drank his down like medicine and tried to order a second round immediately.

'You set quite a pace. Slow down.'

'Are you telling me what to do?' he said distinctly and unpleasantly.

'I'm willing to listen to your story. I want you to be able to tell it.'

'You think I'm an alcoholic or something?'

'I think you're a bundle of nerves. Pour alcohol on a bundle of nerves and it generally turns into a can of worms. While I'm making suggestions you might as well get rid of those chips you're wearing on both shoulders. Somebody's liable to knock them off and take a piece of you with them.'

He sat for a while with his head down. His face had an almost fluorescent pallor, and a faint humming tremor went through him.

'I'm not my usual self. I admit that. I didn't know things like this could happen to people.'

'It's about time you told me what did happen. Why not start at the beginning?'

'You mean when she left the hotel?'

'All right. Start with the hotel.'

'We were staying at the Surf House,' he said, 'right here in Pacific Point. I couldn't really afford it but Dolly wanted the experience of staying there – she never had. I figured a three-day week-end wouldn't break me. It was the Labour Day week-end. I'd already used my vacation time, and we got married that Saturday so that we could have at least a three-day honeymoon.'

'Where were you married?'

'In Long Beach, by a judge.'

'It sounds like one of these spur-of-the-moment weddings.'

'I suppose it was, in a way. We hadn't known each other too long. Dolly was the one, really, who wanted to get married right now. Don't think I wasn't eager. I was. But my parents thought we should wait a bit, until we could find a house and have it furnished and so on. They would have liked a church wedding. But Dolly wanted to be married by a judge.'

'What about her parents?'

'They're dead. She has no living relatives.' He turned his head slowly and met my eyes. 'Or so she claims.'

'You seem to have your doubts about it.'

'Not really. It's just that she got so upset when I asked her about her parents. I naturally wanted to meet them, but she treated my request as though I was prying. Finally she told me her entire family was dead, wiped out in an auto accident.'

'Where?'

'I don't know where. When it comes right down to it, I don't know too much about my wife. Except that she's a wonderful girl,' he added in a rush of loyal feeling slightly flavoured with whisky. 'She's beautiful and intelligent and good and I know she loves me.' He was almost chanting, as though by wishful thinking or sheer incantation he could bend reality back into shape around him.

'What was her maiden name?'

'Dolly McGee. Her name is really Dorothy. She was working in the university library and I was taking a summer course in Business Ad –'

'Just this summer?'

'That's correct.' He swallowed, and his Adam's apple throbbed like a grief in his throat. 'We only knew each other for six weeks – six-and-a-half weeks – before we were married. But we saw each other every day of those six-and-a-half weeks.'

'What did you do together?'

'I don't see that it matters.'

'It could. I'm trying to get a line on her personal habits.

'She had no *bad* habits, if that's what you're looking for. She never let me drink when we were out together. She wasn't very keen on the coffee houses, either, or the movies. She was – she's a very serious girl. Most of our time we talked – we talked and walked. We must have covered most of West Los Angeles.'

'What did you talk about?'

'The meaning of life,' he said, as if this went without saying. 'We were trying to work out a plan to live by, a set of rules for our marriage and our children. The main thing for Dolly was the children. She wanted to bring them up to e real people. She thought it was more important to be an honest individual than to have security and worldly possessions and so on. I don't want to bore you with all this.'

'You're not. I take it she was completely sincere?'

'Nobody was ever more sincere. I mean it. She actually wanted me to give up my job and go back and finish my MA. She didn't think I should take money from my family. She was willing to go on working to help me through. But we decided against that plan, when we made up our minds to get married.'

'It wasn't a forced marriage?'

He looked at me stonily. 'There was nothing like that between us. As a matter of fact we didn't even – I mean, I didn't touch her on our wedding night. The Surf Hotel and Pacific Point seemed to get on her nerves, even though she was the one who wanted to come here. So we decided to postpone the physical bit. A lot of couples do that nowadays.'

'How does Dolly feel about sex?'

'Fine. We talked about it very frankly. If you think she left me because she's afraid of it, you're way off the beam. She's a warm person.'

'Why did she leave you, Alex?'

His eyes clouded with pain, which had scarcely left them. 'I haven't been able to figure it out. It wasn't anything between me and Dolly, I'm sure of that. The man with the beard must have had something to do with it.'

'How does he get into the picture?'

'He came to the hotel that afternoon – the day she left. I was down on the beach having a swim, and afterwards I went to sleep in the sun. I must have been away from the room for a couple of hours. She was gone, bag and baggage, when I got back. The desk clerk told me she had this visitor before she left, a man with a short grey beard who stayed in the room about an hour.'

'No name?'

'He didn't mention his name.'

'Did he and your wife leave together?'

'The desk clerk said they didn't. The man left first. Then Dolly took a taxi to the bus station, but so far as I could find out she didn't buy a ticket. She didn't buy a railroad ticket or an airline ticket, either. She had no car. So I've been going on the assumption that she's still here in Pacific Point. She couldn't walk down the freeway.'

'She could hitchhike.'

'Not Dolly.'

'Where did she live before you were married?'

'In Westwood, in a furnished apartment. She gave it up and we moved her typewriter and things into my apartmen on Saturday morning just before the ceremony. All the stuf is still there, and it's one of the things that worry me. I've been over it with a fine-toothed comb for clues, but she didn' leave any behind – nothing really personal at all.'

'Do you think she planned to marry you and leave you?'

'No, I don't. What would be the point?'

'I can think of several possibilities. Do you carry much insurance, for example?'

'A fair amount. Dad insured me when I was born. But he's still the beneficiary.'

'Does your family have money?'

'Not that much. Dad makes a good living, but he works for it. Anyway, what you're hinting at is out of the question Dolly's completely honest, and she doesn't even care abou money.'

'What does she care about?'

'I thought she cared about me,' he said with his head down 'I still believe she does. Something must have happened to her. She may have gone out of her mind.'

'Is she mentally unstable?'

He considered the question, and his answer to it. 'I don' think so. She had her black spells. I guess most people do. was talking loosely.'

'Keep on talking loosely. You can't tell what may be im portant. You've been making a search for her, of course?'

'As much of a search as I could. But I can't do it all by myself, without any co-operation from the police. They writ down what I say on little pieces of paper and put them away in a drawer and give me pitying looks. They seem to thin Dolly found out something shameful about me on our weddin night.'

'Could there be any truth in that?'

'No! We're crazy about each other. I tried to tell that to the Sheriff this morning. He gave me one of those knowin leers and said he couldn't act unless there was some indicatio of a breach of the peace. I asked him if a missing woma wasn't some indication, and he said no. She was free an twenty-one and she left under her own power and I had n legal right to force her to come back. He advised me to get a annulment. I told him what he could do with his advice, an he ordered two of his men to throw me out of his office. found out where the deputy DA was, in court, and I wa waiting to put in a complaint when I saw you on the stand.'

'Nobody sent you to me, then?'

'No, but I can give you references. My father—'

'You told me about your father. He thinks you should get an annulment, too.'

Alex nodded dolefully. 'Dad thinks I'm wasting my time, on a girl who isn't worth it.'

'He could be right.'

'He couldn't be more wrong. Dolly is the only one I've ever loved and the only one I ever will love. If you won't help me, I'll find somebody who will!'

I liked his insistence. 'My rates are high. A hundred a day and expenses.'

'I've got enough to pay you for at least a week.' He reached for his billfold and slammed it down on the bar, so hard that the bartender looked at him suspiciously. 'Do you want a cash advance?'

'There's no hurry,' I said. 'Do you have a picture of Dolly?'

He removed a folded piece of newspaper from the billfold and handed it to me with a certain reluctance, as if it was more valuable than money. It was a reproduction of a photograph which had been unfolded and refolded many times.

'Among happy honeymooners at the Surf House,' the caption said, 'are Mr and Mrs Alex Kincaid of Long Beach.' Alex and his bride smiled up at me through the murky light. Her face was oval and lovely in a way of its own, with a kind of hooded intelligence in the eyes and humour like a bitter-sweet taste on the mouth.

'When was this taken?'

'Three weeks ago Saturday, when we arrived at the Surf House. They do it for everybody. They printed it in the Sunday morning paper, and I clipped it. I'm glad I did. It's the only picture I have of her.'

'You could get copies.'

'Where?'

'From whoever took it.'

'I never thought of that. I'll see the photographer at the hotel about it. How many copies do you think I should ask him for?'

'Two or three dozen, anyway. It's better to have too many than too few.'

'That will run into money.'

'I know, and so will I.'

'Are you trying to talk yourself out of a job?'

'I don't need the work, and I could use a rest.'

'To hell with you then.'

He snatched at the flimsy picture between my fingers. I tore across the middle. We faced each other like enemies each of us holding a piece of the happy honeymooners.

Alex burst into tears.

CHAPTER TWO

I agreed over lunch to help him find his wife. That and the chicken pot pie calmed him down. He couldn't remember when he had eaten last, and he ate ravenously.

We drove out to the Surf Hotel in separate cars. It was on the sea at the good end of town : a pueblo hotel whose Spanish gardens were dotted with hundred-dollar-a-day cottages. The terraces in front of the main building descended in wide green steps to its own marina. Yachts and launches were bobbing at the slip. Farther out on the water, beyond the curving promontory that gave Pacific Point its name, white sails leaned against a low grey wall of fog.

The desk clerk in the Ivy League suit was very polite, but he wasn't the one who had been on duty on the Sunday I was interested in. That one had been a summer replacement, a college boy who had gone back to school in the East. He himself, he regretted to say, knew nothing about Mrs Kincaid's bearded visitor or her departure.

'I'd like to talk to the hotel photographer. Is he around today?'

'Yes, sir. I believe he's out by the swimming-pool.'

We found him, a thin spry man wearing a heavy camera like an albatross around his neck. Among the coloured beach clothes and bathing costumes, his dark business suit made him look like an undertaker. He was taking some very candid pictures of a middle-aged woman in a bikini who didn't belong in one. Her umbilicus glared at the camera like an eyeless socket.

When he had done his dreadful work, the photographer turned to Alex with a smile. 'Hi. How's the wife?'

'I haven't seen her recently,' Alex said glumly.

'Weren't you on your honeymoon a couple of weeks ago? Didn't I take your picture?'

Alex didn't answer him. He was peering around at the poolside loungers like a ghost trying to remember how it felt to be human. I said:

'We'd like to get some copies made of that picture you took. Mrs Kincaid is on the missing list, and I'm a private detective. My name is Archer.'

'Fargo. Simmy Fargo.' He gave me a quick handshake and the kind of glance a camera gives you when it records you for posterity. 'In what sense on the missing list?'

'We don't know. She left here in a taxi on the afternoon of September the second. Kincaid has been looking for her ever since.'

'That's tough,' Fargo said. 'I suppose you want the prints for circulation. How many do you think you'll be needing?'

'Three dozen?'

He whistled, and slapped himself on his narrow wrinkled forehead. 'I've got a busy week-end coming up, and it's already started. This is Friday. I could let you have them by Monday. But I suppose you want them yesterday?'

'Today will do.'

'Sorry.' He shrugged loosely, making his camera bob against his chest.

'It could be important, Fargo. What do you say we settle for a dozen, in two hours?'

'I'd like to help you. But I've got a job.' Slowly, almost against his will, he turned and looked at Alex. 'Tell you what I'll do. I'll call the wife in, and you can have your pictures. Only don't stand me up, the way the other one did.'

'What other one?' I said.

'Big guy with a beard. He ordered a print of the same picture and never came back for it. I can let you have that print now if you like.'

Alex came out of his dark trance. He took hold of Fargo's arm with both hands and shook it. 'You saw him then. Who is he?'

'I thought maybe you knew him.' Fargo disengaged himself and stepped back. 'As a matter of fact, I thought I knew him, too. I could have sworn I took his picture once. But I couldn't quite place the face. I see too many faces.'

'Did he give you his name?'

'He must have. I don't take orders without a name. I'll see if I can find it for you, eh?'

We followed him into the hotel and through a maze of corridors to his small cluttered windowless office. He phoned his wife, then burrowed into the pile of papers on his desk and came up with a photographer's envelope. Inside, between two sheets of corrugated paper, was a glossy print of the newly-weds. On the front of the envelope Fargo had written in pencil: 'Chuck Begley, Wine Cellar.'

'I remember now,' he said. 'He told me he was working at the Wine Cellar. That's a liquor store not too far from here. When Begley didn't claim his picture I called them. They said Begley wasn't working for them any more.' Fargo looked from me to Alex. 'Does the name Begley mean anything to you?'

We both said that it didn't. 'Can you describe him, Mr Fargo?'

'I can describe the part of him that wasn't covered with seaweed, I mean the beard. His hair is grey, like the beard, and very thick and wavy. Grey eyebrows and grey eyes, an ordinary kind of straight nose, I noticed it was peeling from the sun. He's not bad-looking for an older man, apart from his teeth, which aren't good. And he looks as though he's taken a beating or two in his time. Personally I wouldn't want to go up against him. He's a big man, and he looks pretty rough.'

'How big?'

'Three or four inches taller than I am. That would make him six feet one or two. He was wearing a short-sleeved sport shirt, and I noticed the muscles in his arms.'

'How did he talk?'

'Nothing special. He didn't have a Harvard accent, and he didn't say ain't.'

'Did he give you any reason for wanting the picture?'

'He said he had a sentimental interest. He saw it in the paper, and it reminded him of somebody. I remember thinking he must have dashed right over. The paper with the picture in it came out Sunday morning, and he came in around Sunday noon.'

'He must have gone to see your wife immediately afterwards,' I said to Alex. And to Fargo: 'How did this particular picture happen to be used by the newspaper?'

'They picked it out of a batch I sent over. The *Press* often uses my pictures, as a matter of fact I used to work for them. Why they used this one instead of some of the others I couldn't say.' He held up the print in the fluorescent light, then handed it to me. 'It did turn out well, and Mr Kincaid and his wife make an attractive couple.'

'Thanks very much,' Alex said sardonically.

'I was paying you a compliment, fellow.'

'Sure you were.'

I took the print from Fargo and shunted Alex out of the

place before it got too small for him. Black grief kept flooding up in him, changing to anger when it reached the air. It wasn't just grief for a one-day wife, it was also grief for himself. He didn't seem to know if he was a man or not.

I couldn't blame him for his feelings, but they made him no asset to the kind of work I was trying to do. When I found the Wine Cellar, on a motel strip a few blocks inland, I left him outside in his little red sports car.

The interior of the liquor store was pleasantly cool. I was the only potential customer, and the man behind the counter came out from behind it to greet me.

'What can I do for you, sir?'

He wore a plaid waistcoat, and he had the slightly muzzy voice and liquid eyes and dense complexion of a man who drank all day and into the night.

'I'd like to see Chuck Begley.'

He looked vaguely pained, and his voice took on a note of mild complaint. 'I had to fire Chuck. I'd send him out with a delivery, and sometimes it'd arrive when it was supposed to, and sometimes it wouldn't.'

'How long ago did you fire him?'

'Couple of weeks. He only worked for me a couple of weeks. He isn't cut out for that kind of work. I told him more than once it was beneath his capacity. Chuck Begley is a fairly bright man if he'd straighten up, you know.'

'I don't know.'

'I thought perhaps you were an acquaintance of his.'

I showed him my photostat.

He blew the smell of peppermint in my face. 'Is Begley on the run?'

'He may be. Why?'

'I wondered when he first came in why a man like him would take a part-time delivery job. What's he wanted for?'

'I wouldn't know. Can you give me his home address?'

'I think I can at that.' He stroked his veined nose, watching me over his fingers. 'Don't tell Begley I gave you the word. I don't want him bouncing back on me.'

'I won't.'

'He spends a lot of time in the home of one of my customers. You might say he's a non-paying guest of hers. I certainly wouldn't want to make trouble for her. But then,' he reasoned, 'if Begley's on the run I'm doing her a favour in seeing that he's picked up. Isn't that right?'

'I'd say so. Where does she live?'

'On Shearwater Beach, cottage number seventeen. Her

name's Madge Gerhardi. Take the freeway south and you'll see the Shearwater turnoff about two miles down the line. Only just don't tell either of them that it was me sent you. Okay?'

'Okay.' I left him with his bottles.

CHAPTER THREE

We parked our cars at the top of the access lane, and I persuaded Alex to stay in his, out of sight. Shearwater Beach turned out to be a kind of expensive slum where several dozen cottages stood in a row. The changing blue reflection of the sea glared through the narrow gaps between them. Beyond their peaked rooftops, out over the water, a tern circled on flashing wings, looking for fish.

Number seventeen needed paint, and leaned on its pilings like a man on crutches. I knocked on the scabbed grey door. Slowly, like bodies being dragged, footsteps approached the other side. The bearded man opened it.

He was a man of fifty or so wearing an open-necked black shirt from which his head jutted like weathered stone. The sunlight struck mica glints from his eyes. The fingers with which he was holding the edge of the door were bitten down to the quick. He saw me looking at them and curled them into a fist.

'I'm searching for a missing girl, Mr Begley,' I had decided on the direct approach. 'She may have met with foul play and if she did, you may have been one of the last people who saw her alive.'

He rubbed the side of his face with his clenched knuckles. His face bore marks of old trouble, some of them done by hand: faintly quilted patches around the eyes, a thin scar on his temple divided like a miniature ruler by stitch-marks. Old trouble and the promise of further trouble.

'You must be crazy. I don't even know any girls.'

'You know *me*,' a woman said behind him.

She appeared at his shoulder and leaned on him, waiting for somebody to second the self-administered flattery. She was about Begley's age, and may have been older. Her body was very assertive in shorts and a halter.: Frizzled by repeated dyeings and bleachings, her hair stuck up on her head like a yellow fright wig. Between their deep blue artificial shadows her eyes were the colour of gin.

'I'm very much afraid that you must be mistaken,' she said to me with a cultivated Eastern-seaboard accent which lapsed immediately. 'I swear by all that's holy that Chuck had nothing to do with any girl. He's been too busy looking after little old me.' She draped a plump white arm across the back of his neck. 'Haven't you, darling?'

Begley was immobilized between the woman and me. I showed him Fargo's glossy print of the honeymooners.

'You know this girl, don't you? Her name, her married name, is Dolly Kincaid.'

'I never heard of her in my life.'

'Witnesses tell me different. They say you went to see her at the Surf House three weeks ago this coming Sunday. You saw this picture of her in the paper and ordered a copy of it from a photographer at the Surf House.'

The woman tightened her arm around his neck, more like a wrestling partner than a lover. 'Who is she, Chuck?'

'I have no idea.' But he muttered to himself: 'So it's started all over again.'

'What has started all over again?'

She was stealing my lines. 'Could I please talk to Mr Begley alone?'

'He has no secrets from me.' She looked up at him, proudly, with a wilted edge of anxiety on her pride. 'Have you, darling? We're going to be married, aren't we, darling?'

'Could you stop calling me darling? Just for five minutes? Please?'

She backed away from him, ready to cry, her down-turned red mouth making a lugubrious clown face.

'Please go inside,' he said. 'Let me talk to the man.'

'This is my place. I have a right to know what goes on in my own place.'

'Sure you do, Madge. But I have squatter's privileges, at least. Go in and drink some coffee.'

'Are you in trouble?'

'No. Of course I'm not.' But there was resignation in his voice. 'Beat it, eh, like a good girl?'

His last word seemed to mollify her. Dawdling and turning, she disappeared down the hallway. Begley closed the door and leaned on it.

'Now you can tell me the truth,' I said.

'All right, so I went to see her at the hotel. It was a stupid impulse. It doesn't make me a murderer.'

'Nobody suggested that, except you.'

'I thought I'd save you the trouble.' He spread out his arms as if for instant crucifixion. 'You're the local law, I gather.'

'I'm working with them,' I said hopefully. 'My name is Archer. You haven't explained why you went to see Mrs Kincaid. How well did you know her?'

'I didn't know her at all.' He dropped his outspread arms in emphasis. The sensitive areas around his mouth were hidden by his beard, and I couldn't tell what he was doing with them. His grey eyes were unrevealing. 'I thought I knew her, but I didn't.'

'What do you mean?'

'I thought she might be my daughter. There was quite a resemblance to her in the newspaper picture, but not so much in the flesh. The mistake on my part was natural. I haven't seen my daughter for so long.'

'What's your daughter's name?'

He hesitated. 'Mary. Mary Begley. We haven't been in touch for over ten years. I've been out of the country, on the other side of the world.' He made it sound as remote as the far side of the moon.

'Your daughter must have been quite young when you left.'

'Yeah. Ten or eleven.'

'And you must have been quite fond of her,' I said, 'to order a picture just because it reminded you of her.'

'I was fond of her.'

'Why didn't you go back for the picture then?'

He went into a long silence. I became aware of something impressive in the man, the untouchable still quality of an ageing animal.

'I was afraid that Madge would be jealous,' he said. 'I happen to be living on Madge.'

I suspect he was using the bald statement to tell a lie. But it may have come from a deeper source. Some men spend their lives looking for ways to punish themselves for having been born, and Begley had some of the stigmata of the trouble-prone. He said:

'What do you think happened to Mrs Kincaid?' His question was cold and formal, disclaiming all interest in the answer to it.

'I was hoping you'd have some ideas on the subject. She's been missing for nearly three weeks. I don't like it. It's true that girls are always disappearing, but not on their honeymoons – not when they love their husbands.'

'She loves hers, does she?'

'He thinks so. How was she feeling when you saw her? Was she depressed?'

'I wouldn't say that. She was surprised to see me.'

'Because she hadn't seen you for so long?'

He sneered at me hairily. 'Don't bother trying to trap me. I told you she wasn't my daughter. She didn't know me from Adam.'

'What did you find to talk about with her?'

'We didn't talk.' He paused. 'Maybe I asked her a few questions.'

'Such as?'

'Who her father was. Who her mother was. Where she came from. She said she came from Los Angeles. Her maiden name was Dolly something – forget the name. Her parents were both dead. That's about all.'

'It took you quite a while to get that much out of her.'

'I was only there five or ten minutes, maybe fifteen.'

'The desk clerk said an hour.'

'He made a mistake.'

'Or maybe you did, Mr Begley. Time passes very rapidly sometimes.'

He clutched at this dubious excuse. 'Maybe I did stay longer than I realized. I remember now, she wanted me to stay and meet her husband.' His eyes held steady, but they had taken on a faint lying sheen. 'He didn't come and didn't come, so I left.'

'Did you suggest seeing her again?'

'No. She wasn't that interested in my story.'

'You told her your story?'

'I told her about my daughter, naturally, just like I told you.'

'I don't understand it. You say you were out of the country for ten years. Where?'

'In New Caledonia, mostly. I worked for a chrome mine there. They shut it down last spring and shipped us home.'

'And now you're looking for your daughter?'

'I'd certainly like to put my hands on her.'

'So she can be a bridesmaid at your wedding?' I wanted to see how sharp a needle he would take.

He took this one without a word.

'What happened to your wife?'

'She died.' His eyes were no longer steady. 'Look, do we have to go into all this? It's bad enough losing your loved ones without having it raked up and pushed in your face.'

19

I couldn't tell if his self-pity was false: self-pity always is to some extent.

'It's too bad you lost your family,' I said. 'But what did you expect when you left the country for ten years?'

'It wasn't my choice. How would you like to get shanghaied and not be able to get back?'

'Is that your story? It isn't a likely one.'

'My story is wilder than that, but we won't go into it. You wouldn't believe me, anyway. Nobody else has.'

'You could always try me.'

'It would take all day. You've got better things to do than talk to me.'

'Name one.'

'You said there's a young lady missing. Go and find her.'

'I was hoping you could help me. I still am hoping, Mr Begley.'

He looked down at his feet. He was wearing *huaraches*. 'I've told you all I know about her. I should never have gone to that hotel in the first place. Okay, so I made a mistake. You can't *hang* a man for a little mistake in judgment.'

'You've mentioned murder once, and hanging once. I wonder why.'

'It was just a manner of speaking.' But the confidence was seeping out of him through the holes my needle had made. He said with a rising inflection: 'You think I murdered her?'

'No. I do think this. Something happened between you, or something was said, that might explain why she left so suddenly. Give it some thought, will you?'

Slowly, perhaps involuntarily, he raised his head and looked up at the sun. Under his tilted beard his neck was pale and scrawny. It gave the impression that he was wearing the kind of mask Greek actors wore, covering him completely from my eyes.

'No. Nothing was said like that.'

'Was there any trouble between you?'

'No.'

'Why did she let you come to her room?'

'I guess she was interested in my story. I talked to her on the house phone, said she resembled my daughter. It was just a foolish impulse. I knew as soon as I saw her that she wasn't.'

'Did you make arrangements to see her again?'

'No. I'd certainly like to.'

'Did you wait outside the hotel for her, or agree to meet

her at the bus station?'

'I did not. What are you trying to nail me for? What do you want?'

'Just the truth. I"m not satisfied I've been getting it from you.'

He said in a sudden spurt of fury: 'You've got as much as –' He began to regret the outburst before it was over, and swallowed the rest of his words.

But he turned his back on me and went inside, slamming the door. I waited for a little while, and gave up on him. I walked back along the sandy access lane to our cars.

The blonde woman, Madge Gerhardi, was sitting beside Alex in his red Porsche. He looked up with shining eyes.

'Mrs Gerhardi has seen her. She's seen Dolly.'

'With Begley?'

'No, not with him.' She opened the door and squeezed out of the little car. 'It was at that garage that specialises in fixing foreign cars. I drive an MG myself, and I had it in for a lube job. The girl was there with an old woman. They went away together in an old brown Rolls. The girl was doing the driving.'

'Are you certain of the identification?' I showed her the picture again.

She nodded over it emphatically. 'I'm certain, unless she has a twin. I noticed her because she was so stunning.'

'Do you know who the old woman was?'

'No, but the man at the garage ought to be able to tell you.' She gave us directions, and started to edge away. 'I better get back to the house. I snuck out along the beach, and Chuck will be wondering where I am.'

CHAPTER FOUR

A mechanic lying face up on a creeper rolled out from under the raised front end of a Jaguar sedan. I saw when he stood up that he was a plump Mediterranean type with 'Mario' embroidered on his coverall. He nodded enthusiastically when I asked him about the old Rolls and the old lady.

'That's Mrs Bradshaw. I been looking after her Rolls for the last twelve years, ever since she bought it. It's running as good now as the day she bought it.' He looked at his greasy hands with some satisfaction, like a surgeon recalling a series of difficult but successful operations. 'Some of the girls she gets to drive her don't know how to treat a good car.'

'Do you know the girl who's driving her at present?'

'I don't know her name. Mrs Bradshaw has quite a turn-over with her drivers. She gets them from the college mostly. Her son is Dean at the college, and he won't let the old lady do her own driving. She's crippled with rheumatics, and I think she was in a smash-up at one time.'

I cut in on Mario's complicated explanations and showed him the print. 'This girl?'

'Yeah. She was here with Mrs Bradshaw the other day. She's a new one. Like I said, Mrs Bradshaw has quite a turn-over. She likes to have her own way, and these college girls don't take orders too well. Personally I always hit it off with Mrs Bradshaw –'

'Where does she live?'

Alex sounded anxious, and Mario was slightly infected by his anxiety. 'What is it you want with her?'

'She's not the one I'm interested in. The girl is my wife.'

'You and her are on the outs?'

'I don't know. I have to talk to her.'

Mario looked up at the high corrugated-iron roof of the garage. 'My wife divorced me a couple of years ago. I been putting on weight ever since. A man don't have the same motivation.'

'Where does Mrs Bradshaw live?' I said.

'Foothill Drive, not too far from here. Take the first cross street to the right, it runs into it. You can look up the house number in the phone book, on the desk there. It's in her son's name, Roy Bradshaw.'

I thanked him. He lay down on the creeper and slid back under the Jaguar. The directory was under the telephone on top of the battered desk which stood in a corner. I found the listing: 'Roy Bradshaw, 311 Foothill Drive.'

'We could phone from here,' Alex said.

'It's always better in person.'

In spite of the housing tracts and the smokeless industries proliferating around it, Pacific Point had kept its identity. Foothill Drive was lined with trees, and had a dusty change-less quality. Settled old families still lived here behind mortised walls that had resisted earthquakes, or hedges that had out-lived generations of gardeners.

The towering cypress hedge of 311 masked the house com-pletely from the road. I turned in through the open iron gates with Alex following me. We passed a small white gatehouse with a green door and green shutters, rounded a bend in the driveway, and came in sight of the white Colonial house.

A woman with a wide straw hat tied under her chin was kneeling shoulder deep among the flowers in front of it. She had a pair of clippers in her gloved hands. They snicked in the silence when our engines died.

She rose cumbrously to her feet and came towards us, tucking wisps of grey hair under her hat. She was just an old lady in dirty tennis shoes but her body, indeterminate in a loose blue smock, carried itself with heavy authority, as if it recalled that it had once been powerful or handsome. The architecture of her face had collapsed under the weight of flesh and years. Still her black eyes were alert, like unexpected animal or bird life in the ruins of a building.

'Mrs Bradshaw?' Alex said eagerly.

'I am Mrs Bradshaw. What do you gentlemen want? I'm very busy, as you can see.' She flourished the clippers. 'I never trust anyone else to clip my roses. And still they die, poor things.' Regret rustled in her voice.

'They look very beautiful to me,' I said in an encouraging way. 'Mr Kincaid and I hate to bother you. But he seems to have misplaced his wife, and we have reason to think she's working for you. '

'For me? I employ no one but my Spanish couple. My son,' she added with a trace of pride, 'keeps me to a strict budget.'

'Don't you have a girl driving for you?'

She smiled. 'I completely forgot about her. She's just on a part-time basis. What's her name? Molly? Dolly? I never can remember the girls' names.'

'Dolly,' I said, and showed her the print. 'Is this Dolly?'

She removed one gardening glove to take the picture. Her hand was gnarled by arthritis.

'I do believe it is. But she said nothing to me about being married. I'd never have hired her if I'd known, it makes for too much involvement. I like to take my little drives on schedule.'

Alex interrupted her rather garrulous chatter. 'Where is she now?'

'I couldn't say. She's done her day's stint for me. She may have walked over to the college, or she may be in the gatehouse. I let my girls use the gatehouse. Sometimes they abuse the privilege, but so far this one hasn't.' She gave Alex a sharp black glance. 'I hope she won't begin to, now that you've turned up.'

'I don't expect she'll be going on–'

I cut him short. 'Go and see if she's in the gatehouse.' I turned back to Mrs Bradshaw: 'How long has she been with you?'

'About two weeks. The semester started two weeks ago.'

'Is she attending the college?'

'Yes. I get all my girls from there, except when I have to have a regular attendant, as I did when my son was abroad last summer. I hope I don't lose Dolly. She's brighter than most of them. But if she goes I suppose there are always others. You'll realize, when you've lived as long as I have that the young ones leave the old ones. . . .'

She turned to her roses, glowing red and yellow in the sunlight. She seemed to be looking for some way to finish the thought. None occurred to her. I said:

'What name is she using? What surname?'

'I'm afraid I don't remember. I call them by their first names. My son could tell you.'

'Is he here?'

'Roy is at the college. He happens to be the Dean there.'

'Is it far from here?'

'You can see it from where you stand.'

Her arthritic hand curled on my elbow and turned me gently. Through a gap in the trees I could make out the metal cupola of a small observatory. The old lady spoke close to my ear, in a gossipy way:

'What happened between your young friend and his wife?'

'They came here on their honeymoon and she walked out on him. He's trying to find out why.'

'What a strange thing to do,' she said. 'I'd never have acted like that on my honeymoon. I had too much respect for my husband. But girls are different nowadays, aren't they? Loyalty and respect mean nothing to them. Are you married, young man?'

'I have been.'

'I see. Are you the boy's father?'

'No. My name is Archer. I'm a private detective.'

'Really? What do you make of all this?' She gestured vaguely with her clippers toward the gatehouse.

'Nothing so far. She may have left him on account of a girlish whim. Or she may have had deep dark reasons. All I can do is ask her. By the way, Mrs Bradshaw, have you ever heard her mention a man named Begley?'

'Begley?'

'He's a big man with a short grey beard. He visited her at

24

the Surf House the day she left her husband. There's some possibility that he's her father.'

She wet her seamed lips with the purple tip of her tongue. 'She didn't mention him to me. I don't encourage the girls to unburden themselves to me. Perhaps I should.'

'What kind of a mood has Dolly been in lately?'

'It's hard to say. She's always the same. Quiet. She thinks her own thoughts.'

Alex appeared, walking rapidly around the bend in the driveway. His face was bright.

'It's her definitely. I found her things in the closet.'

'You weren't authorized to go in there,' Mrs Bradshaw said.

'It's her house, isn't it?'

'It happens to be mine.'

'But she has the use of it, hasn't she?'

'She does. You don't.'

A quarrel with Dolly's employer was the last thing Alex needed. I stepped between them, turned him around, and walked him away from trouble for the second time.

'Get lost,' I said when he was in his car. 'You're in my way.'

'But I have to see her.'

'You'll see her. Go and check in at the Mariner's Rest Motel for both of us. It's on the strip between here and the Surf House –'

'I know where it is. But what about Dolly?'

'I'm going over to the college to talk to her. I'll bring her back with me, if she's willing.'

'Why can't I go along to the college?' he said like a spoiled child.

'Because I don't want you to. Dolly has a separate life of her own. You may not like it, but you have no right to jump in and wreck it for her. I'll see you at the motel.'

He drove away rapidly and angrily, spinning the wheels of his car. Mrs Bradshaw was back among her roses. I asked her very politely for permission to examine Dolly's things. She said that would have to be up to Dolly.

CHAPTER FIVE

The campus was an oasis of vivid green under the brown September foothills. Most of the buildings were new and very modern, ornamented with pierced concrete screens and semi-tropical plantings. A barefoot boy sitting under a roadside palm took time out from his Salinger to show me where the Administration Building was.

I parked in the lot behind it, among a scattering of transportation clunks with faculty stickers. A new black Thunderbird stood out among them. It was late Friday afternoon by now, and the long collegiate week-end was setting in. The glass information booth opposite the entrance of the building was empty. The corridors were practically deserted.

I found the Dean's office without much trouble. The panelled anteroom was furnished with convertible Danish pieces, and with a blonde secretary who sat at a typewriter guarding the closed inner door. She had a pale thin face, strained blue eyes that had worked too long under fluorescent light, and a suspicious voice:

'Can I help you, sir?'

'I'd like to see the Dean.'

'Dean Bradshaw is very busy, I'm afraid. Perhaps I can assist you?'

'Perhaps. I'm trying to get in touch with one of your girl students. Her name is Dolly McGee, or Dolly Kincaid.'

'Which?' she said with a little gasp of irritation.

'Her maiden name is McGee, her married name is Kincaid. I don't know which she's using.'

'Are you a parent?' she said delicately.

'No. I'm not her father. But I have good reason for wanting to see her.'

She looked at me as if I was a self-confessed kingpin in the white slave traffic. 'We have a policy of not giving out information about students, except to parents.'

'What about husbands?'

'You're her husband?'

'I represent her husband. I think you'd better let me talk to the Dean about her.'

'I can't do that,' she said in a final tone. 'Dean Bradshaw is in conference with the department heads. About what do you wish to see Miss McGee?'

'It's a private matter.'

'I see.'

We had reached an impasse. I said in the hope of making her smile: 'We have a policy of not giving out information.'

She looked insulted, and went back to her typewriter. I stood and waited. Voices rose and fell behind the door of the inner office. 'Budget' was the word I caught most frequently. After a while the secretary said:

'I suppose you could try Dean Sutherland, if she's in. Dean Sutherland is Dean of Women. Her office is just across the hall.'

Its door was standing open. The woman in it was the well-scrubbed ageless type who looks old in her twenties and young in her forties. She wore her brown hair rolled in a bun at the back of her neck. Her only concession to glamour was a thin pink line of lipstick accenting her straight mouth.

She was a good-looking woman in spite of this. Her face was finely chiselled. The front of her blouse curved out over her desk like a spinnaker going downwind.

'Come in,' she said with a severity that I was getting used to. 'What are you waiting for?'

Her fine eyes had me hypnotized. Looking into them was like looking into the beautiful core of an iceberg, all green ice and cold blazing light.

'Sit down,' she said. 'What is your problem?'

I told her who I was and why I was there.

'But we have no Dolly McGee or Dolly Kincaid on campus.'

'She must be using a third name, then. I know she's a student here. She has a job driving for Dean Bradshaw's mother.' I showed her my photograph.

'But this is Dorothy Smith. Why would she register with us under a false name?'

'That's what her husband would like to know.'

'Is this her husband in the picture with her?'

'Yes.'

'He appears to be a nice enough boy.'

'Apparently she didn't think so.'

'I wonder why.' Her eyes were looking past me, and I felt cheated. 'As a matter of fact, I don't see how she *could* register under a false name, unless she came to us with forged credentials.' She rose abruptly. 'Excuse me for a minute, Mr Archer.'

She went into the next room, where filing cabinets stood like upended metal coffins, and came back with a folder which she opened on her desk. There wasn't much in it.

'I see,' she said more or less to herself. 'She's been admitted provisionally. There's a note here to the effect that her transcript is on the way.'

'How long is provisional admission good for?'

'Until the end of September.' She consulted her desk calendar. 'That gives her nine days to come up with a transcript. But she'll have to come up with an explanation rather sooner. We don't look with favour on this sort of deception. And I had the impression that she was a straight-forward girl.' Her mouth turned down at the corners.

'You know her personally, Dean Sutherland?'

'I make a point of contacting all the new girls. I went out of my way to be useful to Miss or Mrs Smith-Kincaid. In fact I helped to get her a part-time job in the library.'

'And the job with old Mrs Bradshaw?'

She nodded. 'She heard that there was an opening there, and I recommended her.' She looked at her watch. 'She may be over there now.'

'She isn't. I just came from Mrs Bradshaw's. Your Dean lives pretty high on the hog, by the way. I thought academic salaries were too low.'

'They are. Dean Bradshaw comes from a wealthy old family. What was his mother's reaction to this?' She made an impatient gesture which somehow included me.

'She seemed to take it in stride. She's a smart old woman.'

'I'm glad you found her so,' she said, as if she had had other kinds of experience with Mrs Bradshaw. 'Well, I suppose I'd better see if Mrs Smith-Kincaid is in the library.'

'I could go over there and ask.'

'I think not. I had better talk to her first, and try to find out what's going on in her little head.'

'I didn't want to make trouble for her.'

'Of course not, and you didn't. The trouble is and was there. You merely uncovered it. I'm grateful to you for that.'

'Could your gratitude,' I said carefully, 'possibly take the form of letting me talk to her first?'

'I'm afraid not.'

'I've had a lot of experience of getting the facts out of people.'

It was the wrong thing to say. Her mouth turned down at the corners again. Her bosom changed from a promise to a threat.

'I've had experience, too, a good many years of it, and I am a trained counsellor. If you'll be good enough to wait outside, I'm going to try and phone her at the library.' She flung a last shaft as I went out: 'And please don't try to intercept her on the way here.'

'I wouldn't dream of it, Miss Sutherland.'

'Dean Sutherland, if you please.'

I went and read the bulletin board beside the information booth. The jolly promises of student activities, dances and get-togethers and poetry clubs and breakfasts where French was spoken, only saddened me. It was partly because my own attempt at college hadn't worked out, partly because I'd just put the kibosh on Dolly's.

A girl wearing horn-rimmed glasses, and a big young fellow in a varsity sweater drifted in from outside and leaned against the wall. She was explaining something to him, something about Achilles and the tortoise. Achilles was chasing the tortoise, it seemed, but according to Zeno he would never catch it. The space between them was divisible into an infinite number of parts; therefore it would take Achilles an infinite period of time to traverse it. By that time the tortoise would be somewhere else.

The young man nodded. 'I see that.'

'But it isn't so,' the girl cried. 'The infinite divisibility of space is merely theoretical. It doesn't affect actual *movement* across space.'

'I don't get it, Heidi.'

'Of course you do. Imagine yourself on the football field. You're on the twenty-yard line and there's a tortoise crawling away from you toward the thirty-yard line.'

I stopped listening. Dolly was coming up the outside steps toward the glass door, a dark-haired girl in a plaid skirt and a cardigan. She leaned on the door for a moment before she pushed it open. She seemed to have gone to pieces to some extent since Fargo had taken her picture. Her skin was sallow, her hair not recently brushed. Her dark uncertain glance slid over me without appearing to take me in.

She stopped short before she reached Dean Sutherland's office. Turning in a sudden movement, she started for the front door. She stopped again, between me and the two philosophers, and stood considering. I was struck by her faintly sullen beauty, her eyes dark and blind with thought. She turned around once more and trudged back along the hallway to meet her fate.

The office door closed behind her. I strolled past it after a while and heard the murmur of female voices inside, but nothing intelligible. From Dean Bradshaw's office across the hall the heads of departments emerged in a body. In spite of their foreheads and their scholars' stoops, they looked a little like schoolboys let out for recess.

A woman with a short razor-blade haircut came into the building and drew all their eyes. Her ash-blonde hair shone against the deep tan of her face. She attached herself to a man standing by himself in the doorway of the Dean's office.

He seemed less interested in her than she was in him. His good looks were rather gentle and melancholy, the kind that excite maternal passions in women. Though his brown wavy hair was greying at the temples, he looked rather like a college boy who twenty years after graduation glanced up from his books and found himself middle-aged.

Dean Sutherland opened the door of her office and made a sign to him. 'Can you spare me a minute, Dr Bradshaw? Something serious has come up.' She was pale and grim, like a reluctant executioner.

He excused himself. The two Deans shut themselves up with Dolly. The woman with the short and shining haircut frowned at the closed door. Then she gave me an appraising glance, as if she was looking for a substitute for Bradshaw. She had a promising mouth and good legs and a restless predatory air. Her clothes had style.

'Looking for someone?' she said.

'Just waiting.'

'For Lefty or for Godot? It makes a difference.'

'For Lefty Godot. The pitcher.'

'The pitcher in the rye?'

'He prefers bourbon.'

'So do I,' she said. 'You sound like an anti-intellectual to me, Mr –'

'Archer. Didn't I pass the test?'

'It depends on who does the grading.'

'I've been thinking maybe I ought to go back to school. You make it seem attractive, and besides I feel so out of things when my intellectual friends are talking about Jack Kerouac and Eugene Burdick and other great writers, and I can't read. Seriously, if I were thinking of going back to college, would you recommend this place?'

She gave me another of her appraising looks. 'Not for you, Mr Archer. I think you'd feel more at home in some larger urban university, like Berkeley or Chicago. I went to Chicago myself. This college presents quite a contrast.'

'In what way?'

'Innumerable ways. The quotient of sophistication here is

very low, for one thing. This used to be a denominational college, and the moral atmosphere is still in Victorian stays.' As if to demonstrate that she was not, she shifted her pelvis. 'They tell me when Dylan Thomas visited here – but perhaps we'd better not go into that. *De mortuis nil nisi bonum.*'

'Do you teach Latin?'

'No, I have small Latin and less Greek. I try to teach modern languages. My name is Helen Haggerty, by the way. As I was saying, I wouldn't really recommend Pacific Point to you. The standards are improving every year, but there's still a great deal of dead wood around. You can see some of it from here.'

She cast a sardonic glance toward the entrance, where five or six of her fellow professors were conducting a post-mortem of their conference with the Dean.

'That was Dean Bradshaw you were talking to, wasn't it?'

'Yes. Is he the one you want to see?'

'Among others.'

'Don't be put off by his rather forbidding exterior. He's a fine scholar – the only Harvard doctor on the faculty – and he can advise you better than I ever could. But tell me honestly, are you really serious about going back to college? Aren't you kidding me a little?'

'Maybe a little.'

'You could kid me more effectively over a drink. And I could use a drink, preferably bourbon.'

'It's a handsome offer.' And a sudden one, I thought. 'Give me a rain check, will you? Right now I have to wait for Lefty Godot.'

She looked more disappointed that she had any right to be. We parted on fairly good, mutually suspicious terms.

The fatal door I was watching opened at last. Dolly backed out thanking the two Deans effusively, and practically curtseying. But I saw when she turned around and headed for the entrance that her face was white and set.

I went after her feeling a little foolish. The situation reminded me of a girl I used to follow home from Junior High. I never did work up enough nerve to ask her for the privilege of carrying her books. But I began to identify Dolly with that unattainable girl whose name I couldn't even remember now.

She hurried along the mall that bisected the campus, and started up the steps of the library building. I caught up with her.

'Mrs Kincaid?'

She stopped as though I had shot her. I took her arm instinctively. She flung away my hand, and opened her mouth as if to call out for help. No sound came out. The other students around us, passing on the wide mall or chatting on the steps, paid no attention to her silent scream.

'I'd like very much to talk to you, Mrs Kincaid.'

She pushed her hair back, so forcefully that one of her eyes slanted up and gave her a Eurasian look. 'Who are you?'

'A friend of your husband's. You've given Alex a bad three weeks.'

'I suppose I have,' she said, as if she had only just thought of it.

'You must have had a bad three weeks yourself, if you're fond of him at all. Are you?'

'Am I what?' She seemed to be slightly dazed.

'Fond of Alex?'

'I don't know. I haven't had time to think about it. I don't wish to discuss it, with you or anyone. Are you really a friend of Alex's?'

'I think I can claim to be. He doesn't understand what you're doing to him. He's a pretty sad young man.'

'No doubt he caught it from me. Spreading ruin is my specialty.'

'It doesn't have to be. Why don't you call it off, whatever you're doing, and give it another try with Alex? He's waiting for you here in town right now.'

'He can wait till doomsday. I'm not going back to him.'

Her young voice was surprisingly firm, almost harsh. There was something about her eyes I didn't like. They were wide and dry and fixed, eyes which had forgotten how to cry.

'Did Alex hurt you in some way?'

'He wouldn't hurt a fly. You know that, if you're really a friend of his. He's a nice harmless boy, and I don't want to hurt him.' She added with conscious drama: 'Tell him to congratulate himself on his narrow escape.'

'Is that the only message you have for your husband?'

'He isn't my husband, not really. Tell him to get an annulment. Tell him I'm not ready to settle down. Tell him I've decided to finish my education.'

She made it sound like a solitary trip to the moon, one-way.

I went back to the Administrative Building. The imitation flagstone pavement of the mall was flat and smooth, but I had the feeling that I was walking knee-deep in gopher holes. Dean Sutherland's door was closed and, when I knocked, her 'Come in' was delayed and rather muffled.

Dean Bradshaw was still with her, looking more than ever like a college student on whom light frost had fallen during the night.

She was flushed, and her eyes were bright emerald green. 'This is Mr Archer, Brad, the detective I told you about.'

He gave my hand a fiercely competitive grip. 'It's a pleasure to meet you, sir. Actually,' he said with an attempt at a smile, 'it's rather a mixed pleasure under the circumstances. I very much regret the necessity of your coming here to our campus.'

'The kind of work I do has to be done,' I said a little defensively. 'Mrs Kincaid ran out on her husband, and some explanation is due him. Did she give any to you?'

Dean Sutherland put on her grim face. 'She's not returning to him. She found out something on their wedding night so dreadful –'

Bradshaw raised his hand. 'Wait a minute, Laura. The facts she divulged to you are in the nature of professional confidences. We certainly don't want this chap running back to her husband with them. The poor girl is frightened enough as it is.'

'Frightened of her husband? I find that hard to believe,' I said.

'She didn't pour out her heart to you,' Laura Sutherland cried warmly. 'Why do you suppose the poor child used a fake name? She was mortally afraid that he would track her down.'

'You're being melodramatic, you know.' Bradshaw's tone was indulgent. 'The boy can't be as bad as all that.'

'You didn't hear her, Brad. She told me things, as woman to woman, that I haven't even told you, and I don't intend to.'

I said: 'Perhaps she was lying.'

'She most assuredly was not! I know the truth when I hear it. And my advice to you is to go back to that husband of hers, wherever he is, and tell him that you haven't been able to find her. She'll be safer and happier if you do.'

'She seems to be safe enough. She certainly isn't happy. I talked to her outside for a minute.'

Bradshaw tilted his head in my direction. 'What did she say?'

'Nothing sensational. She made no accusations against Kincaid. In fact she blamed herself for the break-up. She says she wants to go on with her education.'

'Good.'

'Are you going to let her stay here?'

Bradshaw nodded. 'We've decided to overlook her little deception. We believe in giving young people a certain amount of leeway, so long as it doesn't impinge on the rights of others. She can stay, at least for the present, and continue to use her pseudonym if she likes.' He added with dry academic humour: ' "A rose by any other name," you know.'

'She's going to have her transcripts sent to us right away,' Dean Sutherland said. 'Apparently she's had two years of junior college and a semester at the university.'

'What's she planning to study here?'

'Dolly is majoring in psychology. According to Professor Haggerty, she has a flair for it.'

'How would Professor Haggerty know that?'

'She's Dolly's academic counsellor. Apparently Dolly is deeply interested in criminal and abnormal psychology.'

For some reason I thought of Chuck Begley's bearded head, with eyes opaque as a statue's. 'When you were talking with Dolly, did she say anything about a man named Begley?'

'Begley?' They looked at each other and then at me. 'Who,' she asked, 'is Begley?'

'It's possible he's her father. At any rate he had something to do with her leaving her husband. Incidentally I wouldn't put too much stock in her husband's Asiatic perversions or whatever it was she accused him of. He's a clean boy, and he respects her.'

'You're entitled to your opinion,' Laura Sutherland said as though I wasn't. 'But please don't act on it precipitately. Dolly is a sensitive young woman, and something has happened to shake her very deeply. You'll be doing them both a service by keeping them apart.'

'I agree,' Bradshaw said solemnly.

'The trouble is, I'm being paid to bring them together. But I'll think about it, and talk it over with Alex.'

CHAPTER SIX

In the parking lot behind the building Professor Helen Haggerty was sitting at the wheel of the new black Thunderbird convertible. She had put the top down and parked it beside my car, as if for contrast. The late afternoon sunshine slanting across the foothills glinted on her hair and eyes and teeth.

'Hello again.'

'Hello again,' I said. 'Are you waiting for me?'

'Only if you're left-handed.'

'I'm ambidextrous.'

'You would be. You threw me a bit of a curve just now.'

'I did?'

'I know who you are.' She patted a folded newspaper on the leather seat beside her. The visible headline said: 'Mrs Perrine Acquitted.' Helen Haggerty said: 'I think it's very exciting. The paper credits you with getting her off. But it's not quite clear how you did it.'

'I simply told the truth, and evidently the jury believed me. At the time the alleged larceny was committed here in Pacific Point, I had Mrs Perrine under close surveillance in Oakland.'

'What for? Another larceny?'

'It wouldn't be fair to say.'

She made a mock-sorrowful mouth, which fitted the lines of her face too well. 'All the interesting facts are confidential. But I happen to be checked out for security. In fact my father is a policeman. So get in and tell me all about Mrs Perrine.'

'I can't do that.'

'Or I have a better idea,' she said with her bright unnatural smile. 'Why don't you come over to my house for a drink?'

'I'm sorry. I have work to do.'

'Detective work?'

'Call it that.'

'Come on.' With a subtle movement, her body joined in the invitation. 'All work and no play makes Jack a dull boy. You don't want to be a dull boy and make me feel rejected. Besides, we have things to talk about.'

'The Perrine case is over. Nothing could interest me less.'

'It was the Dorothy Smith case I had in mind. Isn't that why you're on campus?'

'Who told you that?'

'The grapevine. Colleges have the most marvellously efficient grapevines, second only to penitentiaries.'

'Are you familiar with penitentiaries?'

'Not intimately. But I wasn't lying when I told you my father was a policeman.' A grey pinched expression touched her face. She covered it over with another smile. 'We do have things in common. Why don't you come along?'

'All right. I'll follow you. It will save you driving me back.'

'Wonderful.'

She drove as rapidly as she operated, with a jerky nervousness and a total disregard for the rules of the road. Fortunately the campus was almost empty of cars and people. Diminished by the foothills and by their own long shadows, the buildings resembled a movie lot which had shut down for the night.

She lived back of Foothill Drive in a hillside house made out of aluminium and glass and black enamelled steel. The nearest rooftop floated among the scrub oaks a quarter of a mile down the slope. You could stand in the living-room by the central fireplace and see the blue mountains rising up on one side, the grey ocean falling away on the other. The off-shore fog was pushing in to the land.

'Do you like my little eyrie?'

'Very much.'

'It isn't really mine, alas. I'm only renting at present, though I have hopes. Sit down. What will you drink? I'm going to have a tonic.'

'That will do nicely.'

The polished tile floor was almost bare of furniture. I strolled around the large room, pausing by one of the glass walls to look out. A wild pigeon lay on the patio with its iridescent neck broken. Its faint spreadeagled image outlined in dust showed where it had flown against the glass.

I sat on a rope chair which probably belonged on the patio. Helen Haggerty brought our drinks and disposed herself on a canvas chaise, where the sunlight would catch her hair again, and shine on her polished brown legs.

'I'm really just camping for now,' she said. 'I haven't sent for my furniture, because I don't know if I want it around me any more. I may just leave it in storage and start all over, and to hell with the history. Do you think that's a good idea, Curveball Lefty Lew?'

'Call me anything, I don't mind. I'd have to know the history.'

'Ha. You never will.' She looked at me sternly for a minute, and sipped her drink. 'You might as well call me Helen.'

'All right, Helen.'

'You make is sound so formal. I'm not a formal person, and neither are you. Why should we be formal with each other?'

'You live in a glass house, for one thing,' I said smiling 'I take it you haven't been in it long.'

'A month. Less than a month. It seems longer. You're the

first really interesting man I've met since I arrived here.'

I dodged the compliment. 'Where did you live before?'

'Here and there. There and here. We academic people are such nomads. It doesn't suit me. I'd like to settle down permanently. I'm getting old.'

'It doesn't show.'

'You're being gallant. Old for a woman, I mean. Men never grow old.'

Now that she had me where she apparently wanted me, she wasn't crowding so hard, but she was working. I wished that she would stop, because I liked her. I downed my drink. She brought me a second tonic with all the speed and efficiency of a cocktail waitress. I couldn't get rid of the dismal feeling that each of us was there to use the other.

With the second tonic she let me look down her dress. She was smooth and brown as far as I could see. She arranged herself on the chaise with one hip up, so that I could admire the curve. The sun, in its final yellow flare-up before setting, took possession of the room.

'Shall I pull the drapes?' she said.

'Don't bother for me. It'll be down soon. You were going to tell me about Dolly Kincaid alias Dorothy Smith.'

'Was I?'

'You brought the subject of her up. I understand you're her academic counsellor.'

'And that's why you're interested in me, *n'est-ce pas?*' Her tone was mocking.

'I was interested in you before I knew of your connection with Dolly.'

'Really?'

'Really. Here I am to prove it.'

'Here you are because I lured you with the magic words Dorothy Smith. What's she doing on this campus anyway?' She sounded almost jealous of the girl.

'I was sort of hoping you knew the answer to that.'

'Don't you?'

'Dolly gives conflicting stories, probably derived from romantic fiction –'

'I don't think so,' she said. 'She's a romantic all right – one of these romantic idealists who are always a jump or two behind her unconscious mind. I ought to know, I used to be one myself. But I also think she has some real trouble – appalling trouble.'

'What was her story to you?'

'It was no story. It was the lousy truth. We'll come to it

37

later on, if you're a good boy.' She stirred like an odalisque in the dying light, and recrossed her polished legs. 'How brave are you, Mr Lew?'

'Men don't talk about how brave they are.'

'You're full of copybook maxims,' she said with some malice. 'I want a serious answer.'

'You could always try me.'

'I may at that. I have a use – I mean, I need a man.'

'Is that a proposal, or a business proposition, or are you thinking about some third party?'

'You're the man I have in mind. What would you say if I told you that I'm likely to be killed this week-end.'

'I'd advise you to go away for the week-end.'

She leaned sideways toward me. Her breast hardly sagged. 'Will you take me?'

'I have a prior commitment.'

'If you mean little Mr Alex Kincaid, I can pay you better than he can. Not to mention fringe benefits,' she added irrepressibly.

'That college grapevine is working overtime. Or is Dolly the source of your information?'

'She's one of them. I could tell you things about that girl that would curl your hair.'

'Go ahead. I've always wanted curly hair.'

'Why should I? You don't offer a *quid pro quo*. You don't even take me seriously. I'm not used to being turned down flat, by the way.'

'It's nothing personal. I'm just the phlegmatic type. Anyway, you don't need me. There are roads going in three directions – Mexico, the desert, or Los Angeles – and you have a nice fast car.'

'I'm too nervous to drive any distance.'

'Scared?'

She nodded.

'You put up a good front.'

'A good front is all I have.'

Her face looked closed and dark, perhaps because the sunlight had faded from the room. Only her hair seemed to hold the light. Beyond the slopes of her body I could see the mountains darkening down.

'Who wants to kill you, Helen?'

'I don't know exactly. But I've been threatened.'

'How?'

'Over the telephone. I didn't recognize the voice. I couldn't

tell if it was a man or a woman, or something in between.'
She shuddered.

'Why would anybody threaten you?'

'I don't know,' she said without meeting my eyes.

'Teachers do get threatened from time to time. It usually
isn't too serious. Have you had a run-in with any local
crackpots?'

'I don't even know any local people. Except the ones at
the college, of course.'

'You may have a psychoneurotic in one of your classes.'
She shook her head. 'It's nothing like that. This is serious.'

'How do you know?'

'I have my ways of knowing.'

'Is it anything to do with Dolly Kincaid?'

'Perhaps. I can't say for sure. The situation is so complicated.'

'Tell me about the complicated situation.'

'It goes a long way back,' she said, 'all the way back to
Bridgeton.'

'Bridgeton?'

'The city where I was born and raised. The city where
everything happened. I ran away, but you can't run away
from the landscape of your dreams. My nightmares are still
set in the streets of Bridgeton. That voice on the telephone
threatening to kill me was Bridgeton catching up with me. It
was the voice of Bridgeton talking out of the past.'

She was unconscious of herself, caught in a waking nightmare, but her description of it sounded false. I still didn't
know whether to take her seriously.

'Are you sure you're not talking nonsense out of the
present?'

'I'm not making this up,' she said. 'Bridgeton will be the
death of me. Actually I've always known it would.'

'Towns don't kill people.'

'You don't know the proud city of my birth. It has quite
a record along those lines.'

'Where is it?'

'In Illinois, south of Chicago.'

'You say that everything happened there. What do you
mean?'

'Everything important – it was all over before I knew it
had started. But I don't want to go into the subject.'

'I can't very well help unless you do.'

'I don't believe you have any intention of helping me.

39

You're simply trying to pump me for information.'

It was true. I didn't care for her as she wished to be cared for by someone. I didn't entirely trust her. Her handsome body seemed to contain two alternating persons, one sensitive and candid, one hard and evasive.

She rose and went to the glass wall that faced the mountains. They had turned lavender and plum, with dark nocturnal blue in their clefts and groins. The entire evening, mountains and sky and city, was inundated with blue.

'*Die blaue Stunde*,' she said more or less to herself. 'I used to love this hour. Now it gives me the mortal shivers.'

I got up and stood behind her. 'You're deliberately working on your own emotions.'

'You know so much about me.'

'I know you're an intelligent woman. Act like one. If the place is getting you down leave it, or stay here and take precautions. Ask for police protection.'

'You're very free with brilliant suggestions not involving you. I asked for protection yesterday after I got the threatening telephone call. The Sheriff sent a man out. He said such calls were common, and usually involved teenagers.'

'Could it have been a teenager?'

'I didn't think so. But the deputy said they sometimes disguise their voices. He told me not to worry.'

'So don't worry.'

'I can't help it. I'm afraid, Lew. Stay with me?'

She turned and leaned on my chest, moving her body tentatively against me. The only real feeling I had for her was pity. She was trying to use me, and using herself in order to use me.

'I have to run along,' I said. 'I told you at the start I have a prior commitment. But I'll check back on you.'

'Thanks so much!'

She pulled away from me, so violently that she thudded like a bird against the glass wall.

CHAPTER SEVEN

I drove downhill through deepening twilight towards the Mariner's Rest Motel, telling myself in various tones of voice that I had done the right thing. The trouble was, in the scene I had just walked out of, there was no right thing to do—

only sins of commission or omission.

A keyboy wearing a gold-braided yachting cap who looked as though he had never set foot on a deck told me that Alex Kincaid had registered and gone out again. I went to the Surf House for dinner. The spotlit front of the big hotel reminded me of Fargo and all the useless pictures I had ordered from him.

He was in the dark room adjoining his little office. When he came out he was wearing rectangular dark glasses against the light. I couldn't see his eyes, but his mouth was hostile. He picked up a bulky manila envelope from the desk and thrust it at me.

'I thought you were in a hurry for these prints.'

'I was. Things came up. We found her.'

'So now you don't want 'em? My wife worked in this sweat-box half the afternoon to get 'em ready.'

'I'll take them. Kincaid will have a use for them if I don't. How much?'

'Twenty-five dollars including tax. It's actually $24.96.'

I gave him two tens and a five, and his mouth went through three stages of softening. 'Are they getting back together?'

'I don't know yet.'

'Where did you find her?'

'Attending the local college. She has a job driving for an old lady named Bradshaw.'

'The one with the Rolls?'

'Yes. You know her?'

'I wouldn't say that. She and her son generally eat Sunday buffet lunch in the dining-room. She's quite a character. I took a candid picture of them once, on the chance they'd order some copies, and she threatened to smash my camera with her cane. I felt like telling the old biddy her face was enough to smash it.'

'But you didn't?'

'I can't afford such luxuries.' He spread out his chemical-stained hands. 'She's a local institution, and she could get me fired.'

'I understand she's loaded.'

'Not only that. Her son is a big wheel in educational circles. He seems like a nice enough joe, in spite of the Harvard lah-de-dah. As a matter of fact he calmed her down when she wanted to smash my Leica. But it's hard to figure a guy like that, a good-looking guy in his forties, still tied to his old lady's apron-strings.'

'It happens in the best of families.'

'Yeah, especially in the best. I see a lot of these sad cookies waiting around for the money, and by the time they inherit it's too late. At least Bradshaw had the guts to go out and make a career for himself.' Fargo looked at his watch 'Speaking of careers, I've already put in a twelve-hour day and I've got about two hours of developing to do. See you.'

I started towards the hotel coffee shop. Fargo came running after me along the corridor. The rectangular dark glasses lent his face a robot-like calm which went oddly with the movements of his legs and arms.

'I almost forgot to ask you. You get a line on this Begley?'

'I talked to him for quite a while. He didn't give too much. He's living with a woman on Shearwater Beach.'

'Who's the lucky woman?' Fargo said.

'Madge Gerhardi is her name. Do you know her?'

'No, but I think I know who he is. If I could take another look at him –'

'Come over there now.'

'I can't. I'll tell you who I *think* he is under all that seaweed, if you'll promise not to quote me. There's such a thing as accidental resemblance, and a libel suit is the last thing I need.'

'I promise not to quote you.'

'See that you don't.' He took a deep breath like a skin diver getting ready to go for the bottom. 'I think he's a fellow named Thomas McGee who murdered his wife in Indian Springs about ten years ago. I took a picture of McGee when I was a cub reporter on the paper, but they never used the picture. They never play up those Valley cases.'

'You're sure he murdered his wife?'

'Yeah, it was an open-and-shut case. I don't have time to go into details, in fact they're getting pretty hazy at this late date. But most of the people around the courthouse thought he should have been given first degree. Gil Stevens convinced the jury to go for second degree, which explains how he's out so quick.'

Remembering Begley's story about his ten years on the other side of the world, the other side of the moon, I thought that ten years wasn't so very quick.

The fog was dense along Shearwater Beach. It must have been high tide: I could hear the surf roaring up under the cottages and sucking at their pilings. The smell of iodine

...ung in the chilly air.

Madge Gerhardi answered the door and looked at me rather vaguely. The paint on her eyelids couldn't hide the fact that they were swollen.

'You're the detective, aren't you?'

'Yes. May I come in?'

'Come in if you want. It won't do any good. He's gone.'

I'd already guessed it from her orphaned air. I followed her along a musty hallway into the main room, which was high and raftered. Spiders had been busy in the angles of the rafters, which were webbed and blurred as if fog had seeped in at the corners. The rattan furniture was coming apart at the joints. The glasses and empty bottles and half-empty bottles standing around on the tables and the floor suggested that a party had been going on for some days and might erupt again if I wasn't careful.

The woman kicked over an empty bottle on the way to the settee, where she flung herself down.

'It's your fault he's gone,' she complained. 'He started to pack right after you were here this afternoon.'

I sat on a rattan chair facing her. 'Did Begley say where he was going?'

'Not to me he didn't. He did say I wasn't to expect him back, that it was all off. Why did you have to scare him, anyway? Chuck never did anybody any harm.'

'He scares very easily.'

'Chuck is sensitive. He's had a great deal of trouble. Many's the time he told me that all he wanted was a quiet nook where he could write about his experiences. He's writing an autobiographical novel about his experiences.'

'His experiences in New Caledonia?'

She said with surprising candour: 'I don't think Chuck ever set foot in New Caledonia. He got that business about the chrome mine out of an old *National Geographic* magazine. I don't believe he ever left this country.'

'Where has he been?'

'In the pen,' she said. 'You know that, or you wouldn't be after him. I think it's a dirty crying shame, when a man has paid his debt to society and proved that he can rehabilitate himself –'

It was Begley she was quoting, Begley's anger she was expressing, but she couldn't sustain the anger or remember the end of the quotation. She looked around the wreckage of the room in dim alarm, as if she had begun to suspect that his rehabilitation was not complete.

'Did he tell you what he was in for, Mrs Gerhardi?'

'Not in so many words. He read me a piece from his book the other night. This character in the book was in the pen and he was thinking about the past and how they framed him for a murder he didn't commit. I asked him if the character stood for him. He wouldn't say. He went into one of his deep dark silences.'

She went into one of her own. I could feel the floor trembling under her feet. The sea was surging among the pilings like the blithe mindless forces of dissolution. The woman said :

'Was Chuck in the pen for murder?'

'I was told tonight that he murdered his wife ten years ago. I haven't confirmed it. Can you?'

She shook her head. Her face had lengthened as if by its own weight, like unbaked dough. 'It must be a mistake.'

'I hope so. I was also told that his real name is Thomas McGee. Did he ever use that name?'

'No.'

'It does tie in with another fact,' I said, thinking aloud. 'The girl he went to visit at the Surf House had the same name before she was married. He said the girl resembled his daughter. I think she is his daughter. Did he ever talk about her?'

'Never.'

'Or bring her here?'

'No. If she's his daughter, he wouldn't bring her here.' She reached for the empty bottle she had kicked over, set it on its base, and slumped back on to the settee, as if morally exhausted by the effort.

'How long did Begley, or McGee, live here with you?'

'A couple of weeks is all. We were going to be married. It's lonely living here without a man.'

'I can imagine.'

She drew a little life from the sympathy in my voice. 'They just don't stay with me. I try to make things nice for them, but they don't stay. I should have stuck with my first husband.' Her eyes were far away and long ago. 'He treated me like a queen but I was young and foolish. I didn't know any better than to leave him.'

We listened to the water under the house.

'Do you think Chuck went away with this girl you call his daughter?'

'I doubt it,' I said, 'How did he leave here, Mrs Gerhardi? By car?'

44

'He wouldn't let me drive him. He said he was going up to the corner and catch the LA bus. It stops at the corner if you signal it. He walked up the road with his suitcase and out of sight.' She sounded both regretful and relieved.

'About what time?'

'Around three o'clock.'

'Did he have any money?'

'He must have had some for the bus fare. He couldn't have had much. I've been giving him a little money, but he would only take what he needed from me, and then it always had to be a loan. Which he said he would pay back when he got his book of experiences on the market. But I don't care if he never pays me back. He was nice to have around.'

'Really?'

'Really he was. Chuck is a smart man. I don't care what he's done in the course of his life. A man can change for the better. He never gave me a bad time once.' She had a further break-through into candour: 'I was the one who gave him the bad times. I have a drinking problem. He only drank with me to be sociable. He didn't want me to drink alone.' She blinked her gin-coloured eyes. 'Would you like a drink?'

'No thanks. I have to be on my way.' I got up and stood over her. 'You're sure he didn't tell you where he was going?'

'Los Angeles is all I know. He promised I'd hear from him but I don't expect it. It's over.'

'If he should write or phone will you let me know?'

She nodded. I gave her my card, and told her where I was staying. When I went out, the fog had moved inland as far as the highway.

CHAPTER EIGHT

I stopped at the motel again on my way to the Bradshaw house. The keyboy told me that Alex was still out. I wasn't surprised when I found his red Porsche parked under the Bradshaws' hedge beside the road.

The moon was rising behind the trees. I let my thoughts rise with it imagining that Alex had got together with his bride and they were snug in the gatehouse, talking out their troubles. The sound of the girl's crying wiped out the hopeful image. Her voice was loud and terrible, almost inhuman Its compulsive rhythms rose and fell like the ululations of a hurt cat.

The door of the gatehouse was slightly ajar. Light spilled around its edges, as if extruded by the pressure of the noise inside. I pushed it open.

'Get out of here,' Alex said.

They were on a studio bed in the tiny sitting-room. He had his arms around her, but the scene was not domestic. She seemed to be fighting him, trying to struggle out of his embrace. It was more like a scene in a closed ward where psychiatric nurses will hold their violent patients, sometimes for hours on end, rather than strap them in canvas jackets.

Her blouse was torn, so that one of her breasts was almost naked. She twisted her unkempt head around and let me see her face. It was grey and stunned, and it hardly changed expression when she screamed at me:

'Get out!'

'I think I better stick around,' I said to both of them.

I closed the door and crossed the room. The rhythm of her crying was running down. It wasn't really crying. Her eyes were dry and fixed in her grey flesh. She hid them against her husband's body.

His face was shining white.

'What happened, Alex?'

'I don't really know. I was waiting for her when she got home a few minutes ago. I couldn't get much sense out of her. She's awfully upset about something.'

'She's in shock,' I said, thinking that he was close to it himself. 'Was she in an accident?'

'Something like that.'

His voice trailed off in a mumble. His look was inward, as if he was groping for the strength to handle this new problem.

'Is she hurt, Alex?'

'I don't think so. She came running down the road, and then she tried to run away again. She put up quite a battle when I tried to stop her.'

As if to demonstrate her prowess as a battler, she freed her hands and beat at his chest. There was blood on her hands. It left red dabs on his shirt-front.

'Let me go,' she pleaded. 'I want to die. I deserve to.'

'She's bleeding, Alex.'

He shook his head. 'It's somebody else's blood. A friend of hers was killed.'

46

'And it's all my fault,' she said in a flat voice.

He caught her wrists and held her. I could see manhood biting into his face. 'Be quiet, Dolly. You're talking nonsense.'

'Am I? She's lying in her blood, and I'm the one who put her there.'

'Who is she talking about?' I said to Alex.

'Somebody called Helen. I've never heard of her.'

I had.

The girl began to talk in her wispy monotone, so rapidly and imprecisely that I could hardly follow. She was a devil and so was her father before her and so was Helen's father and they had the bond of murder between them which made them blood sisters and she had betrayed her blood sister and done her in.

'What did you do to Helen?'

'I should have kept away from her. They die when I go near them.'

'That's crazy talk,' Alex said softly. 'You never hurt anybody.'

'What do you know about me?'

'All I need to. I'm in love with you.'

'Don't say that. It only makes me want to kill myself.' Sitting upright in the circle of his arms, she looked at her bloody hands and cried some more of her terrible dry tears. 'I'm a criminal.'

Alex looked up at me, his eyes blue-black. 'Can you make any sense of it?'

'Not much.'

'You can't really think she killed this Helen person?' We were talking past Dolly as if she was deaf or out of her head, and she accepted this status.

'We don't even know that anybody's been killed,' I said. 'Your wife is loaded with some kind of guilt, but it may belong to somebody else. I found out a little tonight about her background, or I think I did.' I sat on the shabby brown studio bed beside them and said to Dolly: 'What's your father's name?'

She didn't seem to hear me.

'Thomas McGee?'

She nodded abruptly, as if she'd been struck from behind. 'He's a lying monster. He made me into a monster.'

'How did he do that?'

The question triggered another nonstop sentence. 'He shot her,' she said with her chin on her shoulder, 'and left her

47

lying in her blood but I told Aunt Alice and the policemen and the court took care of him but now he's done it again.'

'To Helen?'

'Yes, and I'm responsible. I caused it to happen.'

She seemed to take a weird pleasure in acknowledging her guilt. Her grey and jaded looks, her tearless crying, her breathless run-on talking and her silences, were signs of an explosive emotional crisis. Under the raw melodrama of her self-accusations, I had the sense of something valuable and fragile in danger of being permanently broken.

'We'd better not try to question her any more,' I said. 'I doubt right now she can tell the difference between true and false?'

'Can't I?' she said malignly. 'Everything I remember is true and I can remember everything from year one, the quarrels and the beatings, and then he finally shot her in her blood –'

I cut in: 'Shut up, Dolly, or change the record. You need a doctor. Do you have one in town here?'

'No. I don't need a doctor. Call the police. I want to make a confession.'

She was playing a game with us and her own mind, I thought, performing dangerous stunts on the cliff edge of reality, daring the long cloudy fall.

'You want to confess that you're a monster,' I said.

It didn't work. She answered matter-of-factly: 'I am a monster.'

The worst of it was, it was happening physically before my eyes. The chaotic pressures in her were changing the shape of her mouth and jaw. She peered at me dully through a fringe of hair. I'd hardly have recognized her as the girl I talked to on the library steps that day.

I turned to Alex. 'Do you know any doctors in town?'

He shook his head. His short hair stood up straight as if live electricity was running through him from the contact with his wife. He never let go of her.

'I could call Dad in Long Beach.'

'That might be a good idea, later.'

'Couldn't we take her to the hospital?'

'Not without a private doctor to protect her.'

'Protect her from what?'

'The police, or the psycho ward. I don't want her answering any official questions until I have a chance to check on Helen.'

The girl whimpered. 'I don't want to go to the psycho

ward. I had a doctor in town here a long time ago.' She was sane enough to be frightened, and frightened enough to co-operate.

'What's his name?'

'Dr Godwin. Dr James Godwin. He's a psychiatrist. I used to come in and see him when I was a little girl.'

'Do you have a phone in the gatehouse?'

'Mrs Bradshaw lets me use her phone.'

I left them and walked up the driveway to the main house. I could smell fog even at this level now. It was rolling down from the mountains, flooding out the moon, as well as rising from the sea.

The big white house was quiet, but there was light behind some of the windows. I pressed the bell push. Chimes tinkled faintly behind the heavy door. It was opened by a large dark woman in a cotton print dress. She was crudely handsome, in spite of the pitted acne scars on her cheekbones. Before I could say anything she volunteered that Dr Bradshaw was out and Mrs Bradshaw was on her way to bed.

'I just want to use the phone. I'm a friend of the young lady in the gatehouse.'

She looked me over doubtfully. I wondered if Dolly's contagion had given me a wild irrational look.

'It's important,' I said. 'She needs a doctor.'

'Is she sick?'

'Quite sick.'

'You shouldn't ought to leave her alone.'

'She isn't alone. Her husband's with her.'

'But she is not married.'

'We won't argue about it. Are you going to let me call a doctor?'

She stepped back reluctantly and ushered me past the foot of a curved staircase into a book-lined study where a lamp burned like a night light on the desk. She indicated the telephone beside it, and took up a watchful position by the door.

'Could I have a little privacy, please? You can search me on the way out.'

She sniffed, and withdrew out of sight. I thought of calling Helen's house, but she wasn't in the telephone directory. Dr James Godwin fortunately was. I dialled his number. The voice that eventually answered was so quiet and neutral that I couldn't tell if it was male or female.

'May I speak to Dr Godwin?'

'This is Dr Godwin.' He sounded weary of his identity.

'My name is Lew Archer. I've just been talking to a girl who says she used to be your patient. Her maiden name was Dolly or Dorothy McGee. She's not in a good way.'

'Dolly? I haven't see her for ten or eleven years. What's troubling her?'

'You're the doctor, and I think you'd better see her. She's hysterical, to put it mildly, talking incoherently about murder.'

He groaned. With my other ear I could hear Mrs Bradshaw call hoarsely down the stairs:

'What's going on down there, Maria?'

'The girl Dolly is sick, he says.'

'Who says?'

'I dunno. Some man.'

'Why didn't you tell me she was sick?'

'I just did.'

Dr Godwin was talking in a small dead voice that sounded like the whispering ghost of the past: 'I'm not surprised this material should come up. There was a violent death in her family when she was a child, and she was violently exposed to it. She was in the immediate pre-pubic period, and already in a vulnerable state.'

I tried to cut through the medical jargon: 'Her father killed her mother, is that right?'

'Yes.' The word was like a sigh. 'The poor child found the body. Then they made her testify in court. We permit such barbarous things –' He broke off, and said in a sharply different tone: 'Where are you calling from?'

'Roy Bradshaw's house. Dolly is in the gatehouse with her husband. It's on Foothill Drive –'

'I know where it is. In fact I just got in from attending a dinner with Dean Bradshaw. I have another call to make, and then I'll be right with you.'

I hung up and sat quite still for a moment in Bradshaw's leather-cushioned swivel-chair. The walls of books around me, dense with the past, formed a kind of insulation against the present world and its disasters. I hated to get up.

Mrs Bradshaw was waiting in the hallway. Maria had disappeared. The old woman was breathing audibly, as if the excitement was a strain on her heart. She clutched the front of her pink wool bathrobe against her loosely heaving bosom.

'What's the trouble with the girl?'

'She's emotionally upset.'

'Did she have a fight with her husband? He's a hothead, I could hardly blame her.'

'The trouble goes a little deeper than that. I just called Dr Godwin the psychiatrist. She's been his patient before.'

'You mean to tell me the girl is – ?' She tapped her veined temple with a swollen knuckle.

A car had stopped in the driveway, and I didn't have to answer her question. Roy Bradshaw came in the front door. The fog had curled his hair tight, and his thin face was open. It closed up when he saw us standing together at the foot of the stairs.

'You're late,' Mrs Bradshaw said in an accusing tone. 'You go out wining and dining and leave me here to cope all by myself. Where were you anyway?'

'The Alumni banquet. You can't have forgotten that. You know how those banquets drag on, and I'm afraid I made my own contribution to the general boredom.' He hesitated, becoming aware of something in the scene more serious than an old woman's possessiveness. 'What's up, Mother?'

'This man tells me the little girl in the gatehouse has gone out of her mind. Why did you have to send me a girl like that, a psychiatric patient?'

'I didn't send her.'

'Who did?'

I tried to break in on their foolishness, but neither of them heard me. They were intent on their game of emotional ping-pong, which had probably been going on since Roy Bradshaw was a boy.

'It was either Laura Sutherland or Helen Haggerty,' he was saying. 'Professor Haggerty is her counsellor, and it was probably she.'

'Whichever one it was, I want you to instruct her to be more careful next time. If you don't care about my personal safety –'

'I *do* care about your safety. I care very much about your safety.' His voice was strained thin between anger and submissiveness. 'I had no idea there was anything the matter with the girl.'

'There probably wasn't,' I said. 'She's had a shock. I just called a doctor for her. Dr Godwin.'

Bradshaw turned slowly in my direction. His face was strangely soft and empty, like a sleeping boy's.

'I know Dr Godwin,' he said. 'What kind of a shock did she sustain?'

'It isn't clear. I'd like to talk to you in private.'

Mrs Bradshaw announced in a trembling voice: 'This is my house, young man.'

She was telling me, but she was also reminding Bradshaw, flicking the economic whip at him. He felt its sting:

'I live here, too. I have my duties to you, and I try to perform them satisfactorily. I also have my duties to the students.'

'You and your precious students.' Her bright black eyes were scornful. 'Very well. You can have your privacy. I'll go outside.'

She actually started for the front door, drawing her bathrobe around her lumpy body as if she was being cast out into a blizzard. Bradshaw went after her. There were pullings and haulings and cajolings and a final good night embrace, from which I averted my eyes, before she climbed heavily up the stairs, with his assistance.

'You mustn't judge Mother too harshly,' he said when he came down. 'She's getting old, and it makes it hard for her to adjust to crises. She's really a generous-hearted soul, as I have good reason to know.'

I didn't argue with him. He knew her better than I did.

'Well, Mr Archer, shall we go into my study?'

'We can save time if we talk on the road.'

'On the road?'

'I want you to take me to Helen Haggerty's place if you know where it is. I'm not sure I can find it in the dark.'

'Why on earth? Surely you're not taking Mother seriously? She was simply talking to hear herself talk.'

'I know. But Dolly's been doing some talking, too. She says that Helen Haggerty is dead. She has blood on her hands, by way of supporting evidence. I think we'd better go up there and see where the blood came from.'

He gulped. 'Yes. Of course. It isn't far from here. In fact it's only a few minutes by the bridle path. But at night we'll probably get there faster in my car.'

We went out to his car. I asked him to stop at the gatehouse, and glanced in. Dolly was lying on the studio bed with her face turned to the wall. Alex had covered her with a blanket. He was standing by the bed with his hands loose.

'Dr Godwin is on his way,' I said in a low voice. 'Keep him here till I get back, will you?'

He nodded, but he hardly appeared to see me. His look was still inward, peering into depths he hadn't begun to imagine until tonight.

CHAPTER NINE

Bradshaw's compact car was equipped with seat-belts, and he made me fasten mine before we set out. Between his house and Helen's I told him as much as I thought he needed to know about Dolly's outpourings. His response was sympathetic. At my suggestion, he left his car by the mailbox at the foot of Helen's lane. When we got out I could hear a foghorn moaning from the low sea.

Another car, a dark convertible whose shape I could barely make out through the thickening air, was parked without lights down the road. I ought to have shaken it down. But I was pressed by my own private guilt, and eager to see if Helen was alive.

Her house was a faint blur of light high among the trees. We started up the hairpinning gravel driveway. An owl flew low over our heads, silent as a travelling piece of fog. It lit somewhere in the grey darkness, called to its mate, and was answered. The two invisible birds seemed to be mocking us with their sad distant foghorn voices.

I heard a repeated crunching up ahead. It resolved itself into footsteps approaching in the gravel. I touched Bradshaw's sleeve, and we stood still. A man loomed up above us. He had on a topcoat and a snap-brim hat. I couldn't quite see his face.

'Hello.'

He didn't answer me. He must have been young and bold. He ran straight at us, shouldering me, spinning Bradshaw into the bushes. I tried to hold him but his downhill momentum carried him away.

I chased his running footfalls down to the road, and got there in time to see him climbing into the convertible. Its engine roared and its parking lights came on as I ran toward it. Before it leaped away, I caught a glimpse of a Nevada licence and the first four figures of the licence number. I went back to Bradshaw's car and wrote them down in my notebook: FT37.

I climbed up the driveway a second time. Bradshaw had reached the house. He was sitting on the doorstep with a sick look on his face. Lights poured over him from the open door and cast his bowed shadow brokenly on the flagstones.

'She *is* dead, Mr Archer.'

I looked in. Helen was lying on her side behind the door. Blood had run from a round bullet hole in her forehead and formed a pool on the tiles. It was coagulating at the edges, like frost on a dark puddle. I touched her sad face. She was already turning cold. It was nine-seventeen by my watch.

Between the door and the pool of blood I found a faint brown hand-print still sticky to the touch. It was about the size of Dolly's hand. She could have fallen accidentally, but the thought twisted through my head that she was doing her best to be tried for murder. Which didn't necessarily mean that she was innocent.

Bradshaw leaned like a convalescent in the doorway. 'Poor Helen. This is a heinous thing. Do you suppose the fellow who attacked us – ?'

'I'd say she's been dead for at least two hours. Of course he may have come back to wipe out his traces or retrieve his gun. He acted guilty.'

'He certainly did.'

'Did Helen Haggerty ever mention Nevada?'

He looked surprised. 'I don't believe so. Why?'

'The car our friend drove away in had a Nevada licence.'

'I see. Well, I suppose we must call the police.'

'They'll resent it if we don't.'

'Will you? I'm afraid I'm feeling rather shaken.'

'It's better if you do, Bradshaw. She worked for the college, and you can keep the scandal to a minimum.'

'Scandal? I hadn't even thought of that.'

He forced himself to walk past her to the telephone on the far side of the room. I went through the other rooms quickly. One bedroom was completely bare except for a kitchen chair and a plain table which she had been using as a working desk. A sheaf of test papers conjugating French irregular verbs lay on top of the table. Piles of books, French and German dictionaries and grammars and collections of poetry and prose, stood around it. I opened one at the flyleaf. It was rubber-stamped in purple ink: Professor Helen Haggerty, Maple Park College, Maple Park, Illinois.

The other bedroom was furnished in rather fussy elegance with new French Provincial pieces, lambswool rugs on the polished tile floor, soft heavy handwoven drapes at the enormous window. The wardrobe contained a row of dresses and skirts with Magnin and Bullocks labels, and under them a row of new shoes to match. The chest of drawers was stuffed with sweaters and more intimate garments, but nothing really intimate. No letters, no snapshots.

The bathroom had wall-to-wall carpeting and a triangular sunken tub. The medicine chest was well supplied with beauty cream and cosmetics and sleeping pills. The latter had been prescribed by a Dr Otto Schrenk and dispensed by Thompson's Drug Store in Bridgeton, Illinois, on June 17 of this year.

I turned out the bathroom wastebasket on the carpet. Under crumpled wads of used tissue I found a letter in an airmail envelope postmarked in Bridgeton, Illinois, a week ago and addressed to Mrs Helen Haggerty. The single sheet inside was signed simply 'Mother,' and gave no return address.

Dear Helen,

It was thoughtful of you to send me a card from sunny Cal my favourite state of the union even though it is years since I was out there. Your father keeps promising to make the trip with me on his vacation but something always comes up to put it off. Anyway his blood pressure is some better and that is a blessing. I'm glad you're well. I wish you would reconsider about the divorce but I suppose that's all over and done with. It's a pity you and Bert couldn't stay together. He is a good man in his way. But I suppose distant pastures look greenest.

Your father is still furious of course. He won't let me mention your name. He hasn't really forgiven you for when you left home in the first place, or forgiven himself either I guess, it takes two to make a quarrel. Still you are his daughter and you shouldn't have talked to him the way you did. I don't mean to recriminate. I keep hoping for a reconcilement between you two before he dies. He is not getting any younger, you know, and I'm not either, Helen. You're a smart girl with a good education and if you wanted to you could write him a letter that would make him feel different about 'things.' You are his only daughter after all and you've never taken it back that he was a crooked stormtrooper. That is a hard word for a policeman to swallow from anybody and it still rankles him after more than twenty years. Please write.

I put the letter back in the wastebasket with the other discarded paper. Then I washed my hands and returned to the main room. Bradshaw was sitting in the rope chair, stiffly formal even when alone. I wondered if this was his first experience of death. It wasn't mine by a long shot, but this death had hit me especially hard. I could have prevented it.

The fog outside was getting denser. It moved against the glass wall of the house, and gave me the queer sensation that the world had dropped away, and Bradshaw and I were floating together in space, unlikely gemini encapsulated with the dead woman.

'What did you tell the police?'

'I talked to the Sheriff personally. He'll be here shortly. I gave him only the necessary minimum. I didn't know whether or not to say anything about Mrs Kincaid.'

'We have to explain our discovery of the body. But you don't have to repeat anything she said. It's purely hearsay so far as you're concerned.'

'Do you seriously regard her as a suspect in this?'

'I have no opinion yet. We'll see what Dr Godwin has to say about her mental condition. I hope Godwin is good at his job.'

'He's the best we have in town. I saw him to-night, oddly enough. He sat at the speaker's table with me at the Alumni dinner, until he was called away.'

'He mentioned seeing you at dinner.'

'Yes. Jim Godwin and I are old friends.' He seemed to lean on the thought.

I looked around for something to sit on, but there was only Helen's canvas chaise. I squatted on my heels. One of the things in the house that puzzled me was the combination of lavish spending and bare poverty, as if two different women had taken turns furnishing it. A princess and a pauper.

I pointed this out to Bradshaw, and he nodded: 'It struck me when I was here the other evening. She seems to have spent her money on inessentials.'

'Where did the money come from?'

'She gave me to understand she had a private income. Heaven knows she didn't dress as she did on an assistant professor's salary.'

'Did you know Professor Haggerty well?'

'Hardly. I did escort her to one or two college functions, as well as the opening concert of the fall season. We discovered a common passion for Hindemith.' He made a steeple of his fingers. 'She's a – she was a very presentable woman. But I wasn't close to her, in any sense. She didn't encourage intimacy.'

I raised my eyebrows. Bradshaw coloured slightly.

'I don't mean sexual intimacy, for heaven's sake. She wasn't my type at all. I mean that she didn't talk about herself to any extent.'

'Where did she come from?'

'Some small college in the Middle West, Maple Park I believe. She'd already left there and come out here when we appointed her. It was an emergency appointment, necessitated by Dr Farran's coronary. Fortunately Helen was available. I don't know what our Department of Modern Languages will do now, with the semester already under way.'

He sounded faintly resentful of the dead woman's absenteeism. While it was natural enough for him to be thinking of the college and its problems, I didn't like it. I said with deliberate intent to jolt him:

'You and the college are probably going to have worse problems than finding a teacher to take her place.'

'What do you mean?'

'She wasn't an ordinary female professor. I spent some time with her this afternoon. She told me among other things that her life had been threatened.'

'How dreadful,' he said, as though the threat of murder were somehow worse than the fact. 'Who on earth – ?'

'She had no idea, and neither have I. I thought perhaps you might. Did she have enemies on the campus?'

'I certainly can't think of any. You understand, I didn't know Helen at all well.'

'I got to know her pretty well, in a hurry. I gathered she'd had her share of experience, not all of it picked up in graduate seminars and faculty teas. Did you go into her background before you hired her?'

'Not too thoroughly. It was an emergency appointment, as I said, and in any case it wasn't my responsibility. The head of her department, Dr Geisman, was favourably impressed by her credentials and made the appointment.'

Bradshaw seemed to be delicately letting himself off the hook. I wrote down Geisman's name in my notebook.

'Her background ought to be gone into,' I said. 'It seems she was married, and recently divorced. I also want to find out more about her relations with Dolly. Apparently they were close.'

'You're not suggesting a Lesbian attachment? We have had –' He decided not to finish the sentence.

'I'm not suggesting anything. I'm looking for information. How did Professor Haggerty happen to become Dolly's counsellor?'

'In the normal way, I suppose.'

'What is the normal way of acquiring a counsellor?'

'It varies. Mrs Kincaid was an upperclassman, and we

57

usually permit upperclassmen to choose their own counsellors, so long as the counsellor in question has an opening in his or her schedule.'

'Then Dolly probably chose Professor Haggerty, and initiated the friendship herself?'

'She had every chance to. Of course it may have been pure accident.'

As if we had each received a signal on a common wavelength, we turned and looked at Helen Haggerty's body. It seemed small and lonely at the far end of the room. Our joint flight with it through cloudy space had been going on for a long time. I looked at my watch. It was only nine-thirty-one, fourteen minutes since our arrival. Time seemed to have slowed down, dividing itself into innumerable fractions, like Zeno's space or marijuana hours.

With a visible effort, Bradshaw detached his gaze from the body. His moment of communion with it had cost him the last of his boyish look. He leaned toward me with deep lines of puzzlement radiating from his eyes and mouth:

'I don't understand what Mrs Kincaid said to you. Do you mean to say she actually confessed this – this murder?'

'A cop or a prosecutor might say so. Fortunately none was present. I've heard a lot of confessions, good ones and phony ones. Hers was a phony one, in my opinion.'

'What about the blood?'

'She may have slipped and fallen in it.'

'Then you don't think we should mention any of it to the Sheriff?'

'If you don't mind stretching a point.'

His face showed that he minded, but after some hesitation he said: 'We'll keep it to ourselves, at least for the present. After all she was a student of ours, however briefly.'

Bradshaw didn't notice his use of the past tense, but I did, and it depressed me. I think we were both relieved by the sound of the Sheriff's car coming up the hill. It was accompanied by a mobile laboratory. Within a few minutes a fingerprint man and a deputy coroner and a photographer had taken over the room and changed its character. It became impersonal and drab like any room anywhere in which murder had been committed. In a curious way the men in uniform seemed to be doing the murder a second and final time, annulling Helen's rather garish aura, converting her into laboratory meat and courtroom exhibits. My raw nerves jumped when the bulbs flashed in her corner.

Sheriff Herman Crane was a thick-shouldered man in a tan gaberdine suit. His only suggestion of uniform was a slightly broad-brimmed hat with a woven leather band. His voice had an administrative ring, and his manner had the heavy ease of a politician, poised between bullying and flattery. He treated Bradshaw with noisy deference, as if Bradshaw was a sensitive plant of undetermined value but some importance.

Me he treated the way cops always treated me, with occupational suspicion. They suspected me of the misdemeanour of doing my own thinking. I did succeed in getting Sheriff Crane to dispatch a patrol car in pursuit of the convertible with the Nevada licence. He complained that his department was seriously understaffed, and he didn't think road blocks were indicated at this stage of the game. At this stage of the game I made up my mind not to co-operate fully with him.

The Sheriff and I sat in the chaise and the rope chair respectively and had a talk while a deputy who knew speedwriting took notes. I told him that Dolly Kincaid, the wife of a client of mine, had discovered the body of her college counsellor Professor Haggerty and reported the discovery to me. She had been badly shocked, and was under a doctor's care.

Before the Sheriff could press me for further details, I gave him a *verbatim* account, or as close to *verbatim* as I could make it, of my conversation with Helen about the death threat. I mentioned that she had reported it to his office, and he seemed to take this as a criticism:

'We're understaffed, like I said. I can't keep experienced men. Los Angeles lures 'em away with salaries we can't pay and pie in the sky.' I was from Los Angeles, as he knew, and the implication was that I was obscurely to blame. 'If I put a man on guard duty in every house that got a crank telephone call, I wouldn't have anybody left to run the department.'

'I understand that.'

'I'm glad you do. Something I don't understand – how did this conversation you had with the decedent happen to take place?'

'Professor Haggerty approached me and asked me to come up here with her.'

'What time was this?'

'I didn't check the time. It was shortly before sundown. I was here for about an hour.'

'What did she have in mind?'

'She wanted me to stay with her, for protection. I'm sorry I didn't.' Simply having the chance to say this made me feel better.

'You mean she wanted to hire you, as a bodyguard?'

'That was the idea.' There was no use going into the complex interchange that had taken place between Helen and me, and failed.

'How did she know you were in the bodyguard business?'

'I'm not, exactly. She knew I was an investigator because she saw my name in the paper.'

'Sure enough,' he said. 'You testified in the Perrine case this morning. Maybe I ought to congratulate you because Perrine got off.'

'Don't bother.'

'No, I don't think I will. The Perrine broad was guilty as hell and you know it and I know it.'

'The jury didn't think so,' I said mildly.

'Juries can be fooled and witnesses can be bought. Suddenly you're very active in our local crime circles, Mr Archer.' The words had the weight of an implied threat. He flung out a heavy careless hand toward the body. 'This woman, this Professor Haggerty here, you're sure she wasn't a friend of yours?'

'We became friends to a certain extent.'

'In an hour?'

'It can happen in an hour. Anyway, we had a previous conversation at the college today.'

'What about before today? Did you have other previous conversations?'

'No. I met her today for the first time.'

Bradshaw, who had been hanging around us in various anxious attitudes, spoke up: 'I can vouch for the truth of that, Sheriff, if it will save you any time.'

Sheriff Crane thanked him and turned back to me: 'So it was a purely business proposition between her and you?'

'It would have been if I had been interested.' I wasn't telling the precise truth, but there was no way to tell it to Crane without sounding foolish.

'You weren't interested. Why not?'

'I had other business.'

'What other business?'

'Mrs Kincaid had left her husband. He employed me to locate her.'

'I heard something about that this morning. Did you find out why she left him?'

'No. My job was to locate her. I did.'

'Where?'

I glanced up at Bradshaw. He gave me a reluctant nod. I said: 'She's a student at the college.'

'And now you say she's under a doctor's care? What doctor?'

'Dr Godwin.'

'The psychiatrist, eh?' The Sheriff uncrossed his heavy legs and leaned toward me confidentially. 'What does she need a psychiatrist for? Is she out of her head?'

'She was hysterical. It seemed like a good idea to call one.'

'Where is she now?'

I looked at Bradshaw again. He said: 'At my house. My mother employed her as a driver.'

The Sheriff got up with a rowing motion of his arms. 'Let's get over there and talk to her.'

'I'm afraid that won't be possible,' Bradshaw said.

'Who says so?'

'I do, and I'm sure the doctor would concur.'

'Naturally Godwin says what his patients pay him to say. I've had trouble with him before.'

'I know that.' Bradshaw had turned pale, but his voice was under rigid control. 'You're not a professional man, Sheriff, and I rather doubt that you understand Dr Godwin's code of ethics.'

Crane reddened under the insult. He couldn't think of anything to say. Bradshaw went on:

'I very seriously doubt that Mrs Kincaid can or should be questioned at the present time. What's the point of it? If she had anything to hide, she wouldn't have rushed to the nearest detective with her dreadful news. I'm sure we don't want to subject the girl to cruel and unusual punishment, simply for doing her duty as a citizen.'

'What do you mean, cruel and unusual punishment? I'm not planning to third-degree her.'

'I hope and trust you're not planning to go near the child tonight. That would be cruel and unusual punishment in my opinion, Sheriff, and I believe I speak for informed opinion in this county.'

Crane opened his mouth to expostulate, perhaps realized the hopelessness of trying to out-talk Bradshaw, and shut it again. Bradshaw and I walked out unaccompanied. I said when we were out of hearing of the house:

'That was quite a job you did of facing down the Sheriff.'

'I've always disliked that blustering bag of wind. Fortunately he's vulnerable. His majority slipped badly in the last election. A great many people in this county, including Dr Godwin and myself, would like to see more enlightened and efficient law enforcement. And we may get it yet.'

Nothing had changed visibly in the gatehouse. Dolly was still lying on the studio bed with her face turned to the wall. Bradshaw and I hesitated at the door. Walking with his head down, Alex crossed the room to speak to us.

'Dr Godwin went up to the house to make a phone call. He thinks she ought to be in a nursing home, temporarily.'

Dolly spoke in a monotone: 'I know what you're saying. You might as well say it out loud. You want to put me away.'

'Hush, darling.' It was a brave word.

The girl relapsed into silence. She hadn't moved at all. Alex drew us outside, keeping the door open so that he could watch her. He said in a low voice:

'Dr Godwin doesn't want to run the risk of suicide.'

'It's that bad, eh?' I said.

'I don't think so. Neither does Dr Godwin, really. He says it's simply a matter of taking reasonable security precautions. I told him I could sit up with her, but he doesn't think I should try to do it myself.'

'You shouldn't,' Bradshaw said. 'You'll need to have something left for tomorrow.'

'Yeah. Tomorrow.' Alex kicked at the rusty boot-scraper attached to the side of the doorstep. 'I better call Dad. Tomorrow's Saturday, he ought to be able to come.'

Footsteps approached from the direction of the main house. A big man in an alligator coat emerged from the fog, his bald head gleaming in the light from the doorway. He greeted Bradshaw warmly:

'Hello, Roy. I enjoyed your speech, what I heard of it. You'll elevate us yet into the Athens of the West. Unfortunately a patient dragged me out in the middle of it. She wanted to know if it was safe for her to see a Tennessee Williams movie all by herself. She really wanted me to go along with her and protect her from bad thoughts.' He turned to me. 'Mr Archer? I'm Dr Godwin.'

We shook hands. He gave me a look of lingering intensity, as if he was going to paint my portrait from memory. Godwin had a heavy, powerful face, with eyes that changed from bright to dark like lamps being turned down. He had authority, which he was being careful not to use.

'I'm glad you called me. Miss McGee – Mrs Kincaid needed something to calm her down.' He glanced in through the doorway. 'I hope she's feeling better now.'

'She's much quieter,' Alex said. 'Don't you think it will be all right for her to stay here with me?'

Godwin made a commiserating face. His mouth was very flexible, like an actor's. 'It wouldn't be wise, Mr Kincaid. I've made arrangements for a bed in a nursing home I use. We don't want to take any chances with her life.'

'But why should she try to kill herself?'

'She has a lot on her mind, poor girl. I always pay attention to suicide threats, or even the slightest hint of them.'

'Have you found out just what she does have on her mind?' Bradshaw said.

'She didn't want to talk much. She's very tired. It can wait till morning.'

'I hope so,' Bradshaw said. 'The Sheriff wants to question her about the shooting. I did my best to hold him off.'

Godwin's mobile face became grave. 'There actually has been a murder then? Another murder?'

'One of our new professors, Helen Haggerty, was shot in her home tonight. Mrs Kincaid apparently stumbled on the body.'

'She's had dreadful luck.' Godwin looked up at the low sky. 'I sometimes feel as though the gods have turned their backs on certain people.'

I asked him to explain what he meant. He shook his head: 'I'm much too tired to tell you the bloody saga of the McGees. A lot of it has faded out of my memory, mercifully. Why don't you ask the courthouse people for the details?'

'That wouldn't be a good idea, under the circumstances.'

'It wouldn't, would it? You can see how tired I am. By the time I get my patient safely disposed of for the night I'll have just enough energy left to make it home and to bed.'

'We still need to talk, doctor.'

'What about?'

I didn't like to say it in front of Alex but I said it, watching him: 'The possibility that she committed this second murder, or let's say the possibility that she'll be accused of it. She seems to want to be.'

Alex rose to her defence: 'She was out of her head, temporarily, and you can't use what she said –'

Godwin laid a hand on his shoulder. 'Take it easy, Mr Kincaid. We can't settle anything now. What we all need is a night's sleep – especially your wife. I want you to come along with me to the nursing home in case I need help with her on the way. You,' he said to me, 'can follow along in your car and bring him back. You'll want to know where the nursing home is, anyway, because I'll meet you there tomorrow morning at eight, after I've had an opportunity to talk to Mrs Kincaid. Got that?'

'Tomorrow morning at eight.'

He turned to Bradshaw. 'Roy, if I were you I'd go and see how Mrs Bradshaw is feeling. I gave her a sedative, but she's alarmed. She thinks, or pretends to think, that she's surrounded by maniacal assassins. You can talk her out of it better than I could.'

Godwin seemed to be a wise and careful man. At any rate, his authority imposed itself. All three of us did as he said.

So did Dolly. Propped between him and Alex, she came out to his car. She didn't struggle or make a sound, but she walked as though she was on her way to the execution chamber.

CHAPTER TEN

An hour later I was sitting on one of the twin beds in my motel room. There was nothing more I could do right now, except possibly stir up trouble if I went for information to the local authorities. But my mind kept projecting on the plaster wall rapid movies of actions I could be performing. Run down Begley-McGee. Capture the man from Nevada.

I shut off the violent images with an effort of will and forced myself to think about Zeno, who said that Achilles could never traverse the space between him and the tortoise. It was a soothing thought, if you were a tortoise, or maybe even if you were Achilles.

I had a pint of whisky in my bag. I was getting it out of its sock when I thought of Arnie Walters, a Reno colleague of mine who had split more than one pint with me. I put in a long-distance call to his office, which happened to be the front room of his house. Arnie was at home.

'Walters Detective Agency,' he said in a reluctant midnight voice.

'This is Lew Archer.'

'Oh. Good. I didn't really want to go to bed. I was only modelling my pyjamas.'

'Irony isn't your forte, so drop it. All I'm asking for is a small service which I will repay in kind at the earliest opportunity. Are you recording?'

I heard the click of the machine, and told it and Arnie about Helen's death. 'A couple of hours after the shooting, the man I'm interested in came out of the murder house and drove away in a black or dark blue convertible, I think a late-model Ford with a Nevada licence. I think I got the first four figures –'

'You think?'

'It's foggy here and it was dark. First four figures are probably FT37. The subject is young and athletic, height about five-eleven, wearing a dark topcoat and dark snap-brim fedora. I couldn't make out his face.'

'Have you seen your oculist lately?'

'You can do better than that, Arnie. Try.'

'I hear senior citizens can get free glaucoma tests nowa-days.'

Arnie was older than I was, but he didn't like to have this pointed out. 'What's bugging you? Trouble with the wife?'

'No trouble,' he said cheerfully. 'She's waiting for me in bed.'

'Give Phyllis my love.'

'I'll give her my own. In case I come up with anything, which seems unlikely in view of the fragmentary information, where do I contact you?'

'I'm staying at the Mariner's Rest Motel in Pacific Point. But you better call my answering service in Hollywood.'

He said he would. As I hung up, I heard a gentle tapping on my door. It turned out to be Alex. He had pulled on his trousers over his pyjamas.

'I heard you talking in here.'

'I was on the phone.'

'I didn't mean to interrupt.'

'I'm through phoning. Come in and have a drink.'

He entered the room cautiously, as if it might be booby-trapped. In the last few hours his movements had become very tentative. His bare feet made no sound on the carpet.

The bathroom cupboard contained two glasses wrapped in wax paper. I unwrapped and filled them. We sat on the twin beds, drinking to nothing in particular. We faced each other like mirror images separated by an invisible wall of glass.

I was conscious of the differences between us, particularly of Alex's youth and lack of experience. He was at the age when everything hurts.

'I was thinking of calling Dad,' he said. 'Now I don't know whether I should or not.'

There was another silence.

'He won't say "I told you so," in so many words. But that will be the general idea. Fools rush in where angels fear to tread and all that jazz.'

'I think it makes just as much sense if you reverse it. Angels rush in where fools are afraid to tread. Not that I know any angels.'

He got the message. 'You don't think I'm a fool?'

'You've handled yourself very well.'

'Thank you,' he said formally. 'Even if it isn't actually true.'

'It is, though. It must have taken some doing.'

Whisky and the beginnings of human warmth had dissolved the glass wall between us. 'The worst of it,' he said, 'was when I put her in the nursing home just now. I felt as if I was – you know, consigning her to oblivion. The place is like something out of Dante, with people crying and groaning. Dolly's a sensitive girl. I don't see how she'll be able to take it.'

'She can take it better than some other things, such as wandering around loose in her condition.'

'You think she's insane, don't you?'

'What I think doesn't matter. We'll get an expert opinion tomorrow. There's no doubt she's temporarily off base. I've seen people further off, and I've seen them come back.'

'You think she'll be all right then?'

He'd grabbed at what I said like a flying trapeze and swung up into hopefulness. Which I didn't think ought to be encouraged:

'I'm more concerned about the legal situation than the psychiatric one.'

'You can't really believe she killed this friend of hers – Helen? I know she said so, but it isn't possible. You see, I know Dolly. She isn't aggressive at all. She's one of the really pro-life people. She doesn't even like to kill a spider.'

'It is possible, Alex, and that was all I said. I wanted Godwin to be aware of the possibility from the start. He's in a position to do a lot for your wife.'

Alex said, 'My wife,' with a kind of wonder.

'She is your wife, legally. But nobody would consider that you owe her much. You have an out, if you want to use it.'

The whisky slopped in his glass. I think he barely restrained himself from throwing it in my face.

'I'm not going to ditch her,' he said. 'If you think I ought to, you can go to hell.'

I hadn't liked him thoroughly until now. 'Somebody had to mention the fact that you have an out. A lot of people would take it.'

'I'm not a lot of people.'

'So I gather.'

'Dad would probably call me a fool, but I don't care if she's guilty of murder. I'm staying.'

'It's going to cost money.'

'You want more money, is that it?'

'I can wait. So can Godwin. I was thinking about the future. Also there's the strong possibility that you'll need a lawyer to-morrow.'

'What for?' He was a good boy, but a little slow on the uptake.

'Judging by tonight, your main problem is going to be to prevent Dolly from talking herself into deep trouble. That means keeping her out of the hands of the authorities, in a place where she can be properly looked after. A good lawyer can be a help in that. Lawyers generally don't wait for their money in criminal cases.'

'Do you really think she's in such danger – such legal jeopardy? Or are you just trying to put the iron in my soul?'

'I talked to the local sheriff tonight, and I didn't like the gleam in his eye when we got on the subject of Dolly. Sheriff Crane isn't stupid. He knew that I was holding back on him. He's going to bear down on her when he catches on to the family connection.'

'The family connection?'

'The fact that her father murdered her mother.' It was cruel to hit him with it again, on top of everything else. Still it was better for him to hear it from me than from the dreary voice that talks from under the twisted pillow at three o'clock in the morning. 'Apparently he was tried and convicted in the local courts. Sheriff Crane probably gathered the evidence for the prosecution.'

'It's almost as though history is repeating itself.' There was something approaching awe in Alex's voice. 'Did I hear you say that this Chuck Begley character, the man with the beard, is actually her father?'

'He seems to be.'

'He was the one who started the whole thing off,' he said, as much to himself as to me. 'It was after he visited her that Sunday that she walked out on me. What do you think happened between them, to make her do that?'

'I don't know, Alex. Maybe he bawled her out for testifying against him. In any case he brought back the past. She couldn't handle the old mess and her new marriage together, so she left you.'

'I still don't get it,' he said. 'How could Dolly have a father like that?'

'I'm not a geneticist. But I do know most non-professional killers aren't criminal types. I intend to find out more about Begley-McGee and his murder. I suppose it's no use asking if Dolly ever talked about it to you?'

'She never said a word about either of her parents, except that they were dead. Now I can understand why. I don't blame her for lying –' He cut the sentence short, and amended it: 'I mean, for not telling me certain things.'

'She made up for it tonight.'

'Yeah. It's been quite a night.' He nodded several times, as though he was still absorbing its repercussions. 'Tell me the honest truth, Mr Archer. Do you believe the things she said about being responsible for this woman's death? And her mother?'

'I can't even remember half of them.'

'That's not an answer.'

'Maybe we'll get some better answers tomorrow. It's a complex world. The human mind is the most complex thing in it.'

'You don't give me much comfort.'

'It's not my job to.'

Making a bitter face over this and the last of his whisky, he rose slowly. 'Well, you need your sleep, and I have a phone call to make. Thanks for the drink.' He turned with his hand on the doorknob. 'And thanks for the conversation.'

'Any time. Are you going to call your father?'

'No. I've decided not to.'

I felt vaguely gratified. I was old enough to be his father, with no son of my own, and that may have had something to do with my feeling.

'Who are you going to call, or is that a private matter?'

'Dolly asked me to try and get in touch with her Aunt Alice. I guess I've been putting it off. I don't know what to say to her aunt. I didn't even know she had an Aunt Alice until tonight.'

'I remember she mentioned her. When did Dolly ask you to make the call?'

'In the nursing home, the last thing. She wants her aunt to come and see her. I didn't know if that was a good idea or not.'

68

'It would depend on the aunt. Does she live here in town?'

'She lives in the Valley, in Indian Springs. Dolly said she's in the county directory. Miss Alice Jenks.'

'Let's try her.'

I found her name and number in the phone book, placed the toll call, and handed the receiver to Alex. He sat on the bed, looking at the instrument as if he had never seen one before.

'What am I going to say to her?'

'You'll know what to say. I want to talk to her when you're finished.'

A voice rasped from the receiver: 'Yes? Who is this?'

'I'm Alex Kincaid. Is that Miss Jenks? . . . We don't know each other, Miss Jenks, but I married your niece a few weeks ago . . . Your niece, Dolly McGee. We were married a few weeks ago, and she's come down with a rather serious illness . . . No, it's more emotional. She's emotionally disturbed, and she wants to see you. She's in the Whitmore Nursing Home here in Pacific Point. Dr Godwin is looking after her.'

He paused again. There was sweat on his forehead. The voice at the other end went on for some time.

'She says she can't come tomorrow,' he said to me; and into the receiver: 'Perhaps Sunday would be possible? . . . Yes, fine. You can contact me at the Mariner's Rest Motel, or . . . Alex Kincaid. I'll look forward to meeting you.'

'Let me talk to her,' I said.

'Just a minute, Miss Jenks. The gentleman here with me, Mr Archer, has something to say to you.' He handed over the receiver.

'Hello, Miss Jenks.'

'Hello, Mr Archer. And who are you, may I ask, at one o'clock in the morning?' It wasn't a light question. The woman sounded anxious and irritated, but she had both feelings under reasonable control.

'I'm a private detective. I'm sorry to disrupt your sleep with this, but there's more to the situation than simple emotional illness. A woman has been murdered here.'

She gasped, but made no other comment.

'Your niece is a material witness to the murder. She may be more deeply involved than that, and in any case she's going to need support. So far as I know you're her only relative, apart from her father—'

'You can leave him out. He doesn't count. He never has,

except in a negative way.' Her voice was flat and harsh. 'Who was killed?'

'A friend and counsellor of your niece's, Professor Helen Haggerty.'

'I never heard of the woman,' she said with combined impatience and relief.

'You'll be hearing a great deal about her, if you're at all interested in your niece. Are you close to her?'

'I was, before she grew away from me. I brought her up after her mother's death.' Her voice became flat again: 'Does Tom McGee have anything to do with this new killing?'

'He may have. He's in town here, or he was.'

'I knew it!' she cried in bleak triumph. 'They had no business letting him out. They should have put him in the gas chamber for what he did to my little sister.'

She was choked with sudden emotion. I waited for her to go on. When she didn't, I said:

'I'm anxious to go into the details of that case with you, but I don't think we should do it over the phone. It really would be helpful if you could come here to-morrow.'

'I simply can't. There's no use badgering me. I have a terribly important meeting tomorrow afternoon. Several state officials will be here from Sacramento, and it will probably go on into the evening.'

'What about the morning?'

'I have to prepare for them in the morning. We're shifting over to a new state-county welfare programme.' Latent hysteria buzzed in her voice, the hysteria of a middle-aged spinster who has to make a change. 'If I walked out on this project, I could lose my position.'

'We don't want that to happen, Miss Jenks. How far is it from there to Pacific Point?'

'Seventy miles, but I tell you I can't make it.'

'I can. Will you give me an hour in the morning, say around eleven?'

She hesitated. 'Yes, if it's important. I'll get up an hour earlier and do my paperwork. I'll be home at eleven. You have my address? It's just off the main street of Indian Springs.'

I thanked her and got rid of Alex and went to bed, setting my mental alarm for six-thirty.

CHAPTER ELEVEN

Alex was still sleeping when I was ready to leave in the morning. I let him sleep, partly for selfish reasons, and partly because sleep was kinder to him than waking was likely to be.

The fog was thick outside. Its watery mass overlay Pacific Point and transformed it into a kind of suburb of the sea. I drove out of the motel enclosure into a grey world without perspective, came abruptly to an access ramp, descended on to the freeway where headlights swam in pairs like deep-sea fish, and arrived at a truck stop on the east side without any real sense that I had driven across the city.

I'd been having a little too much talk with people whose business was talking. It was good to sit at the counter of a working-class restaurant where men spoke when they wanted something, or simply to kid the waitress. I kidded her a little myself. Her name was Stella, and she was so efficient that she threatened to take the place of automation. She said with a flashing smile that this was her aim in life.

My destination was near the highway, on a heavily used thoroughfare lined mainly with new apartment buildings. Their faddish pastel colours and scant transplanted palms seemed dingy and desolate in the fog.

The nursing home was a beige stucco one-storeyed building taking up most of a narrow deep lot. I rang the bell at eight o'clock precisely. Dr Godwin must have been waiting behind the door. He unlocked it and let me in himself.

'You're a punctual man, Mr Archer.'

His changeable eyes had taken the stony colour of the morning. I noticed when he turned to shut the door behind us that his shoulders were permanently stooped. He was wearing a fresh white smock.

'Sit down, won't you? This is as good a place to talk as any.'

We were in a small reception room or lounge. I sat in one of several worn armchairs aimed at a silent television set in one corner. Through the inner door I could hear the rattle of dishes and the bright voices of nurses beginning the day.

'Is this your place, doctor?'

'I have an interest in it. Most of the patients here are

mine. I've just been giving some shock treatments.' He smoothed the front of his smock. 'I'd feel less like a witch-doctor if I knew why electric shocks make depressed people feel better. So much of our science, or art, is still in the empirical stage. But the people do get better,' he said with a sudden grin, too sudden to touch his watching, waiting eyes.

'Is Dolly?'

'Yes, I think she's somewhat better. We don't have over-night cures, of course. I want to keep an eye on her for at least a week. Here.'

'Is she fit to be questioned?'

'I don't want you to question her, or anyone else remotely connected with the – the world of crime and punishment.' As if to remove the curse from his refusal, he flung himself loosely into the armchair beside me, asked me for a cigarette and let me light it.

'Why not?'

'I do not love the law in its current primitive state, where sick people are trapped into betraying themselves in their sickness and then treated by the courts as if they were well. I've been fighting the situation for a long time.' He rested his ponderous bald head on the back of the chair, and blew smoke toward the ceiling.

'What you say suggests that Dolly is in danger from the law.'

'I was making a general statement.'

'Which applied specifically to Dolly. We don't have to play games, doctor. We're both on the same side. I don't assume the girl is guilty of anything. I do think she has information which may help me to clear up a murder.'

'But what if she's guilty?' he said, watching for my reaction.

'Then I'd want to co-operate with you in getting charges reduced, finding mitigating circumstances, making a case for merciful treatment by the court. Remember I'm working for her husband. Is she guilty?'

'I don't know.'

'You have talked to her this morning?'

'She did most of the talking. I don't ask many questions. I wait and I listen. In the end you learn more that way.' He gave me a meaningful look, as if I should start applying this principle.

I waited and listened. Nothing happened. A plump woman with long black hair straggling down the back of her cotton robe appeared in the inside doorway. She stretched out her arms to the doctor.

He lifted his hand like a weary king. 'Good morning, Nell.'

She gave him a bright agonized smile and softly withdrew, like a woman walking backward in her sleep. Her outstretched arms were the last I saw of her.

'It would be helpful if you told me what Dolly had to say this morning.'

'And possibly dangerous.' Godwin crushed out his cigarette in a blue ceramic ashtray which looked home-made. 'There is after all a difference between you and me. What a patient says to me is a professional confidence. You have no professional standing. If you refused to repeat information in court you could be jailed for contempt. I could, under the law, but I'm not likely to be.'

'I've sweated out contempt before. And the police won't get anything out of me that I don't choose to tell them. That's a guarantee.'

'Very well.' Godwin nodded his head once, decisively. 'I'm concerned about Dolly and I'll try to tell you why without any professional jargon. You may be able to put together the objective jigsaw puzzle while I'm reconstructing the subjective one.'

'You said no professional jargon, doctor.'

'Sorry. First there's her history. Her mother Constance McGee brought her to me at the instigation of her sister Alice, a woman I know slightly, when Dolly was ten years old. She wasn't a happy child. In fact she was in some danger of becoming really withdrawn, for good reason. There's always good reason. Her father McGee was an irresponsible and violent man who couldn't handle the duties of fatherhood. He blew hot and cold on the child, spoiled her and punished her, constantly fought with his wife and eventually left her, or was left, it hardly matters. I would have preferred to treat him instead of Dolly, since he was the main source of the trouble in the family. But he was unreachable.'

'Did you ever see him?'

'He wouldn't even come in for an interview,' Godwin said with regret. 'If I could have reached him, I might have been able to prevent a murder. Perhaps not. From what I've been told he was a severely maladjusted man who needed help but never got it. You can understand my bitterness about the gap between psychiatry and the law. People like McGee are allowed to run around loose, without preventive action of any kind, until they commit a crime. Then of course they're hauled into court and sent away for ten or twenty years. But not

73

to a hospital. To a prison.'

'McGee's out now. He's been in town here. Did you know that?'

'Dolly told me this morning. It's one of the many severe pressures on her. You can understand how a sensitive child brought up in an atmosphere of violence and instability would be plagued by anxiety and guilt. The worst guilt often arises when a child is forced, by sheer instinctive self-preservation, to turn against her parents. A clinical psychologist I work with helped Dolly to express her feelings in clay and doll-play and so on. There wasn't too much I could do for her myself, since children don't have the mental equipment to be analysed. But I did try to assume the role of the calm and patient father, provide some of the stability that was missing in her young life. And she was doing pretty well, until the disaster occurred.'

'You mean the murder?'

He swung his head in sorrow. 'McGee worked himself into a self-pitying rage one night, came to the aunt's house in Indian Springs where they were staying, and shot Constance through the head. Dolly was alone in the house with her mother. She heard the shot and saw McGee taking off. Then she discovered the body.'

His head went on swinging slowly like a heavy silent bell. I said:

'What was her reaction at the time?'

'I don't know. One of the peculiar difficulties of my work is that I often have to perform a public function with private means. I can't go out and lasso patients. Dolly never came back to me. She no longer had her mother to bring her in from the Valley, and Miss Jenks, her aunt, is a busy woman.'

'But didn't you say that Alice Jenks suggested treatment for Dolly in the first place?'

'She did. She also paid for it. Perhaps with all the trouble in the family she felt she couldn't afford it any longer. At any rate, I didn't see Dolly again until last night, with one exception. I went to the court the day she testified against McGee. As a matter of fact I bearded the judge in his chambers and told him that it shouldn't be allowed. But she was a key witness, and they had her aunt's permission, and they put her through her sad little paces. She acted like a pale little automaton lost in a world of hostile adults.'

His large body trembled with feeling. His hands burrowed under his smock, searching for a cigarette. I gave him one and lit it, and lit one for myself.

'What did she say in court?'

'It was very short and simple. I suspect that she was thoroughly rehearsed. She heard the shot and looked out her bedroom window and saw her father running away with the gun in his hand. One other question had to do with whether McGee had threatened Constance with bodily harm. He had. That was all.'

'You're sure?'

'Yes. This isn't my unaided recollection, as they say. I took written notes at the time, and I scanned them this morning.'

'Why?'

'They're part of her history, evidently a crucial part.' He blew out smoke and looked at me through it, long and cautiously.

I said: 'Does she tell a different story now?'

His face was working with complex passion. He was a man of feeling, and Dolly was his office daughter lost for many years.

'She tells an absurd story,' he burst out. 'I not only can't believe it, I can't believe that she believes it. She isn't that sick.'

He paused, drawing deep on his cigarette, trying to get himself under full control. I waited and listened. This time he did go on:

'She claims now that she didn't see McGee that night, and that in fact he had nothing to do with the murder. She says she lied on the witness stand because the various adults wanted her to.'

'Why would she say that now?'

'I don't pretend to understand her. After an interval of ten years we've naturally lost what rapport we had. And of course she hasn't forgiven me for what she considers my betrayal – my failure to look after her in the disaster. But what could I do? I couldn't go to Indian Springs and kidnap her out of her aunt's house.'

'You care about your patients, doctor.'

'Yes, I care. It keeps me tired.' He stubbed his cigarette in the ceramic ashtray. 'Nell made this ashtray, by the way. It's rather good for a first attempt.'

I murmured something in agreement. Above the subsiding clamour of dishes, a wild old complaining voice rose in the depths of the building.

'That story of hers,' I said, 'may not be so very absurd. It fits in with the fact that McGee visited her on the second day of her honeymoon and hit her so hard with something that it knocked her right off the tracks.'

'You're acute, Mr Archer. That's precisely what happened. He treated her to a long tirade on the subject of his innocence. You mustn't forget that she loved her father, however ambivalently. He was able to convince her that her memory was at fault, that he was innocent and she was guilty. Childhood memories are powerfully influenced by emotion.'

'That she was guilty of perjury, you mean?'

'Murder.' He leaned toward me. 'She told me this morning she killed her mother herself.'

'With a gun?'

'With her tongue. That's the absurd part. She claims she killed her mother and her friend Helen, and sent her father to prison into the bargain, all with her poisonous tongue.'

'Does she explain what she means by that?'

'She hasn't yet. It's an expression of guilt which may be only superficially connected with these murders.'

'You mean she's using the murders to unload guilt which she feels about something else?'

'More or less. It's a common enough mechanism. I know for a fact that she didn't kill her mother, or lie about her father, essentially. I'm certain McGee was guilty.'

'Courts can make mistakes, even in a capital case.'

He said with a kind of muted arrogance: 'I know more about that case than ever came out in court.'

'From Dolly?'

'From various sources.'

'I'd be obliged if you'd let me in on it.'

His eyes veiled themselves. 'I can't do that. I have to respect the confidences of my patients. But you can take my word for it that McGee killed his wife.'

'Then what's Dolly feeling so guilty about?'

'I'm sure that will come out, in time. It probably has to do with her resentment against her parents. It's natural she'd want to punish them for the ugly failure of their marriage. She may well have fantasied her mother's death, her father's imprisonment, before those things emerged into reality. When the poor child's vengeful dreams came true, how else could she feel but guilty? McGee's tirade the other week-end stirred up the old feelings, and then this dreadful accident last night—' He ran out of words and spread his hands, palms upward and fingers curling, on his heavy thighs.

'The Haggerty shooting was no accident, doctor. The gun is missing, for one thing.'

'I realize that. I was referring to Dolly's discovery of the body, which was certainly accidental.'

'I wonder. She blames herself for that killing, too. I don't see how you can explain that in terms of childhood resentments.'

'I wasn't attempting to.' There was irritation in his voice. It made him pull a little professional rank with me: 'Nor is there any need for you to understand the psychic situation. You stick to the objective facts, and I'll handle the subjective.' He softened this with a bit of philosophy: 'Objective and subjective, the outer world and the inner, do correspond of course. But sometimes you have to follow the parallel lines almost to infinity before they touch.'

'Let's stick to the objective facts then. Dolly said she killed Helen Haggerty with her poisonous tongue. Is that all she said on the subject?'

'There was more, a good deal more, of a rather confused nature. Dolly seems to feel that her friendship with Miss Haggerty was somehow responsible for the latter's death.'

'The two women were friends?'

'I'd say so, yes, though there was twenty years' difference in their ages. Dolly confided in her, poured out everything, and Miss Haggerty reciprocated. Apparently she'd had severe emotional problems involving her own father, and she couldn't resist the parallel with Dolly. They both let down their back hair. It wasn't a healthy situation,' he said drily.

'Does she have anything to say about Helen's father?'

'Dolly seems to think he was a crooked policeman involved in a murder – but that may be sheer fantasy – a kind of secondary image of her own father.'

'It isn't. Helen's father is a policeman, and Helen at least regarded him as a crook.'

'How in the world would you know that?'

'I read a letter from her mother on the subject. I'd like to have a chance to talk to her parents.'

'Why don't you?'

'They live in Bridgeton, Illinois.'

It was a long jump, but not so long as the jump my mind made into blank possibility. I had handled cases which opened up gradually like fissures in the firm ground of the present, cleaving far down through the strata of the past. Perhaps Helen's murder was connected with an obscure murder in Illinois more than twenty years ago before Dolly was born. It was a wishful thought, and I didn't mention it to Dr Godwin.

'I'm sorry I can't be more help to you,' he was saying. 'I have to go now, I'm already overdue for my hospital rounds.'

The sound of a motor detached itself from the traffic in the street, and slowed down. A car door was opened and closed. Men's footsteps came up the walk. Moving quickly for a big man, Godwin opened the door before they rang.

I couldn't see who his visitors were, but they were unwelcome ones. Godwin went rigid with hostility.

'Good morning, Sheriff,' he said.

Crane responded folksily: 'It's a hell of a morning and you know it. September's supposed to be our best month, but the bloody fog's so thick the airport's socked in.'

'You didn't come here to discuss the weather.'

'That's right, I didn't. I heard you got a fugitive from justice holed up here.'

'Where did you hear that?'

'I have my sources.'

'You'd better fire them, Sheriff. They're giving you misleading information.'

'Somebody is, doctor. Are you denying that Mrs Dolly Kincaid née McGee is in the building?'

Godwin hesitated. His heavy jaw got heavier. 'She is.'

'You said a minute ago she wasn't. What are you trying to pull, doc?'

'What are you trying to pull? Mrs Kincaird is not a fugitive. She's here because she's ill.'

'I wonder what made her ill. Can't she stand the sight of blood?'

Godwin's lips curled outward. He looked ready to spit in the other man's face. I couldn't see the Sheriff from where I sat, and I made no attempt to. I thought it was best for me to stay out of sight.

'It isn't just the weather that makes it a lousy day, doc. We had a lousy murder in town last night. I guess you know that, too. Probably Mrs Kincaid told you all about it.'

'Are you accusing her?' Godwin said.

'I wouldn't say that. Not yet, anyway.'

'Then beat it.'

'You can't talk like that to me.'

Godwin held himself motionless but his breath shook him as though he had a racing engine inside of him. 'You accused me in the presence of witnesses of harbouring a fugitive from justice. I could sue you for slander and by God I will if you don't stop harassing me and my patients.'

'I didn't mean it that way.' Crane's voice was much less.

confident. 'Anyway, I got a right to question a witness.'

'At some later time perhaps you have. At the present time Mrs Kincaid is under heavy sedation. I can't permit her to be questioned for at least a week.'

'A week?'

'It may be longer. I strongly advise you not to press the point. I'm prepared to go before a judge and certify that police questioning at the present time would endanger her health and perhaps her life.'

'I don't believe it.'

'I don't care what you believe.'

Godwin slammed the door and leaned on it, breathing like a runner. A couple of white-uniformed nurses who had been peeking through the inner door tried to look as if they had business there. He waved them away.

I said with unfeigned admiration: 'You really went to bat for her.'

'They did enough damage to her when she was a child. They're not going to compound it if I can help it.'

'How did they know she was here?'

'I have no idea. I can usually trust the staff to keep their mouths shut.' He gave me a probing look. 'Did you tell anyone?'

'Nobody connected with the law. Alex did mention to Alice Jenks that Dolly was here.'

'Perhaps he shouldn't have. Miss Jenks has worked for the county a long time, and Crane and she are old acquaintances.'

'She wouldn't tattle on her own niece, would she?'

'I don't know what she'd do.' Godwin tore off his smock and threw it at the chair where I had been sitting. 'Well, shall I let you out?'

He shook his keys like a jailer.

CHAPTER TWELVE

About half-way up the pass road I came out into sunlight. The fog below was like a sea of white water surging into the inlets of the mountains From the summit of the pass, where I paused for a moment, further mountains were visible on the inland horizon.

The wide valley between was full of light. Cattle grazed among the live oaks on the hillsides. A covey of quail marched across the road in front of my car like small plumed tipsy soldiers. I could smell newmown hay, and had the feeling that I had dropped down into a pastoral scene where nothing much had changed in a hundred years.

The town of Indian Springs didn't entirely dispel the feeling, though it had its service stations and its drive-ins offering hamburgers and *tacos*. It had a bit of old-time Western atmosphere, and more than a bit of the old-time sun-baked poverty of the West. Prematurely ageing women watched over their brown children in the dooryards of crumbling adobes. Most of the loiterers in the main street had Indian faces under their broad-brimmed hats. Banners advertising Old Rodeo Days hung limply over their heads.

Alice Jenks lived in one of the best houses on what appeared to be the best street. It was a two-storeyed white frame house, with deep porches upstairs and down, standing far back from the street behind a smooth green lawn. I stepped on to the grass and leaned on a pepper tree, fanning myself with my hat. I was five minutes early.

A rather imposing woman in a blue dress came out on the veranda. She looked me over as if I might possibly be a burglar cleverly creeping up on her house at eleven o'clock in the morning. She came down the steps and along the walk toward me. The sun flashed on her glasses and lent her searchlight eyes.

Close up, she wasn't so alarming. The brown eyes behind the glasses were strained and anxious. Her hair was streaked with grey. Her mouth was unexpectedly generous and even soft, but it was tweezered like a live thing between the harsh lines that thrust down from the base of her nose. The stiff blue dress that curved like armour plate over her monolithic bosom was old-fashioned in cut, and gave her a dowdy look. The valley sun had parched and roughened her skin.

'Are you Mr Archer?'

'Yes. How are you, Miss Jenks?'

'I'll survive.' Her handshake was like a man's. 'Come up on the porch, we can talk there.'

Her movements, like her speech, were so abrupt that they suggested the jitters. The jitters under firm, perhaps lifelong, control. She motioned me into a canvas glider and sat on a reed chair facing me, her back to the street. Three Mexican boys on one battered bicycle rode by precariously like high-wire artists.

'I don't know just what you want from me, Mr Archer. My niece appears to be in very serious trouble. I talked to a friend in the courthouse this morning –'

'The Sheriff?'

'Yes. He seems to think that Dolly is hiding from him.'

'Did you tell Sheriff Crane where she was?'

'Yes. Shouldn't I have?'

'He trotted right over to the nursing home to question her. Dr Godwin wouldn't let him.'

'Dr Godwin is a great one for taking matters into his own hands. I don't believe myself that people in trouble should be coddled and swaddled in cotton-wool, and what I believe for the rest of the world holds true for my own family. We've always been a law-abiding family, and if Dolly is holding something back, she ought to come out with it. I say the truth be told, and the chips fall where they may.'

It was quite a speech. She seemed to be renewing her old disagreement with Godwin about Dolly's testimony at the trial.

'Those chips can fall pretty hard, sometimes, when they fall on people you love.'

She watched me, her sensitive mouth held tight, as if I had accused her of a weakness. 'People I love?'

I had only an hour, and no sure intuition of how to reach her. 'I'm assuming you love Dolly.'

'I haven't seen her lately – she seems to have turned against me – but I'll always be fond of her. That doesn't mean' – and the deep lines reasserted themselves at the corners of her mouth – 'that I'll condone any wrongdoing on her part. I have a public position –'

'Just what is your position?'

'I'm senior county welfare worker for this area,' she announced. Then she looked anxiously behind her at the empty street, as if a posse might be on its way to relieve her of her post.

'Welfare begins at home.'

'Are you instructing me in the conduct of my private life?' She didn't wait for an answer. 'Let me tell you, you don't have to. Who do you think took the child in when my sister's marriage broke up? I did, of course. I gave them both a home, and after my sister was killed I brought my niece up as if she was my own daughter. I gave her the best of food and clothes, the best of education. When she wanted her own independence, I gave her that, too. I gave her the money to go and study in Los Angeles. What more could I do for her?'

'You can give her the benefit of the doubt right now. I don't know what the Sheriff said to you, but I'm pretty sure he was talking through his little pointed hat.'

Her face hardened. 'Sheriff Crane does not make mistakes.'

I had the sense of doubleness again, of talking on two levels. On the surface we were talking about Dolly's connection with the Haggerty killing but underneath this, though McGee had not been mentioned, we were arguing the question of McGee's guilt.

'All policemen make mistakes,' I said. 'All human beings make mistakes. It's possible that you and Sheriff Crane and the judge and the twelve jurors and everybody else were mistaken about Thomas McGee, and convicted an innocent man.'

She laughed in my face, not riotously. 'That's ridiculous, you didn't know Tom McGee. He was capable of anything. Ask anybody in this town. He used to get drunk and come home and beat her. More than once I had to stand him off with a gun, with the child holding on to my legs. More than once, after Constance left him, he came to this house and battered on the door and said he would drag her out of here by the hair. But I wouldn't let him.' She shook her head vehemently, and a strand of iron-grey hair fell like twisted wire across her cheek.

'What did he want from her?'

'He wanted domination. He wanted her under his thumb. But he had no right to her. We Jenks are the oldest family in town. The McGees across the river are the scum of the earth, most of them are on welfare to this day. He was one of the worst of them but my sister couldn't see it when he came courting her in his white sailor suit. He married her against Father's bitter objections. He gave her a dozen years of hell on earth and then he finally killed her. Don't tell me he was innocent. You don't know him. '

A scrub jay in the pepper tree heard her harsh obsessive voice and raised his own voice in counter-complaint. I said under his noise:

'Why did he kill your sister?'

'Out of sheer diabolical devilment. What he couldn't have he chose to destroy. It was as simple as that. It wasn't true that there was another man. She was faithful to him to the day she died. Even though they were living in separate houses, my sister kept herself pure.'

'Who said there was another man?'

She looked at me. The hot blood left her face. She seemed to lose the confidence that her righteous anger had given her.

'There were rumours,' she said weakly. 'Foul, dirty

rumours. There always are when there's bad blood between a husband and wife. Tom McGee may have started them himself. I know his lawyer kept hammering away at the idea of another man. It was all I could do to sit there and listen to him, trying to destroy my sister's reputation after that murdering client of his had already destroyed her life. But Judge Gahagan made it clear in his instructions to the jury that it was just a story he invented, with no basis in fact.'

'Who was McGee's lawyer?'

'An old fox named Gil Stevens. People don't go to him unless they're guilty, and he takes everything they have to get them off.'

'But he didn't get McGee off.'

'He practically did. Ten years is a small price to pay for first-degree murder. It should have been first-degree. He should have been executed.'

The woman was implacable. With a firm hand she pressed her stray lock of hair back into place. Her greying head was marcelled in neat little waves, all alike, like the sea in old steel engravings. Such implacability as hers, I thought, could rise from either one of two sources: righteous certainty, or a guilty dubious fear that she was wrong. I hesitated to tell her what Dolly had said, that she had lied her father into prison. But I intended to tell her before I left.

'I'm interested in the details of the murder. Would it be too painful for you to go into them?'

'I can stand a lot of pain. What do you want to know?'

'Just how it happened.'

'I wasn't here myself. I was at a meeting of the Native Daughters. I was president of the local group that year.' The memory of this helped to restore her composure.

'Still I'm sure you know as much about it as anyone.'

'No doubt I do. Except Tom McGee,' she reminded me.

'And Dolly.'

'Yes, and Dolly. The child was here in the house with Constance. They'd been living with me for some months. It was past nine o'clock, and she'd already gone to bed. Constance was downstairs sewing. My sister was a fine seamstress, and she made most of the child's clothes. She was making a dress for her that night. It got all spotted with blood. They made it an exhibit at the trial.'

Miss Jenks couldn't seem to forget the trial. Her eyes went vague, as if she could see it like a ritual continually being repeated in the courtroom of her mind.

'What were the circumstances of the shooting?'

'It was simple enough. He came to the front door. He talked her into opening it.'

'It's strange that he could do that, after her bad experiences with him.'

She brushed my objection aside with a flat movement of her hand. 'He could talk a bird out of a tree when he wanted to. At any rate, they had an argument. I suppose he wanted her to come back with him, as usual, and she refused. Dolly heard their voices raised in anger.'

'Where was she?'

'Upstairs in the front bedroom, which she shared with her mother.' Miss Jenks pointed upward at the boarded ceiling of the veranda. 'The argument woke the child up, and then she heard the shot. She went to the window and saw him run out to the street with the smoking gun in his hand. She came downstairs and found her mother in her blood.'

'Was she still alive?'

'She was dead. She died instantaneously, shot through the heart.'

'With what kind of a gun?'

'A medium-calibre hand-gun, the Sheriff thought. It was never found. McGee probably threw it in the sea. He was in Pacific Point when they arrested him next.'

'On Dolly's word?'

'She was the only witness, poor child.'

We seemed to have an unspoken agreement that Dolly existed only in the past. Perhaps because we were both avoiding the problem of Dolly's present situation, some of the tension between us had evaporated. I took advantage of this to ask Miss Jenks if I could look over the house.

'I don't see what for.'

'You've given me a very clear account of the murder. I want to try and relate it to the physical layout.'

She said doubtfully: 'I don't have much more time, and frankly I don't know how much more of this I can stand. My sister was very dear to me.'

'I know.'

'What are you trying to prove?'

'Nothing. I just want to understand what happened. It's my job.'

A job and its imperatives meant something to her. She got up, opened the front door, and pointed out the place just inside it where her sister's body had lain. There was of course no trace of the ten-year-old crime on the braided rag rug in the hall. No trace of it anywhere, except for the blind red smear it had left in Dolly's mind, and possibly in her aunt's.

I was struck by the fact that Dolly's mother and her friend Helen had both been shot at the front door of their homes by the same calibre gun, possibly held by the same person. I didn't mention this to Miss Jenks. It would only bring on another outburst against her brother-in-law McGee.

'Would you like a cup of tea?' she said unexpectedly.

'No thanks.'

'Or coffee? I use instant. It won't take long.'

'All right. You're very kind.'

She left me in the living-room. It was divided by sliding doors from the dining-room, and furnished with stiff old dark pieces reminiscent of a nineteenth-century parlour. There were mottoes on the walls instead of pictures, and one of them brought back with a rush and a pang my grandmother's house in Martinez. It said: 'He is the Silent Listener at Every Conversation.' My grandmother had hand-embroidered the same motto and hung it in her bedroom. She always whispered.

An upright grand piano with a closed keyboard stood in one corner of the room. I tried to open it, but it was locked. A photograph of two women and a child stood in the place of honour on the piano top. One of the women was Miss Jenks, younger but just as stout and overbearing. The other woman was still younger and much prettier. She held herself with the naïve sophistication of a small-town belle. The child between them, with one hand in each of theirs, was Dolly aged about ten.

Miss Jenks had come through the sliding doors with a coffee tray. 'That's the three of us.' As if two women and a little girl made a complete family. 'And that's my sister's piano. She played beautifully. I never could master the instrument myself.'

She wiped her glasses. I didn't know whether they were clouded by emotion or by the steam from the coffee. Over it she related some of Constance's girlhood triumphs. She had won a prize for piano, another for voice. She did extremely well in high school, especially in French, and she was all set to go to college, as Alice had gone before her, when that smooth-talking devil of a Tom McGee —

I left most of my coffee and went out into the hallway. It smelled of the mould that invades old houses. I caught a glimpse of myself in the clouded mirror beside the deer-horn hat-rack. I looked like a ghost from the present haunting a bloody moment in the past. Even the woman behind me had an insubstantial quality, as if her large body was a husk or shell from which the essential being had departed. I found myself associating the smell of mould with her.

A rubber-treaded staircase rose at the rear of the hall. I was moving toward it as I said:

'Do you mind if I look at the room Dolly occupied?'

She allowed my momentum to carry her along and up the stairs. 'It's my room now.'

'I won't disturb anything.'

The blinds were drawn, and she turned on the overhead light for me. It had a pink shade which suffused the room with pinkness. The floor was thickly carpeted with a soft loose pink material. A pink decorated spread covered the queen-sized bed. The elaborate three-mirrored dressing-table was trimmed with pink silk flounces, and so was the upholstered chair in front of it.

A quilted pink long chair stood by the window with an open magazine across its foot. Miss Jenks picked up the magazine and rolled it in her hands so that its cover wasn't visible. But I knew a *True Romance* when I saw one.

I crossed the room, sinking to the ankles in the deep pink pile of her fantasy, and raised the blind over the front window. I could see the wide flat second-storey porch, and through its railings the pepper tree, and my car in the street. The three Mexican boys came by on their bicycle, one on the handlebars, one on the seat, one on the carrier, trailed by a red mongrel which had joined the act.

'They have no right to be riding like that,' Miss Jenks said at my shoulder. 'I have a good mind to report them to the deputy. And that dog shouldn't be running around loose.'

'He's doing no harm.'

'Maybe not, but we had a case of hydrophobia two years ago.'

'I'm more interested in ten years ago. How tall was your niece at that time?'

'She was a good big girl for her age. About four feet and a half. Why?'

I adjusted my height by getting down on my knees. From this position I could see the lacy branches of the pepper tree, and through them most of my car, but nothing nearer. A man leaving the house would scarcely be visible until he passed the pepper tree, at least forty feet away. A gun in his hand could not be seen until he reached the street. It was a hasty and haphazard experiment, but its result underlined the question in my mind.

I got up off my knees. 'Was it dark that night?'

She knew which night I meant. 'Yes. It was dark.'

'I don't see any street lights.'

'No. We have none. This is a poor town, Mr Archer.'

'Was there a moon?'

'No. I don't believe so. But my niece has excellent eye-sight. She can spot the markings on a bird –'

'At night?'

'There's always some light. Anyway, she'd know her own father.' Miss Jenks corrected herself: 'She *knew* her own father.'

'Did she tell you this?'

'Yes. I was the first one she told.'

'Did you question her about it in any detail?'

'I didn't, no. She was quite broken up, naturally. I didn't want to subject her to the strain.'

'But you didn't mind subjecting her to the strain of testify-ing to these things in court.'

'It was necessary, necessary to the prosecution's case. And it did her no harm.'

'Dr Godwin thinks it did her a lot of harm, that the strain she went through then is partly responsible for her break-down.'

'Dr Godwin has his ideas and I have mine. If you want my opinion, he's a dangerous man, a troublemaker. He has no respect for authority, and I have no respect for a man like that.'

'You used to respect him. You sent your niece to him for treatment.'

'I know more about him now than I did then.'

'Do you mind telling me why she needed treatment?'

'No, I don't mind.' She was still trying to preserve a friendly surface, though we were both conscious of the dis-agreement simmering under it. 'Dolly wasn't doing well in school. She wasn't happy or popular. Which was natural enough with her parents – I mean, her father, making a shambles of their home together.

'This isn't the backwoods,' she said as if she suspected maybe it was, 'and I thought the least I could do was see that she got a little help. Even the people on welfare get family counselling when they need it. So I persuaded my sister to take her into Pacific Point to see Dr Godwin. He was the best we had at that time. Constance drove her in every Saturday morning for about a year. The child showed con-siderable improvement, I'll say that much for Godwin. So did

Constance. She seemed brighter and happier and surer of herself.'

'Was she getting treatment, too?'

'I guess she had a little, and of course it did her good to get into town every Saturday. She wanted to move into town but there was no money for it. She left McGee and moved in with me instead. That took some of the strain off her. He couldn't stand to see that. He couldn't stand to see her getting her dignity back. He killed her like a dog in the manger.'

After ten years her mind was still buzzing like a fly around the bloody moment.

'Why didn't you continue Dolly's therapy? She probably needed it more than ever afterward?'

'It wasn't possible. I work Saturday mornings. I have to get my paperwork done some time.' She fell silent, confused and tongue-tied as honest people can be by their own deviousness.

'Also you had a disagreement with Godwin about your niece's testimony at the trial.'

'I'm not ashamed of it, no matter what *he* says. It did her no harm to speak out about her father. It probably did her good. She had to get it out of her system somehow.'

'It isn't out of her system, though. She's still hung up on it.' Just as you are, Miss Jenks. 'But now she's changed her story.'

'Changed her story?'

'She says now that she didn't see her father the night of the murder. She denies that he had anything to do with it.'

'Who told you that?'

'Godwin. He'd just been talking to her. She told him she lied in court to please the adults.' I was tempted to say more, but remembered in time that it would almost certainly be relayed to her friend the Sheriff.

She was looking at me as if I had questioned a basic faith of her life. 'He's twisting what she said, I'm sure. He's using her to prove that he was right when he was wrong.'

'I doubt that, Miss Jenks. Godwin doesn't believe her new story himself.'

'You see! She's either crazy or she's lying! Don't forget she's got McGee blood in her!' She was appalled by her own outburst. She turned her eyes away, glancing around the pink room as though it might somehow vouch for the girlish innocence of her intentions. 'I didn't really mean that,' she said. 'I love my niece. It's just — it's harder than I thought to rake over the past like this.'

'I'm sorry, and I'm sure you love your niece. Feeling about her the way you do, and did, you couldn't have fed her a false story to tell in court.'

'Who says I did?'

'No one. I'm saying you couldn't have. You're not the sort of woman who could bring herself to corrupt the mind of a twelve-year-old child.'

'No,' she said. 'I had nothing to do with Dolly's accusation against her father. She came to me with it, the night it happened, within half an hour of the *time* it happened. I never questioned it for a minute. It had all the accents of truth.'

But she had not. I didn't think she was lying, exactly. More likely she was suppressing something. She spoke carefully and in a low voice, so that the motto in the living-room wouldn't hear her. She still wasn't meeting my eyes. A slow dull flush rose from her heavy neck to her face. I said:

'I doubt that it was physically possible for her to identify anyone, even her own father, at this distance on a dark night – let alone pick out a smoking gun in his hand.'

'But the police accepted it. Sheriff Crane and the DA both believed her.'

'Policemen and prosecutors are usually glad to accept the facts, or the pseudo-facts, that fit their case.'

'But Tom McGee was guilty. He was guilty.'

'He may have been.'

'Then why are you trying to convince me that he wasn't?' The flush of shame in her face was going through the usual conversion into a flush of anger. 'I won't listen.'

'You might as well listen. What can you lose? I'm trying to open up that old case because it's connected, through Dolly, with the Haggerty case.'

'Do you believe she killed Miss Haggerty?' she said.

'No. Do you?'

'Sheriff Crane seems to regard her as the main suspect.'

'Did he say so to you, Miss Jenks?'

'He as much as said so. He was feeling me out on what my reaction would be if he took her in for questioning.'

'And what was your reaction?'

'I hardly know, I was so upset. I haven't seen Dolly for some time. She went and married behind my back. She was always a good girl, but she may have changed.'

I had the feeling that Miss Jenks was talking out of her deepest sense of herself: She had always been a good girl, but she might have changed.

'Why don't you call Crane up and tell him to lay off? Your niece needs delicate handling.'

'You don't believe she's guilty of this murder?'

'I said I didn't. Tell him to lay off or he'll lose the next election.'

'I couldn't do that. He's my senior in county work.' But she was thinking about it. She shook the thought off. 'Speaking of which, I've given you all the time I possibly can. It must be past twelve.'

I was ready to leave. It had been a long hour. She followed me downstairs and out on to the veranda. I had the impression as we said goodbye that she wanted to say something more. Her face was expectant. But nothing came.

CHAPTER THIRTEEN

The fog had thinned out a little along the coastline, but you still couldn't see the sun, only a sourceless white glare that hurt the eyes. The keyboy at the Mariner's Rest told me that Alex had driven away with an older man in a new Chrysler. His own red sports car was still in the parking enclosure, and he hadn't checked out.

I bought a sandwich at a drive-in down the street and ate it in my room. Then I made a couple of frustrating phone calls. The switchboard operator at the courthouse said there wasn't a chance of getting hold of a trial transcript this afternoon: everything was locked up tight for the week-end. I called the office of Gil Stevens, the lawyer who had unsuccessfully defended Tom McGee. His answering service said he was in Balboa. No, I couldn't reach him there. Mr Stevens was racing his yacht today and tomorrow.

I decided to drop in on Jerry Marks, the young lawyer who had acted as Mrs Perrine's defence counsel. His office was in a new shopping centre not too far from the motel strip. Jerry was unmarried and ambitious, and he might be in it, even on a Saturday afternoon.

The front door was open and I walked into the waiting-room, which was furnished with maple and chintz. The secretary's cubicle behind the glass half-wall on the left was deserted for the week-end, but Jerry Marks was in the inner office.

'How are you, Jerry?'

'I'm all right.'

He looked at me guardedly over the book he was reading, an enormous tome entitled *Rules of Evidence*. He wasn't very experienced in criminal practice, but he was competent and honest. His homely Middle-European face was warmed and lit by intelligent brown eyes.

'How's Mrs Perrine?' I said.

'I haven't seen her since she was released, and I don't expect to. I seldom see much of my ex-clients. I smell of the courtroom to them. '

'I have the same experience. Are you free?'

'Yeah, and I'm going to stay that way. I promised myself a clear week-end of study, murder or no murder.'

'You know about the Haggerty murder then.'

'Naturally, it's all over town.'

'What have you heard?'

'Really not very much. Somebody at the courthouse told my secretary that this lady professor was shot by a girl student at the college. I forget her name.'

'Dolly Kincaid. Her husband is my client. She's in a nursing home, under a doctor's care.'

'Psycho?'

'It depends on your definition of psycho. It's a complex situation, Jerry. I doubt that she's legally insane under the McNaghten rule. On the other hand I very much doubt that she did the shooting at all.'

'You're trying to get me interested in the case,' he said suspiciously.

'I'm not trying to do anything to you. Actually I came to you for information. What's your opinion of Gil Stevens?'

'He's the local old master. Get him.'

'He's out of town. Seriously, is he a good lawyer?'

'Stevens is the most successful criminal lawyer in the county. He has to be good. He knows law, and he knows juries. He does pull some old-fashioned courtroom shenanigans that I wouldn't use myself. He's quite an actor, heavy with the emotion. It works, though. I can't remember when he's lost an important case.'

'I can. About ten years ago he defended a man named Tom McGee who was convicted of shooting his wife.'

'That was before my time.'

'Dolly Kincaid is McGee's daughter. Also, she was the key witness for the prosecution at her father's trial.'

Jerry whistled. 'I see what you mean by complex.' After

a pause, he said: 'Who's her doctor?'

'Godwin.'

He pushed out his heavy lips. 'I'd go easy with him.'

'What do you mean?'

'I'm sure he's a good psychiatrist, but maybe not so much in the forensic department. He's a very bright man and he doesn't hide his light under a bushel, in fact he sometimes acts like a mastermind. Which puts people's backs up, especially if their name is Gahagan and they're sitting on the Superior Court bench. So I'd use him sparingly.'

'I can't control the use that's made of him.'

'No, but you can warn her attorney —'

'It would be a lot simpler if you were her attorney. I haven't had a chance to talk to her husband today, but I think he'll go along with my recommendation. His family isn't poverty-stricken, by the way.'

'It wasn't the money I was thinking about,' Jerry said coldly. 'I promised myself that I'd spend this week-end with my books.'

'Helen Haggerty should have picked another week-end to get herself shot.'

It came out harsher than I intended. My own failure to do anything for Helen was eating me.

Jerry regarded me quizzically. 'This case is a personal matter with you?'

'It seems to be.'

'Okay, okay,' he said. 'What do you want me to do?'

'Just hold yourself in readiness for the present.'

'I'll be here all afternoon. After that my answering service will be able to contact me.'

I thanked him and went back to the motel. Alex's room next to mine was still empty. I checked with my own answering service in Hollywood. Arnie Walters had left his number for me and I called Reno.

Arnie was out of the office, but his wife and partner Phyllis took the call. Her exuberant femininity bounced along the wires:

'I never *see* you, Lew. All I hear is your voice on the telephone. For all I know you don't exist any more, but simply made some tapes a number of years ago and somebody plays them to me from time to time.'

'How do you explain the fact that I'm responsive? Like now.'

'Electronics. I explain everything I don't understand electronically. It saves me no end of trouble. But when am I oing to *see* you?'

'This week-end, if Arnie's tabbed the driver of the con-
ertible.'

'He hasn't quite done that, but he does have a line on the
>wner. She's a Mrs Sally Burke and she lives right here in
Reno. She claims her car was stolen a couple of days ago. But
Arnie doesn't believe her.'

'Why not?'

'He's very intuitive. Also she didn't report the alleged
heft. Also she has boy-friends of various types. Arnie's out
loing leg-work on them now.'

'Good.'

'I gather this is important,' Phyllis said.

'It's a double murder case, maybe a triple. My client's a
'oung girl with emotional problems. She's probably going to
>e arrested today or tomorrow, for something she almost
>ertainly didn't do.'

'You sound very intense.'

'This case has gotten under my skin. Also I don't know
where I'm at.'

'I never heard you admit that before, Lew. Anyway, I was
hinking before you called, maybe I could strike up an ac-
>uaintance with Mrs Sally Burke. Does that sound like a
>ood idea to you?'

'An excellent idea.' Phyllis was an ex-Pinkerton operative
vho looked like an ex-chorus girl. 'Remember Mrs Burke
nd her playmates may be highly dangerous. They may have
illed a woman last night.'

'Not this woman. I've got too much to live for.' She
neant Arnie.

We exchanged some further pleasantries in the course of
vhich I heard people coming into Alex's room next door.
After I said goodbye to Phyllis I stood by the wall and
stened. Alex's voice and the voice of another man were raised
n argument, and I didn't need a contact mike to tell what the
rgument was about. The other man wanted Alex to clear out
f this unfortunate mess and come home.

I knocked on his door.

'Let me handle them,' the other man said, as if he was
xpecting the police.

He stepped outside, a man of about my age, good-looking
n a greyish way, with a thin face, narrow light eyes, a pugna-
ious chin. The mark of organization was on him, like an
nvisible harness worn under his conservative grey suit.

There was some kind of desperation in him, too. He didn't

even ask who I was before he said: 'I'm Frederick Kincaid
and you have no right to chivvy my son around. He has
nothing to do with that girl and her crimes. She married him
under false pretences. The marriage didn't last twenty-four
hours. My son is a respectable boy –'

Alex stepped out and pulled at the older man's arm. His
face was miserable with embarrassment. 'You'd better come
inside, Dad. This is Mr Archer.'

'Archer, eh? I understand you've involved my son in this
thing –'

'On the contrary, he hired me.'

'I'm firing you.' His voice sounded as if it had often performed this function.

'We'll talk it over,' I said.

The three of us jostled each other in the doorway. Kincaid
senior didn't want me to come in. It was very close to turning
into a brawl. Each of us was ready to hit at least one of the
others.

I bulled my way into the room and sat down in a chair with
my back to the wall. 'What's happened, Alex?'

'Dad heard about me on the radio. He phoned the Sheriff
and found out where I was. The Sheriff called us over there
just now. They found the murder gun.'

'Where?'

Alex was slow in answering, as though the words in his
mouth would make the whole thing more real when he let
them out. His father answered for him:

'Where she hid it, under the mattress of the bed in that
little hut she's been living in –'

'It isn't a hut,' Alex said. 'It's a gatehouse.'

'Don't contradict me, Alex.'

'Did you see the gun?' I said.

'We did. The Sheriff wanted Alex to identify it, which
naturally he couldn't do. He didn't even know she had a gun.'

'What kind of a gun is it?'

'It's a Smith and Wesson revolver, .38 calibre, with walnut
grips. Old, but in pretty fair condition. She probably bought
it at a pawn shop.'

'Is this the police theory?'

'The Sheriff mentioned the possibility.'

'How does he know it's hers?'

'They found it under her mattress, didn't they?' Kincaid
talked like a prosecutor making a case, using it to bring his
son into line. 'Who else could have hidden it there?'

'Practically anybody else. The gatehouse was standing

open last night, wasn't it, Alex?'

'It was when I got there.'

'Let me do the talking,' his father said. 'I've had more experience in these matters.'

'It hasn't done you a hell of a lot of good. Your son is a witness, and I'm trying to get at the facts.'

He stood over me with his hands on his hips, vibrating. 'My son has nothing whatever to do with this case.'

'Don't kid yourself. He's married to the girl.'

'The marriage is meaningless – a boyish impulse that didn't last one full day. I'm having it annulled. It wasn't even consummated, he tells me.'

'You can't annul it.'

'Don't tell me what I can do.'

'I think I will, though. All you can do is annul yourself and your son. There's more to a marriage than sexual consummation or legal technicalities. The marriage is real because it's real for Alex.'

'He wants out of it now.'

'I don't believe you.'

'It's true, isn't it, Alex, you want to come home with me and Mother? She's terribly worried about you. Her heart is kicking up again.' Kincaid was throwing everything but the kitchen sink.

Alex looked from him to me. 'I don't know. I just want to do what's right.'

Kincaid started to say something, probably having to do with the kitchen sink, but I talked over him:

'Then answer another question or two, Alex. Was Dolly carrying a gun when she came running back to the gatehouse last night?'

'I didn't see one.'

Kincaid said: 'She probably had it concealed under her clothes.'

'Shut up, Kincaid,' I said calmly from my sitting position. 'I don't object to the fact that you're a bloodless bastard. You obviously can't help it. I do object to your trying to make Alex into one. Leave him a choice, at least.'

Kincaid sputtered a couple of times, and walked away from me. Alex said without looking at either of us: 'Don't talk to my father that way, Mr Archer.'

'All right. She was wearing a cardigan and a blouse and skirt. Anything else?'

'No.'

'Carrying a bag?'

'I don't think so.'

'Think.'

'She wasn't.'

'Then she couldn't have been carrying a concealed .38 calibre revolver. You didn't see her hide it under the mattress?'

'No.'

'And were you with her all the time, between the time she got back and the time she left for the nursing home?'

'Yes, I was with her all the time.'

'Then it's pretty clear it isn't Dolly's gun, or at least it wasn't Dolly who hid it under the mattress. Do you have any idea who it could have been?'

'No.'

'You said it was the murder gun. How did they establish that? They haven't had time for ballistics tests.'

Kincaid spoke up from the far corner where he had been sulking: 'It's the right calibre to fit the wound, and one shell had been fired, recently. It stands to reason it's the gun she used.'

'Do you believe that, Alex?'

'I don't know.'

'Have they questioned her?'

'They intend to. The Sheriff said something about waiting until they nailed it down with ballistic evidence. Monday.' That gave me a little time, if I could believe Alex. The pressures of the night and morning, on top of the uncertainties of the last three weeks, had left him punchy. He looked almost out on his feet.

'I think we all should wait,' I said, 'before we make up our minds about your wife. Even if she's guilty, which I very strongly doubt, you owe her all the help and support you can give her.'

'He owes her nothing,' Kincaid said. 'Not a thing. She married him fraudulently. She lied to him again and again.'

I kept my voice and temper down, for contrast. 'She still needs medical care, and she needs a lawyer. I have a good local lawyer waiting to step in, but I can't retain him myself.'

'You're taking quite a lot into your hands, aren't you?'

'Somebody has to assume responsibility. There's a lot of it floating around loose at the moment. You can't avoid it by crawling into a hole and pulling the hole in after you. The girl's in trouble, and whether you like it or not she's a member of your family.'

Alex appeared to be listening. I didn't know if he was hearing me. His father shook his narrow grey head:

'She's no member of my family, and I'll tell you one thing for certain. She's not going to drag my son down into the underworld. And neither are you.' He turned to Alex. 'How much have you already paid this man?'

'A couple of hundred.'

Kincaird said to me: 'You've been amply paid, exorbitantly paid. You heard me fire you. This is a private room and if you persist in intruding I'll call the management. If they can't handle you I'll call the police.'

Alex looked at me and lifted his hands, not very far, in a helpless movement. His father put an arm around his shoulders.

'I'm only doing what's best for you, son. You don't belong with these people. We'll go home and cheer up Mother. After all you don't want to drive her into her grave.'

It came out smooth and pat, and it was the clincher. Alex didn't look at me again. I went back to my own room and phoned Jerry Marks and told him I had lost a client and so had he. Jerry seemed disappointed.

CHAPTER FOURTEEN

Alex and his father vacated their room and drove away. I didn't go out to see them off but I could hear the sound of their engines, quickly muffled by the fog. I sat and let my stomach unknot, telling myself I should have handled them better. Kincaid was a frightened man who valued his status the way some previous generations valued their souls.

I drove up Foothill to the Bradshaw house. The Dean was probably another breakable reed, but he had money, and he had shown some sympathy for Dolly, over and above his official interest in the case. I had no desire to continue it on my own. I needed a principal, preferable one who swung some weight locally. Alice Jenks met this requirement, more or less, but I didn't want her for a client.

A deputy was standing guard at the gatehouse. He wouldn't let me in to look around but he didn't object to my going up to the main house. The Spanish woman Maria answered the door.

'Is Dr Bradshaw home?'

'No sir.'

'Where can I find him?'

She shrugged. 'I dunno. I think Mrs Bradshaw said he's gone for the week-end.'

'That's queer. I'd like to talk to Mrs Bradshaw.'

'I'll see if she's busy.'

I stepped inside uninvited and sat on a gilt chair in the entrance hall while Maria went upstairs. She came down and told me that Mrs Bradshaw would be with me shortly.

It was at least half an hour before she came limping down. She had primped her grey head and rouged her cheeks and put on a dress with lace at her slack throat held in place by a diamond brooch. I wondered, as she made me the dubious gift of her hand, if all this had been done for my benefit.

The old lady seemed glad to see me. 'How are you, Mr – it's Mr Archer, isn't it? I've been so hoping somebody would call. This fog makes one feel so isolated, and with my driver gone –' She seemed to hear the note of complaint rising in her voice, and cut it off. 'How is the girl?' she said briskly.

'She's being taken care of. Dr Godwin thinks she's better than she was last night.'

'Good. You'll be glad to know,' she said with a bright ironic stare, 'that I'm somewhat better myself than I was last night. My son informed me this morning that I staged one of my exhibitions, as he calls them. Frankly, I was upset. Nights aren't my best season.'

'It was a rough night for everybody.'

'And I'm a selfish old woman. Isn't that what you're thinking?'

'People don't seem to change much as they get older.'

'That has all the earmarks of an insult.' But she was smiling, almost flirtatiously. 'You imply that I've always been this way.'

'You'd know better than I would.'

She laughed outright. It wasn't a joyous sound, but there was humour in it. 'You're a bold young man, and a bright one. I like bright young men. Come into the study and I'll see that you get a drink.'

'Thank you, but I can't stay –'

'Then I'll sit here.' She lowered herself carefully on to the gilt chair. 'My moral qualities may not have altered for the worse. My physical capabilities certainly have. This fog is very bad for my arthritis.' She added, with a gingerly shake of her head: 'But I mustn't complain. I promised my son, in penance for last night, that I would go through an entire day without uttering a word of complaint.'

'How are you doing?'

'Not so well,' she said with her wry and wrinkled smile. 'It's like solitaire, you always cheat a little. Or don't you?'

'I don't play the game.'

'You're not missing a great deal, but it helps to pass the days for me. Well, I won't keep you if you have business.'

'I have business with Dr Bradshaw. Do you know where I can contact him?'

'Roy flew to Reno this morning.'

'Reno?'

'Not to gamble, I assure you. He hasn't an iota of gambling instinct. In fact I sometimes think he's excessively cautious. Roy is a bit of a mother's boy, wouldn't you say?' She looked up at me with complex irony, unembarrassed by his condition or her complicity in it.

'I'm a little surprised that he'd go away in the middle of his murder case.'

'So was I, but there was no stopping him. He isn't exactly running away from it. They're holding a conference of small-college deans at the University of Nevada. It's been planned for months, and Roy is slated as one of the principal speakers. He felt it was his duty to be there. But I could see very well that he was eager to go. He loves the public eye, you know – he's always been a bit of an actor – but he isn't so terribly fond of the responsibilities that go with it.'

I was amused and intrigued and a little appalled by her realism. She seemed to be enjoying it herself. Conversation was better than solitaire.

Mrs Bradshaw rose creakingly and leaned on my arm. 'You might as well come into the study. It's draughty here. I've taken a fancy to you, young man.'

I didn't know if this was a blessing or a curse. She grinned up into my face as if she could read my doubts there. 'Don't worry, I won't eat you.' She placed the emphasis on the final word, as though she had already eaten her son for breakfast.

We went into the study together and sat in facing high-backed leather chairs. She rang for Maria and ordered me a highball. Then she leaned back and scanned the bookshelves. The phalanxes of books seemed to remind her of Bradshaw's importance.

'Don't misunderstand me. I love my son profoundly and I'm proud of him. I'm proud of his good looks and I'm proud of his brains. He graduated *summa cum laude* from Harvard and went on to take a most distinguished doctorate. One of

99

these days he's going to be the president of a major university or a great foundation.'

'Is he ambitious, or are you?'

'I used to be, for him. As Roy became more ambitious, became less so. There are better things in life than climbing an endless ladder. I haven't entirely given up hope that he'll marry.' She cocked a bright old eye at me. 'He *likes* women, you know.'

'I'm sure he does.'

'In fact I was beginning to persuade myself that he was interested in Miss Haggerty. I've never known him to pay so much attention to any other woman.' She dropped the statement so that it became a question.

'He mentioned to me that he took her out several times. But he also said that they were never close in any way. His reaction to her death confirmed that.'

'What was his reaction to her death?'

I'd done a lot of pumping in my time, and I knew when it was being done to me. 'I mean his general reaction. He wouldn't have flown to Reno this morning, deans' conference or no deans' conference, if he had been really fond of Helen Haggerty. He'd be here in Pacific Point trying to find out who did her in.'

'You seem quite let down about it.'

'I was looking for his help. He seemed genuinely concerned about Dolly Kincaid.'

'He is. We both are. In fact Roy asked me at breakfast to do what I could for the girl. But what can I do?' She displayed her crumpled hands, making a show of her helplessness.

Maria came in with my clinking highball, handed it to me unceremoniously, and asked her employer if there was anything else. There wasn't. I sipped my drink, wondering if Mrs Bradshaw was a client I could possibly handle, if she became my client. She had the money, all right. The diamond winking at her throat would have bought my services for several years.

'You can hire me,' I said.

'Hire you?'

'If you really want to do something for Dolly, and not just sit there paying lip-service to the idea. Do you think we could get along?'

'I was getting along with men when you were in the cradle, Mr Archer. Are you implying I can't get along with people?—'

'I seem to be the one who can't. Alex Kincaid just fired me, with a strong assist from his father. They want no part of Dolly and her problems, now that the chips are down.'

Her black eyes flashed. 'I saw through that boy immediately. He's a mollycoddle.'

'I don't have the resources to go on by myself. It isn't good practice, anyway. I need somebody to back me, preferably somebody with local standing and – I'll be frank – a substantial bank balance.'

'How much would it cost me?'

'It depends on how long the case goes on and how many ramifications develop. I get a hundred a day and expenses. Also I have a team of detectives in Reno working on a lead that may be a hot one.'

'A lead in Reno?'

'It originated here, last night.'

I told her about the man in the convertible which belonged to Mrs Sally Burke, a woman with many boy-friends. She leaned forward in her chair with mounting interest:

'Why aren't the police working on that lead?'

'They may be. If they are, I don't know about it. They seem to have settled for the idea that Dolly's guilty and everything else is irrelevant. It's simpler that way.'

'You don't accept that idea?'

'No.'

'In spite of the gun they found in her bed?'

'You know about that, then.'

'Sheriff Crane showed it to me this morning. He wanted to know if I recognized it. Of course I didn't. I abhor the very sight of guns myself. I've never permitted Roy to own a gun.'

'And you have no idea who owned that one?'

'No, but the Sheriff appeared to take it for granted that it was Dolly's, and that it tied her to the murder.'

'We have no reason to think it was hers. If it was, the last place she'd put it would be under her own mattress. Her husband denies she did, and he was with her continuously once she got back to the gatehouse. There's the further point that there's no definite proof it's the murder weapon.'

'Really?'

'Really. It will take ballistics tests, and they're not scheduled until Monday. If my luck holds, I think I can throw more light on the situation by then.'

'Do you have a definite theory of your own, Mr Archer?'

'I have an idea that the ramifications of this thing go far back beyond Dolly. It wasn't Dolly who threatened Miss Haggerty's life. She would have recognized her voice, they were close friends. I think Dolly walked up to her house simply to ask her advice about whether to go back to her husband. She stumbled over the body and panicked. She's still in panic.'

'Why?'

'I'm not prepared to explain it. I want to go into her background further. I also want to go into Miss Haggerty's background.'

'That might be interesting,' she said, as if she was considering attending a double-feature movie. 'How much is all this going to cost me?'

'I'll keep it as low as I can. But it could mount up in the thousands, two or three or even four.'

'That's rather an expensive penance.'

'Penance?'

'For all my selfishness, past and present and future. I'll think about it, Mr Archer.'

'How long do you need to think about it?'

'Call me to-night. Roy will be telephoning me around dinner-time – he telephones me every night when he's away – and I couldn't possibly give you an answer before I discuss it with him. We live on a tighter budget than you might think,' she said earnestly, fingering the diamonds at her throat.

CHAPTER FIFTEEN

I drove up under the dripping trees to Helen Haggerty's place. Two deputies messing around outside the front door wouldn't let me in or answer any questions. It was turning out to be a bad day.

I drifted over to the campus and into the Administration Building. I had some idea of talking to Laura Sutherland, the Dean of Women, but her office was locked. All the offices were locked. The building was deserted except for a white-headed man in blue jeans who was sweeping the corridor with a long-handled push-broom. He looked like Father Time, and I had a nightmare moment of thinking that he was sweeping Helen's last vestiges away.

In a kind of defensive reflex I got out my notebook and looked up the name of the chairman of the modern languages department. Dr Geisman. The old man with the push-broom knew where his office was:

'It's in the new Humanities Building, down the line.' He pointed. 'But he won't be there on a Saturday afternoon.'

The old man was mistaken. I found Geisman in the department office on the first floor of the Humanities Building, sitting with a telephone receiver in one hand and a pencil in the other. I had seen him coming out of Bradshaw's conference the day before, a heavy middle-aged man with thick spectacles imperfectly masking anxious little eyes.

'One moment,' he said to me; and into the telephone: 'I'm sorry you can't help us, Mr Bass. I realize you have your family responsibilities and of course the remuneration is not great for a special lecturer.'

He sounded foreign, though he had no accent. His voice was denatured, as if English was just another language he had learned.

'I am Dr Geisman,' he said as he hung up and stroked out a name on the list in front of him. 'Are you Dr de Falla?'

'No. My name is Archer.'

'What are your qualifications? Do you have an advanced degree?'

'In the university of hard knocks.'

He didn't respond to my smile. 'A member of our faculty is defunct, as you must know, and I've had to give up my Saturday to an attempt to find a replacement for her. If you expect me to take your application seriously –'

'I'm not applying for anything, doctor, except possibly a little information. I'm a private detective investigating Professor Haggerty's death, and I'm interested in how she happened to land here.'

'I have no time to go into all that again. There are classes which must be met on Monday. If this Dr de Falla doesn't arrive, or proves impossible, I don't know what to do.' He peered at his wristwatch. 'I'm due at the Los Angeles airport at six-thirty.'

'You can spare five minutes, anybody can.'

'Very well. Five minutes.' He tapped the crystal of his watch. 'You wish to know how Miss Haggerty came here? I can't say, except that she appeared in my office one day and asked for a position. She had heard about Professor Farrand's heart attack. This is our second emergency in a month.'

'Who told her about the heart attack?'

'I don't know. Perhaps Dean Sutherland. She gave Dean Sutherland as a local reference. But it was common knowledge, it was in the paper.'

'Was she living here before she applied for a job with you?'

'I believe so. Yes, she was. She told me she already had a house. She liked the place, and wished to remain. She was very eager for the post. Frankly, I had some doubts about her. She had a master's degree from Chicago but she wasn't fully qualified. The school where she had been teaching, Maple Park, is not credentialled on our level. But Dean Sutherland told me she needed the position and I let her have it, unfortunately.'

'I understood she had a private income.'

He pursed his lips and shook his head. 'Ladies with a private income don't take on four sections of French and German, plus counselling duties, at a salary of less than five thousand dollars. Perhaps she meant her alimony. She told me she was having difficulty collecting her alimony.' His spectacles glinted as he looked up. 'You knew that she had been recently divorced?'

'I heard that. Do you know where her ex-husband is?'

'No. I had very few words with her at any time. Do you suspect him?'

'I have no reason to. But when a woman is killed you normally look for a man who had a motive to kill her. The local police have other ideas.'

'You don't agree with them?'

'I'm keeping my mind open, doctor.'

'I see. They tell me one of our students is under suspicion.'

'So I hear. Do you know the girl?'

'No. She was registered for none of our departmental courses, fortunately.'

'Why "fortunately"?'

'She is psychoneurotic, they tell me.' His myopic eyes looked as vulnerable as open oysters under the thick lenses of his glasses. 'If the administration employed proper screening procedures we would not have students of that sort on the campus, endangering our lives. But we are very backward here in some respects.' He tapped the crystal of his watch again. 'You've had your five minutes.'

'One more question, doctor. Have you been in touch with Helen Haggerty's family?'

'Yes. I phoned her mother early this morning. Dean Bradshaw asked me to perform that duty, though properly I should think it was his duty. The mother, Mrs Hoffman, is flying out here and I have to meet her at the Los Angeles airport.'

'At six-thirty?'

He nodded dismally. 'There seems to be no one else available. Both our deans are out of town –'

'Dean Sutherland, too?'

'Dean Sutherland, too. They've gone off and left the whole business on my shoulders.' His glasses blurred with self-pity, and he took them off to wipe them. 'It's foggy, and I can't see to drive properly. My eyesight is so poor that without my glasses I can't tell the difference between you and the Good Lord Himself.'

'There isn't much difference.'

He put on his glasses, saw that this was a joke, and emitted a short barking laugh.

'What plane is Mrs Hoffman coming in on, doctor?'

'United, from Chicago. I promised to meet her at the United baggage counter.'

'Let me.'

'Are you serious?'

'It will give me a chance to talk to her. Where do you want me to bring her?'

'I reserved her a room at the Pacific Hotel. I could meet you there, at eight, say.'

'Fine.'

He got up and came around the desk and shook my hand vigorously. As I was leaving the building, a small, old man in a black hat and a greenish black cloak came sidling out of the fog. He had a dyed-looking black moustache, hectic blue eyes, a wine flush on his hollow cheeks.

'Dr de Falla?'

He nodded. I held the door for him. He swept off his hat and bowed.

'Merci beaucoup.'

His rubber-soled shoes made no more sound than a spider. I had another one of my little nightmare moments. This one was Doctor Death.

CHAPTER SIXTEEN

It was a slow drive up the coast but the fog lifted before I reached the airport, leaving a thickish twilight in the air. I parked my car at the United building. It was exactly six-twenty-five, according to the ticket the girl in the parking lot handed me. I crossed the road to the bright enormous building and found the baggage carousel, besieged by travellers.

A woman who looked like a dried-up older Helen was standing on the edge of the crowd beside her suitcase. She had on a black dress under a black coat with a ratty fur collar, black hat, and black gloves.

Only her garish red hair was out of keeping with the occasion. Her eyes were swollen, and she seemed dazed, as if a part of her mind was still back in Illinois.

'Mrs Hoffman?'

'Yes. I am Mrs Earl Hoffman.'

'My name is Archer. Your daughter's department head, Dr Geisman, asked me to pick you up.'

'That was nice of him,' she said with a poor vague smile. 'And nice of you.'

I picked up her suitcase, which was small and light. 'Would you like something to eat, or drink? There's a pretty good restaurant here.'

'Oh no thanks. I had dinner on the plane. Swiss steak. It was a very interesting flight. I never flew in a jet before. But I wasn't the least bit frightened.'

She didn't know what she was. She stared around at the bright lights and the people. The muscles of her face were tensing up as if she might be getting ready to cry some more. I got hold of her thin upper arm and hustled her out of there and across the road to my car. We circled the parking lot and got on to the freeway.

'They didn't have this when I was here before. I'm glad you decided to meet me. I'd get lost,' she said in a lost voice.

'How long is it since you were here before?'

'Nearly twenty years. It was when Hoffman was in the Navy, he was a warrant officer in the Shore Patrol. They assigned him to San Diego and Helen had already run — left home, and I thought I might as well get the benefit of the travel. We lived in San Diego for over a year, and it was very nice.' I could hear her breathing as if she was struggling up to the rim of the present. She said carefully: 'Pacific Point is quite near San Diego, isn't it?'

'About fifty miles.'

'Is that right?' After another pause, she said: 'Are you with the college?'

'I happen to be a detective.'

'Isn't that interesting? My husband is a detective. He's been on the Bridgeton force for thirty-four years. He's due to retire next year. We've talked about retiring in California but this will probably turn him against it. He pretends not to care, but he cares. I think he cares just as much as I do.' Her voice floated along above the highway noises like a disembodied spirit talking to itself.

'It's too bad he couldn't fly out with you today.'

'He could have, if he'd wanted to. He could have taken time off. I think he was afraid he couldn't face it. And he has his blood pressure to consider.' She hesitated again. 'Are you investigating my daughter's murder?'

'Yes.'

'Dr Geisman said it was practically open and shut.' The sorrow in her voice had changed into a kind of vengeful justice.

'That may be.' I had no desire to argue with a potentially valuable witness. 'I'm investigating other angles, and you may be able to help me.'

'How is that?'

'Your daughter's life was threatened. She talked to me about it before she was shot. Somebody called her on the telephone. It was a voice she didn't recognize, but she said a strange thing about it. She said it sounded like the voice of Bridgeton.'

'Bridgeton? That's where we live.'

'I know that, Mrs Hoffman. Helen said it was Bridgeton catching up with her. Do you have any idea what she meant?'

'She always hated Bridgeton. From the time that she was in high school she blamed it for everything that went wrong with her life. She couldn't wait to get out of Bridgeton.'

'I understand she ran away from home.'

'I wouldn't put it that way,' although she almost had. 'She only dropped out of sight for the one summer, and she was working all the time. She had a job with a newspaper in Chicago. Then she started in at the university, and she let me know where she was. It was just her father—' She cut this sentence off short. 'I used to help her out of my house-keeping money until we went into the Navy.'

'What was the trouble between her and her father?'

'It had to do with his professional work. At least that was what the final big battle was about.'

'When Helen called him a crooked stormtrooper?'

She turned in the seat to look at me. 'Helen told you that, eh? Are you – were you her boy-friend or something like that?'

'We were friends.' I found that I could say it with some conviction. We had spent a single angry hour together but her death had turned a light on it which hurt my eyes.

She leaned closer to study my face. 'What else did she tell you?'

'There was murder involved in her quarrel with her father.'

'That's a lie. I don't mean Helen was lying, but she was mistaken. The Deloney shooting was an accident pure and simple. If Helen thought she knew more about it than her father, she was dead wrong.'

'Dead' and 'wrong' were heavy words to lay on the dead. Her black-gloved hand flew up to her mouth. She rode for a while in hunched and fearful silence, a thin dry cricket of a woman who had lost her chirp.

'Tell me about the Deloney shooting, Mrs Hoffman.'

'I don't see the point of doing that. I never talk about my husband's cases. He doesn't like me to.'

'But he isn't here.'

'In a way he is. We've been together so long. Anyway it's all past history.'

'History is always connected with the present. That case may have something to do with Helen's death.'

'How could that be? It was twenty years ago, longer than that, and it didn't amount to anything at the time. The only reason it made an impression on Helen was that it happened in our apartment building. Mr Deloney was cleaning a gun, and it went off and shot him, and that was the whole story.'

'Are you sure?'

'Hoffman said so, and Hoffman doesn't lie.' It sounded like an incantation which she had used before.

'What made Helen think he was lying?'

'Imagination pure and simple. She said she talked to a witness who saw somebody shoot Mr Deloney, but I say she dreamed it. No witness ever turned up, and Hoffman said there couldn't have been a witness. Mr Deloney was alone in the apartment when it happened. He tried to clean a loaded gun and shot himself in the face. Helen must have dreamed the other. She had a bit of a crush on Mr Deloney. He was a good-looking man, and you know how young girls are.'

'How old was she?'

'Nineteen. That was the summer she left home.'

It was full dark now. Away off to the right the lights of Long Beach, where I had spent my own uneasy youth, were reflected like a dying red fire from the overcast.

'Who was Mr Deloney?'

'Luke Deloney,' she said. 'He was a very successful contractor in Bridgeton and throughout the state. He owned our apartment building and other buildings in town. Mrs Deloney still owns them. They're worth a lot more than they were then, and even then he was close to a millionaire.'

'Deloney has a surviving widow?'

'Yes, but don't go jumping to conclusions. She was miles away, in their main house, when it happened. Sure there was a lot of talk in town, but she was as innocent as a newborn babe. She came from a very good family. She was one of the famous Osborne sisters in Bridgeton.'

'What were they famous for.'

'Their father was the US Senator. I remember when I was in grade school, back before the World War One, they used to ride to hounds in red coats. But they were always very democratic.'

'Good for them.' I brought her back to the Deloney case. 'You say Deloney was shot in the building where you had your own apartment?'

'Yes. We were in an apartment on the ground floor. We got it dirt cheap because we used to collect the rent for Mr Deloney. He kept the roof apartment for himself. He used it for a kind of private office, and a place to throw parties for visiting firemen and so on. A lot of big men from the state house were friends of his. We used to see them coming and going,' she said in a privileged way.

'And he shot himself in this penthouse apartment?'

'The gun shot him,' she corrected me. 'It was an accident.'

'What sort of a man was Deloney?'

'He was a self-made man, I guess you'd say. He came from the same section of town Hoffman and I did, which is how we got the job collecting rent for him, and that *helped*, in the depression. The depression didn't faze Luke Deloney. He borrowed the money to start his own contracting business and came up fast on his own initiative, and married Senator Osborne's older daughter. There's no telling where he might have got to. He was only a young man of forty when he died.'

'Helen was interested in him, you say?'

'Not seriously, I don't mean that. I doubt if they ever said two words to each other. But you know how young girls are, dreaming about older men. He was the most successful man around, and Helen was always very ambitious. It's funny, she blamed her father for being a failure, which he isn't. But when she finally got around to marrying she had to pick Bert Haggerty, and he's a failure if there ever was one.'

She was talking much more freely, but her loquacity tended to fly off in all directions. It was natural enough. Her daughter's murder had dropped a depth charge into her life.

'Assume there is a connection,' I said, 'between Helen's death and the Deloney shooting – do you have any notion what it could be?'

'No, she must have been imagining things. She was always a great one for that.'

'But she said she knew a witness who saw Deloney shot by someone else?'

'She was talking foolishness.'

'Why?'

'You mean why would she say such things to her father? To get under his skin. There was always bad blood between them, from the time that Hoffman first raised his hand to her. Once they got arguing, there wasn't anything she wouldn't say.'

'Did she name the witness?'

'How could she? There was no such person. Her father challenged her to mention a name. She admitted that she couldn't, that she was just talking.'

'She admitted it?'

'She had to. Hoffman made her. But she never took back the hard words she spoke to him.'

'Is it possible that Helen herself was the witness?'

'That's crazy and you know it. How could she be a witness to something that never happened?' But there was a shrill edge on her certitude.

'Deloney's dead, remember. So is she. It tends to confirm the things she told her friends before she died.'

'About Bridgeton, you mean?'

'Yes.'

She lapsed into silence again. Below the harbour cities we entered the fog zone. I was afraid of running into a pile-up and I slowed down. Mrs Hoffman kept looking back as if she could feel Bridgeton catching up.

'I hope Hoffman isn't drinking,' she said after a while 'It isn't good for his blood pressure. I'll blame myself if anything happens to him.'

'One of you had to come out here.'

'I suppose so. Anyway Bert is with him and whatever else he may be Bert is no drunk.'

'Helen's ex-husband is staying with her father?'

'Yes. He came over from Maple Park this morning and drove me to the airport. Bert's a good boy. I shouldn't call him a boy, he's a grown man in his forties, but he always seems younger than he is.'

'Does he teach at Maple Park?'

'That's right, only he hasn't got his degree. He's been working on it for years. He teaches journalism and English, and he helps put out the school paper. He used to be a newspaperman, that was how Helen met him.'

'When she was nineteen?'

'You have a good memory. You and Hoffman would get along. Hoffman's middle name is memory. There was a time before we got our wartime expansion when he knew every building in Bridgeton. Every factory, every warehouse, every residence. Pick any house on any street and he could tell you who built it and who owned it. He could tell you who lived there and who used to live there and how many children they had and how much income and anything else you wanted to know about them. I'm not exaggerating, ask any of his fellow officers. They used to predict great things for him, but he never made it higher than Lieutenant.'

I wondered why the great things hadn't materialized. She gave me a kind of answer, which I suspected was more of a legend than a fact:

'Helen got her memory from him. They were more alike than either of them admitted. And they were crazy about each other, under all the trouble there was between them. It broke his heart when Helen left home and never wrote. He never asked about her eyes, but he did a lot of brooding. He was never the same man again.'

'Did she marry Bert Haggerty right away?'

'No, she kept him dangling for five or six years. He was away in the army part of that time. Bert did well in the war – a lot of men did well in the war that never did so well before or since – and he was full of confidence for a while. He was going to write a book, start his own newspaper, take her to Europe on their honeymoon. They did get to Europe, on the

GI Bill – I gave them part of the money to make the trip – but that was all that ever came of his plans. He never could settle down to any one thing, and when he finally did it was too late. Last spring they came to the parting of the ways. I didn't like it, but I can hardly blame her. She always did better than he did, from the time that they were married. And one thing I'll say for Helen, she always had class.'

'I agree.'

'But maybe she should have stuck with Bert. Who knows? Maybe this wouldn't have happened. I sometimes think that any man is better than no man at all.'

Later, as we were entering Pacific Point, she said: 'Why couldn't Helen marry an upstanding husband? It's funny. She had brains and looks *and* class, but she never could attract an upstanding man.'

I could feel her eyes on my profile, trying to chart the lost continent of her daughter's life.

CHAPTER SEVENTEEN

The Pacific Hotel stood on a corner just above the economic equator that divided the main street into a prosperous section and a not so prosperous one. The lobby was almost empty on this Saturday night. Four old men were playing bridge in the light of a standing lamp. The only other human being in sight was Dr Geisman, if he qualified.

He got up out of a shabby green plastic armchair and shook hands formally with Mrs Hoffman.

'I see that you've arrived safely. How are you?'

'I'm all right, thanks.'

'Your daughter's unexpected demise came as quite a blow to us.'

'To me, too.'

'In fact I've been endeavouring all day to find a replacement for her. I still haven't succeeded. This is the worst possible time of year to try to recruit teaching personnel.'

'That's too bad.'

I left them trying to breathe life into their stillborn conversation and went into the bar for a drink. A single customer sat trading sorrows with the fat lugubrious bartender. Her hair was dyed black, with a greenish sheen on it like certain ducks.

I recognized the woman – I could have spotted Mrs Perrine at a thousand yards – and I started to back out of the room. She turned and saw me.

'Fancy meeting you here.' She made a large gesture which almost upset the empty glass in front of her, and said to the bartender: 'This is my friend Mr Archer. Pour my friend a drink.'

'What'll you have?'

'Bourbon. I'm paying. What is the lady drinking?'

'Planter's punch,' she said, 'and thanks for the "lady." Thanks for everything in fact. I'm celebrating, been celebrating all day.'

I wished she hadn't been. The granite front she had kept up at her trial had eroded, and the inner ruin of her life showed through. While I didn't know all of Mrs Perrine's secrets, I knew the record she had left on the police blotters of twenty cities. She had been innocent of this one particular crime, but she was a hustler who had worked the coasts from Acapulco to Seattle and from Montreal to Key West.

The bartender limped away to make our drinks. I sat on the stool beside her. 'You should pick another town to celebrate in.'

'I know. This town is a graveyard. I felt like the last living inhabitant, until you sashayed in.'

'That isn't what I mean, Mrs Perrine.'

'Hell, call me Bridget, you're my pal, you've earned the right.'

'Okay, Bridget. The police didn't like your acquittal, you couldn't expect them to. They'll pick you up for any little thing.'

'I haven't stepped out of line. I have my own money.'

'I'm thinking about what you might do if you go on celebrating. You can't afford to jaywalk in this town.'

She considered this problem, and her twisting face mimicked the efforts of her mind. 'You may be right at that. I been thinking of going to Vegas in the morning. I have a friend in Vegas.'

The bartender brought our drinks. Mrs Perrine sipped at hers, making a sour face, as if she'd suddenly lost her taste for it. Her gaze strayed to the mirror behind the bar.

'My gosh,' she said, 'is that me? I look like the wrath of God.'

'Take a bath and get some sleep.'

'It isn't so easy to sleep. I get lonely at night.' She ogled me, more or less automatically.

She wasn't my baby. I finished my drink and put two dollar bills on the bar.

'Good night, Bridget. Take it easy. I have to make a phone call.'

'Sure you do. See you at Epworth League.'

The bartender limped toward her as I walked out. Mrs Hoffman and Dr Geisman were no longer in the lobby. I found the telephone booths in a cul-de-sac behind the main desk and called the Bradshaw house.

Before the phone had rung more than once, the old lady's voice came quavering over the line. 'Roy? Is that you, Roy?'

'This is Archer.'

'I was so hoping it would be Roy. He always telephones by this time. You don't suppose something has happened to him?'

'No. I don't.'

'Have you seen the paper?'

'No.'

'There's an item to the effect that Laura Sutherland went to the Reno conference with him. Roy didn't tell me that. Do you suppose he's interested in Laura?'

'I wouldn't know.'

'She's a lovely young woman, don't you think?'

I wondered if she'd had some wine at dinner that made her silly. 'I have no opinion on the subject, Mrs Bradshaw. I called to see if you're willing to follow through on our conversation this afternoon.'

'I'm afraid I couldn't possibly, not without Roy's consent. He handles the money in the family, you know. Now I'm going to ask you to cut this short, Mr Archer. I'm expecting to hear from Roy at any moment.'

She hung up on me. I seemed to be losing my touch with little old ladies. I went into the washroom and looked at my face in the mirror above the row of basins. Someone had written in pencil on the wall: Support Mental Health or I'll kill you.

A small brown newsboy came into the washroom and caught me grinning at my reflection. I pretended to be examining my teeth. He looked about ten years old, and conducted himself like a miniature adult.

'Read all about the murder,' he suggested.

I bought a local paper from him. The lead story was head-lined: 'PPC Teacher Shot,' with the subhead: 'Mystery Student to be Questioned.' In effect, it tried and convicted

114

Dolly. She had 'registered fraudulently, using an alias.' Her friendship with Helen was described as 'a strange relationship.' The S and W thirty-eight found in her bed was 'the murder weapon.' She had 'a dark secret in her past'—the McGee killing—and was 'avoiding questioning by the police.'

No other possible suspect was mentioned. The man from Reno didn't appear in the story.

In lieu of doing something constructive I tore the paper to pieces and dropped the pieces in the trash bucket. Then I went back to the telephone booths. Dr Godwin's answering service wanted to know if it was an emergency.

'Yes. It has to do with a patient of Dr Godwin's.'

'Are you the patient, sir?'

'Yes,' I lied, wondering if this meant I needed help.

The switchboard girl said in a gentler voice: 'The last time the doctor called in he was at home.'

She recited his number but I didn't use it. I wanted to talk to Godwin face to face. I got his address out of the directory and drove across town to his house.

It was one of a number of large houses set on the edge of a mesa which normally overlooked the harbour and the city. Tonight it was islanded by the fog.

Behind the Arizona fieldstone front of the house a tenor and a soprano were singing a heartbreaking duet from *La Bohème*.

The door was answered by a handsome woman wearing a red silk brocade coat and the semi-professional smile that doctors' wives acquire. She seemed to recognize my name.

'I'm sorry, Mr Archer. My husband was here until just a few minutes ago. We were actually listening to music for a change. Then a young man called—the husband of one of his patients—and he agreed to meet him at the nursing home.'

'It wasn't Alex Kincaid who called?'

'I believe it was. Mr Archer?' She stepped outside, a brilliant and very feminine figure in her red coat. 'My husband has spoken of you. I understand you're working on this criminal case he's involved with.'

'Yes.'

Her hand touched my arm. 'I'm worried about him. He's taking this thing so seriously. He seems to think that he let the girl down when she was his patient before, and that it makes him responsible for everything that's happened.' Her fine long eyes looked up at me, asking for reassurance.

'He isn't,' I said.

'Will you tell him so? He won't listen to me. There are

very few people he will listen to. But he seems to have some respect for you, Mr Archer.'

'It's mutual. I doubt that he'd want my opinion on the subject of his responsibility, though. He's a very powerful and temperamental man, easy to cross.'

'You're telling me,' she said. 'I suppose I had no right to ask you to speak to him. But the way he pours his life away into those patients of his –' Her hand moved from her breast in an outward gesture.

'He seems to thrive on it.'

'I don't.' She made a wry face. 'Physician's wife, heal thyself, eh?'

'You're thriving by all appearances,' I said. 'That's a nice coat, by the way.'

'Thank you. Jim bought it for me in Paris last summer.'

I left her smiling less professionally, and went to the nursing home. Alex's red Porsche was standing at the curb in front of the big plain stucco building. I felt my heartbeat pounding in my ears. Something good could still happen.

A Spanish American nurse's aide in a blue and white uniform unlocked the door and let me into the front room to wait for Dr Godwin. Nell and several other bathrobed patients were watching a television drama about a pair of lawyers, father and son. They paid no attention to me. I was only a real-life detective, unemployed at the moment. But not, I hoped, for long.

I sat in an empty chair to one side. The drama was well directed and well played but I couldn't keep my mind on it. I began to watch the four people who were watching it. Nell the somnambulist, her black hair hanging like tangled sorrows down her back, held cupped in her hands the blue ceramic ashtray she had made. A young man with an untrimmed beard and rebellious eyes looked like a conscientious objector to everything. A thin-haired man, who was trembling with excitement, went on trembling right through the commercial. An old woman had a translucent face through which her life burned like a guttering candle. Step back a little and you could almost imagine that they were three generations of one family, grandmother, parents, and son, at home on a Saturday night.

Dr Godwin appeared in the inner doorway and crooked his finger at me. I followed him down the hallway through a thickening hospital odour, into a small cramped office. He switched on a lamp over the desk and sat behind it. I took the only other chair.

'Is Alex Kincaid with his wife?'

'Yes. He called me at home and seemed very eager to see her, though he hasn't been around all day. He also wanted to talk to me.'

'Did he say anything about running out on her?'

'No.'

'I hope he's changed his mind.' I told Godwin about my meeting with Kincaid senior, and Alex's departure with his father.

'You can't entirely blame him for falling by the wayside momentarily. He's young, and under great strain.' Godwin's changeable eyes lit up. 'The important thing, for him as well as Dolly, is that he decided to come back.'

'How is she?'

'Calmer, I think. She didn't want to talk tonight, at least not to me.'

'Will you let me have a try at her?'

'No.'

'I almost regret bringing you into this case, doctor.'

'I've been told that before, and less politely,' he said with a stubborn smile. 'But once I'm in I'm in, and I'll continue to do as I think best.'

'I'm sure you will. Did you see the evening paper?'

'I saw it.'

'Does Dolly know what's going on outside? About the gun, for instance?'

'No.'

'Don't you think she should be told?'

He spread out his hands on the scarred desk-top. 'I'm trying to simplify her problems, not add to them. She had so many pressures on her last night, both from the past and the present, that she was on the verge of a psychotic breakthrough. We don't want that to happen.'

'Will you be able to protect her from police questioning?'

'Not indefinitely. The best possible protection would be a solution to this case absolving her.'

'I'm working on it. I talked to her Aunt Alice this morning, and looked over the scene of the McGee killing. I became pretty well convinced that even if McGee did kill his wife, which I doubt, Dolly couldn't have identified him as he left the house. In other words her testimony at his trial was cooked.'

'Alice Jenks convinced you of this?'

'The physical layout did. Miss Jenks did her best to convince me of the opposite, that McGee was guilty. I wouldn't be surprised if she was the main motive power behind the case against him.'

'He *was* guilty.'

'So you've said. I wish you'd go into your reasons for believing that.'

'I'm afraid I can't. It has to do with the confidences of a patient.'

'Constance McGee?'

'Mrs McGee wasn't formally a patient. But you can't treat a child without treating the parents.'

'And she confided in you?'

'Naturally, to some extent. For the most part we talked about her family problems.' Godwin was feeling his way carefully. His face was bland. Under the lamp his bald head gleamed like a metal dome in moonlight.

'Her sister Alice made an interesting slip. She said there was no other man in Constance's life. I didn't ask her. Alice volunteered the information.'

'Interesting.'

'I thought so. Was Constance in love with another man at the time she was shot?'

Godwin nodded almost imperceptibly.

'Who was he?'

'I have no intention of telling you. He's suffered enough.' A shadow of the suffering passed across his own face. 'I've told you this much because I want you to understand that McGee had a motive, and was certainly guilty.'

'I think he was framed, just as Dolly is being framed.'

'We agree on the latter point. Why can't we settle for that?'

'Because there have been three killings, and they're connected. They're connected subjectively, as you would say, in Dolly's mind. I believe they're objectively connected, too. They may all have been done by the same person.'

Godwin didn't ask me who. It was just as well. I was talking over my head, and I had no suspect.

'What third killing are you referring to?'

'The death of Luke Deloney, a man I never heard of until tonight. I met Helen Haggerty's mother at the LA airport and had a talk with her on the way down here. According to her, Deloney shot himself by accident while cleaning a gun. But Helen claimed he was murdered and said she knew a witness. The witness may have been herself. At any rate she quarrelled with her father on the issue – he seems to have been the detective in charge of the case – and ran away from home.

All this was over twenty years ago.'

'You seriously think it's connected with the present case?'

'Helen thought so. Her death makes her an authority on he subject.'

'What do you propose to do about it?'

'I'd like to fly to Illinois tonight and talk to Helen's ather. But I can't afford to do it on my own hook.'

'You could phone him.'

'I could. My sense of the situation is that it would do nore harm than good. He may be a tough nut to crack.'

Godwin said after a minute's thought: 'I might consider backing you.'

'You're a generous man.'

'A curious one,' he said. 'Remember I've been living with this case for over ten years. I'd give a good deal to see it ended.'

'Let me talk to Alex first, and ask him how he feels about laying out more money.'

Godwin inclined his head and remained bowing as he stood up. He wasn't bowing to me. It was more of a general and habitual bow, as if he could feel the weight of the stars and was asking their permission to take part of the weight on human shoulders.

'I'll get him out of there. He's stayed long enough.'

Godwin disappeared down the hallway. A few minutes later Alex came back alone. He walked like a man in a tunnel underground, but his face was more serene than I'd ever seen it.

He paused in the doorway. 'Dr Godwin said you were here.'

'I'm surprised to see you.'

Hurt and embarrassment flickered across the upper part of his face. He brushed at it impatiently with his fingers. Then he stepped into the office, shutting the door behind him and leaning on it.

'I made a fool of myself today. I tried to chicken out.'

'It takes guts to admit it.'

'Don't gloss it over,' he said sharply. 'I was really lousy. It's funny, when Dad gets upset it has a peculiar effect on me. It's like sympathetic vibrations: he goes to pieces, I go to pieces. Not that I'm blaming *him*.'

'I'm blaming him.'

'Please don't. You have no right to.' His eyebrows knitted. 'The company's talking about bringing in computers to handle most of the work in the office. Dad's afraid he can't adjust, and I guess it makes him afraid of things in general.'

'You've been doing some thinking.'

'I had to. You started me off with what you said about annulling myself. I felt that way when I went home with Dad – as though I wasn't a man any more.' He pushed himself clear of the door and balanced himself on his feet, his arms swinging slightly at his sides. 'It's really amazing, you know? You really can make a decision inside yourself. You can decide to be one thing or the other.'

The only trouble was that you had to make the decision every hour on the hour. But he would have to find that out for himself.

'How is your wife?' I said.

'She actually seemed glad to see me. Have you talked to her?'

'Dr Godwin wouldn't let me.'

'He wouldn't let me, either, till I promised not to ask her any questions. I didn't, but the subject of the revolver came up. She'd heard two of the aides talking about some newspaper story – '

'It's in the local paper. What did she have to say about the gun?'

'It isn't hers. Somebody must have hidden it under her mattress. She asked me to describe it, and she said it sounded like her Aunt Alice's revolver. Her aunt used to keep it on her bedside table at night. Dolly was sort of fascinated by it when she was a little girl.' He breathed deeply. 'Apparently she saw her aunt threaten her father with it. I didn't want her to go into all that stuff but I couldn't prevent her. She calmed down again after a while.'

'At least she's stopped blaming herself for Helen Haggerty's death.'

'She hasn't though. She still says it was her fault. Everything's her fault.'

'In what way?'

'She didn't go into it. I didn't want her to.'

'You mean Dr Godwin didn't want you to.'

'That's right. He's calling the shots. I guess he knows more about her than I ever will.'

'I take it you're going on with your marriage?' I said.

'We have to. I realized that today. People can't walk out on each other when they're in this kind of trouble. I think maybe Dolly realizes it, too. She didn't turn her back on me or anything.'

'What else did you talk about?'

'Nothing important. The other patients, mostly. There's one old lady with a broken hip who doesn't want to stay in bed. Dolly's been sort of looking after her.' It seemed important to him. 'She can't be so very sick herself.' It was an implied question.

'You'll have to take that up with the doctor.'

'He isn't saying much. He wants to give her some psychological tests tomorrow. I told him to go ahead.'

'Do I have your go-ahead, too?'

'Naturally. I was hoping you'd take that for granted. I want you to do everything you can to settle this thing. I'll give you a written contract–'

'That won't be necessary. But it's going to cost you money.'

'How much money?'

'A couple of thousand, maybe a good deal more.'

I told him about the Reno end of the case, which Arnie and Phyllis Walters were handling, and about the Bridgeton situation which I wanted to explore. I also advised him to talk to Jerry Marks first thing in the morning.

'Will Mr Marks be available on a Sunday?'

'Yes. I've already set him up for you. Of course you're going to have to give him a retainer.'

'I have some savings bonds,' he said thoughtfully, 'and I can borrow on my insurance policy. Meantime I can sell the car. It's paid for, and I've been offered two five for it. I was getting pretty tired of sports car rallies and all that jazz. It's kid stuff.'

CHAPTER EIGHTEEN

The front-door bell rang. Someone trotted past the office door to answer it. It was getting late for visitors, and I went out and followed the aide along the hallway. The four patients were still watching the television screen as if it was a window on the outside world.

Whoever had rung the bell was knocking now, rather violently.

'Just a minute,' the aide said through the door. She got her key into the lock and opened it partly. 'Who is it? Who do you want to see?'

It was Alice Jenks. She tried to push her way in, but the

aide had her white shoe against the door.

'I wish to see my niece, Dolly McGee.'

'We have no such patient.'

'She calls herself Dolly Kincaid now.'

'I can't let you in to see anyone without doctor's permission.'

'Is Godwin here?'

'I think so.'

'Get him,' Miss Jenks said peremptorily.

The girl's Latin temper flared. 'I don't take orders from you,' she said in a hissing whisper. 'And keep your voice down. We have people trying to rest.'

'Get Dr Godwin.'

'Don't worry, I intend to. But you'll have to wait outside.'

'It will be a pleasure.'

I stepped between them before the nurse closed the door and said to Miss Jenks: 'May I speak to you for a minute?'

She peered at me through fogged glasses. 'So you're here, too.'

'I'm here, too.'

I stepped out under the outside light and heard the door shut behind me. The air was chilly after the hot-house atmosphere of the nursing home. Miss Jenks had on a thick fur-collared coat which made her figure massive in the gloom. Droplets of water glistened in the fur, and in her greying hair.

'What do you want with Dolly?'

'It's none of your business. She's my flesh and blood, not yours.'

'Dolly has a husband. I represent him.'

'You can go and represent him in some other constituency. I'm not interested in you or her husband.'

'But suddenly you're interested in Dolly. Does it have anything to do with the story in the paper?'

'Maybe it has and maybe it hasn't.' In her language, that meant yes. She added defensively: 'I've been interested in Dolly since she was born. I know better than a lot of strangers what's good for her.'

'Dr Godwin isn't a stranger.'

'No. I wish he was.'

'I hope you're not thinking of taking her out of here.'

'Maybe I am and maybe I'm not.' She dug some Kleenex out of her purse and used it to clean her glasses. I could see a newspaper folded small in the purse.

'Miss Jenks, did you read the description of the revolver

that was found in Dolly's bed?'

She replaced her glasses quickly, as though to cover the startled look in her eyes. 'Naturally I read it.'

'Did it ring any bell with you?'

'Yes. It sounded like the revolver I used to have, so I came into town to the courthouse to have a look at it. It looks like mine all right.'

'You admit that?'

'Why shouldn't I? I haven't seen it for over ten years.'

'Can you prove it?'

'Of course I can prove it. It was stolen from my house before Constance was shot. Sheriff Crane theorized at the time that it might have been the gun McGee used on her. He still thinks so. McGee could easily have taken it. He knew where it was in my bedroom.'

'You didn't tell me all this this morning.'

'I didn't think of it. It was only theory, anyway. You were interested in facts.'

'I'm interested in both, Miss Jenks. What's the police theory now? That McGee killed Miss Haggerty and tried to frame his daughter?'

'I wouldn't put it past him. A man who would do what he did to his wife—' Her voice sank out of hearing in her throat.

'And they want to use his daughter to nail McGee again?'

She didn't answer me. Lights went on inside, and there were sounds of movement culminating in Godwin's opening the door. He shook his keys at us, grinning fiercely.

'Come inside, Miss Jenks.'

She stamped up the concrete steps. Godwin had cleared the front room of everyone but Alex, who was sitting on a chair against the wall. I stood unobtrusively in the corner beside the silent television set.

She faced him, almost as tall in heels as he was, almost as wide in her coat, almost as stubborn in her pride. 'I don't approve of what you're doing, Dr Godwin.'

'What am I doing?' He sat on the arm of a chair and crossed his legs.

'You know what I'm referring to. My niece. Keeping her cooped up here in defiance of the constituted authorities.'

'There's no defiance involved. I try to do my duty, the Sheriff tries to do his. Sometimes we come into conflict. It doesn't necessarily mean that Sheriff Crane is right and I'm wrong.'

'It does to me.'

'I'm not surprised. We've disagreed before, on a similar issue. You and your friend the Sheriff had your way on that occasion, unfortunately for your niece.'

'It did her no harm to testify. Truth is truth.'

'And trauma is trauma. It did her incalculable harm, which she's still suffering under.'

'I'd like to see that for myself.'

'So you can make a full report to the Sheriff?'

'Good citizens co-operate with the law,' she said sententiously. 'But I'm not here on the Sheriff's behalf. I came here to help my niece.'

'How do you propose to help her?'

'I'm going to take her home with me.'

Godwin stood up shaking his head.

'You can't stop me. I've been her guardian since her mother died. The law will back me up.'

'I think not,' Godwin said coldly. 'Dolly's of age, and she's here of her own free will.'

'I'd like to ask her that question for myself.'

'You're not going to ask her any questions.'

The woman took a step toward him and thrust her head forward on her neck. 'You think you're a little tin god, don't you, masterminding my family's affairs? I say you've got no right to keep her here under duress, making us all look bad. I've got a position to keep up in this county. I spent the day with some very high-level people from Sacramento.'

'I'm afraid I don't follow your logic. But keep your voice down, please.' Godwin himself was using the slow weary monotone that I had first heard on the telephone twenty-four hours before. 'And let me assure you again, your niece is here of her own free will.'

'That's right.' Alex came forward into the verbal line of fire. 'I don't believe we've met. I'm Alex Kincaid, Dolly's husband.'

She disregarded his hand.

'I think it's important for her to stay here,' he said. 'I have confidence in the doctor, and so has my wife.'

'I'm sorry for you then. He had me bamboozled, too, until I found out what went on in his office.'

Alex looked inquiringly at Godwin. The doctor turned his hands out as if he was feeling for rain. He said to Miss Jenks:

'You graduated in sociology, I believe.'

'What if I did?'

'From a woman of your training and background, I'd

124

expect a more professional attitude toward the practice of psychiatry.'

'I'm not talking about the practice of psychiatry. I'm talking about the practice of other things.'

'What other things?'

'I wouldn't soil my tongue with them. But please don't think I don't know my sister and what went on in her life. I've been remembering things – the way she used to primp and preen Saturday mornings before she came in to town. And then she wanted to move here, to be closer.'

'Closer to me?'

'So she told me.'

Godwin's face was white, as if all its colour had been drawn into the darkness of his eyes. 'You're a silly woman, Miss Jenks, and I've had enough of you. I'll ask you to leave now.'

'I'm staying here till I see my niece. I want to know what you're practising on her.'

'It would do her no good. In your present mood you'd do no good to anyone.' He moved around her to the door and held it open. 'Good night.'

She didn't move or look at him. She stood with her head down, a little dazed by the anger that had gone through her like a storm.

'Do you wish to be forcibly removed?'

'Try it. You'll end up in court.'

But a kind of shame had begun to invade her face. Her mouth was twitching like a small injured thing. It had said more than she intended.

When I took her by the arm and said, 'Come on, Miss Jenks,' she let me lead her to the door. Godwin closed it on her.

'I have no patience with fools,' he said.

'Have a little patience with me, though, will you, doctor?'

'I'll give it a try, Archer.' He took a deep breath and let it out as a sigh. 'You want to know if there's any truth in her innuendo.'

'You make it easy for me.'

'Why not? I love the truth. My entire life is a search for it.'

'Okay, was Constance McGee in love with you?'

'I suppose she was, in a way. Women patients traditionally fall in love with their doctors, particularly in my field. It didn't persist in her case.'

'This may strike you as a foolish question, but did you love her?'

'I'll give you a foolish answer, Mr Archer. Of course I loved her. I love her the way a doctor loves his patients, if he's any good. Its a love that's more maternal than erotic.' He spread his large hands on his chest, and spoke from there: 'I wanted to serve her. I didn't succeed too well.'

I was silenced.

'And now, gentlemen, if you'll excuse me, I have hospital rounds in the morning.' He swung his keys.

Alex said to me in the street: 'Do you believe him?'

'Unless or until I have proof that he's lying. He's not telling all he knows but people seldom do, let alone doctors. I'd take his word ahead of Alice Jenks's.'

He started to climb into his car, then turned back toward me, gesturing in the direction of the nursing home. Its plain rectangular façade loomed in the fog like a blockhouse, the visible part of an underground fortress.

'You think she's safe there, Mr Archer?'

'Safer than she'd be on the streets, or in jail, or in a psycho ward with a police psychiatrist quizzing her.'

'Or at her aunt's?'

'Or at her aunt's. Miss Jenks is one of these righteous women who doesn't let her left lobe know what her right lobe is doing. She's quite a tiger.'

His eyes were still on the front of the nursing home.

Deep inside the building, the wild old voice I had heard that morning rose again. It faded like the cry of a seabird flying away, intermitted by wind.

'I wish I could stay with Dolly, and protect her,' Alex said.

He was a good boy.

I broached the subject of money. He gave me most of the money in his wallet. I used it to buy an airline ticket to Chicago and return, and caught a late flight from International Airport.

CHAPTER NINETEEN

I left the toll road, which bypassed Bridgeton, and drove my rented car through the blocks of housing tracts on the outskirts of the city. I could see the clump of sawed-off skyscrapers in the business district ahead, and off to the left, across the whole south side, the factories. It was Sunday morning, and only one of their stacks was pouring smoke into the deep blue sky.

I stopped for gas at a service station and looked up Earl Hoffman's address in the telephone directory. When I asked the attendant how to get to Cherry Street, where Hoffman lived, he pointed in the general direction of the factories.

It was a middle-class street of substantial two-storey houses which had been touched but not destroyed by the blight that creeps outward from the centres of cities. Hoffman's house was of grimy white brick like the others, but the front porch had been painted within living memory. An old Chevrolet coupé stood at the curb in front of it.

The doorbell didn't work. I knocked on the screen door. An old young man with more nose than chin opened the inner door and looked at me through the screen in a sad way.

'Mr Haggerty?'

'Yes.'

I told him my name and trade and where I was from. 'I was with your wife – your ex-wife – shortly before she was killed.'

'It's a dreadful thing.'

He stood absently in the doorway, forgetting to ask me in. He had a frowzy sleepless look as if he'd been up most of the night. Though there was no grey on his head, white hairs glistened in his day-old beard. His small eyes had the kind of incandescence that goes with conscious suffering.

'May I come in, Mr Haggerty?'

'I don't know if it's such a good idea. Earl's pretty broken up.'

'I thought he and his daughter had been on the outs for a long time.'

'They were. It only makes it harder for him, I think. When you're angry with someone you love, you always expect at the back of your mind there'll be a reconciliation some day.

But now there will never be anything.'

He was speaking for his father-in-law but also for himself. His empty hands moved aimlessly at his sides. The fingers of his right hand were stained dark yellow by nicotine.

'I'm sorry,' I said, 'that Mr Hoffman isn't feeling well. I'm afraid I'll have to talk to him anyway. I didn't come from California for the ride.'

'No. Obviously not. What is it you have to discuss with him?'

'His daughter's murder. He may be able to help me understand it.'

'I thought it was already solved.'

'It isn't.'

'Has the girl student been cleared?'

'She's in process of being cleared,' I said with deliberate vagueness. 'You and I can go into all that later. Right now I'm very eager to talk to Hoffman.'

'If you insist. I only hope you can get some sense out of him. '

I saw what he meant when he took me through the house to 'Earl's den,' as Haggerty called it. It was furnished with a closed roll-top desk, an armchair, a studio couch. Through a haze compounded of whisky fumes and smoke I could see a big old man sprawled in orange pyjamas on the couch, his head propped up by bolsters. A strong reading light shone on his stunned face. His eyes seemed out of focus, but he was holding a magazine with an orange cover that almost matched his pyjamas. The wall above him was decorated with rifles and shotguns and hand guns.

'When I recall the loss of all my perished years,' he said huskily.

Old cops didn't talk like that, and Earl Hoffman looked like no exception to the rule. His body was massive, and could have belonged to a professional football player or a wrestler gone to pot. His nose had once been broken. He had a clipped grey head and a mouth like bent iron.

'That's beautiful poetry, Bert,' the iron mouth said.

'I suppose it is.'

'Who's your friend, Bert?'

'Mr Archer, from California.'

'California, eh? That's where my poor little Helen got knocked off.'

He sobbed, or hiccuped, once. Then he swung himself on to the edge of the couch, letting his bare feet fall heavily to the floor.

'Do you know – did you know my little daughter Helen?'
'I knew her.'
'Isn't that remarkable.' He rose swaying and clasped my hands in both of his, using me to support him. 'Helen was a remarkable girl. I've just been reading over one of her poems. Wrote it when she was just a teen-age girl at City College. Here, I'll show you.'

He made a fairly elaborate search for the orange-covered magazine, which was lying in plain sight on the floor where he had dropped it. The name of it was the *Bridgeton Blazer*, and it looked like a school production.

Haggerty picked it up and handed it to him: 'Please don't bother with it, Earl. Helen didn't write it anyway.'

'Didn't write it? 'Course she wrote it. It's her initials on it.' Hoffman flipped through the pages. 'See?'

'But she was only translating from Verlaine.'

'Never heard of him.' Hoffman turned to me, thrusting the magazine into my hands. 'Here, read this. See what a remarkable gift poor little Helen had.'

I read:

> When the violins
> Of the autumn winds
> Begin to sigh
> My heart is torn
> With their forlorn
> Monotony
>
> And when the hour
> Sounds from the tower
> I weep tears
> For I recall
> The loss of all
> My perished years.
>
> And then I go
> With the winds that blow
> And carry me
> There and here
> Like a withered and sere
> Leaf from a tree. – H.H.

Hoffman looked at me with one of his unfocused eyes. Isn't that beautiful poetry, Mr Arthur?'

'Beautiful.'

'I only wisht I understood it. Do you understand it?'

'I think so.'

'Then keep it. Keep it in memory of poor little Helen.'

'I couldn't do that.'

'Sure you can. Keep it.' He snatched it out of my hands rolled it up, and thrust it into my jacket pocket, breathing whisky in my face.

'Keep it,' Haggerty whispered at my shoulder. 'You don't want to cross him.'

'You heard him. You don't want to cross me.'

Hoffman grinned loosely at me. He clenched his left fist, examined it for defects, then used it to strike himself on the chest. He walked on spraddled legs to the roll-top desk and opened it. There were bottles and a single smeared tumbler inside. He half-filled the tumbler from a fifth of bourbon and drank most of it down. His son-in-law said something under his breath, but made no move to stop him.

The heavy jolt squeezed sweat out on Hoffman's face. It seemed to sober him a little. His eyes focused on me.

'Have a drink?'

'All right. I'll take water and ice in mine, please.' I didn't normally drink in the morning but this was an abnormal occasion.

'Get some ice and a glass, Bert. Mr Arthur wants a drink. If you're too mucky-muck to drink with me, Mr Arthur isn't.'

'The name is Archer.'

'Get two glasses,' he said with his foolish grin. 'Mr Archer wants a drink, too. Sit down,' he said to me. 'Take the load off your feet. Tell me about poor little Helen.'

We sat on the couch. I filled him in quickly on the circumstances of the murder, including the threat that preceded it, and Helen's feeling that Bridgeton was catching up with her.

'What did she mean by that?' The lines of the grin were still in his face like clown marks but the grin had become a rictus.

'I've come a long way to see if you can help me answer that question.'

'Me? Why come to me? I never knew what went on in her mind, she never let me know. She was too bright for me.' His mood swayed into heavy drunken self-pity. 'I sweated and slaved to buy her an education like I never had, but she wouldn't give her poor old father the time of day.'

'I understand you had a bad quarrel and she left home.'

'She told you, eh?'

I nodded. I had decided to keep Mrs Hoffman out of it. He was the kind of man who wouldn't want his wife ahead of him in anything.

'She tell you the names she called me, crook and Nazi, when all I was doing was my bounden duty? You're a cop, you know how a man feels when your own family undermines you.' He peered at me sideways. 'You are a cop, aren't you?'

'I have been.'

'What do you do for a living now?'

'Private investigation.'

'Who for?'

'A man named Kincaid, nobody you know. I knew your daughter slightly, and I have a personal interest in finding out who killed her. I think the answer may be here in Bridgeton.'

'I don't see how. She never set foot in this town for twenty years, until last spring. She only came home then to tell her mother she was getting a divorce. From *him*.' He gestured toward the back of the house, where I could hear ice being chipped.

'Did she do any talking to you?'

'I only saw her the once. She said hello-how-are-you and that was about it. She told her mother that she'd had it with Bert and her mother couldn't talk her out of it. Bert even followed her out to Reno to try and convince her to come back, but it was no go. He isn't enough of a man to hold a woman.'

Hoffman finished his drink and set his tumbler down on the floor. He remained slumped forward for about a minute, and I was afraid he was going to get sick or pass out on me. But he came back up to a sitting position and muttered something about wanting to help me.

'Fine. Who was Luke Deloney?'

'Friend of mine. Big man in town back before the war. She told you about him, too, eh?'

'You could tell me more, Lieutenant. I hear you have a memory like an elephant.'

'Did Helen say that?'

'Yes.' The lie didn't cost me anything, not even a pang of conscience.

'At least she had some respect for her old man, eh?'

'A good deal.'

He breathed with enormous relief. It would pass, as everything passes when a man is drinking seriously to kill awareness. But for the moment he was feeling good. He believed his daughter had conceded a point in their bitter life-long struggle.

'Luke was born in nineteen-oh-three on Spring Street,' he said with great care, 'in the twenty-one-hundred block, way out on the south side – two blocks over from where I lived when I was a kid. I knew him in grade school. He was the kind of a kid who saved up his paper-route money to buy a Valentine for everybody in his class. He actually did that. The principal used to take him around to the various rooms to show off his mental arithmetic. He did have a good head on his shoulders. I'll give him that. He skipped two grades. He was a comer.

'Old man Deloney was a cement finisher, and cement started to come in strong for construction after the World War. Luke bought himself a mixer with money he'd saved and went into business for himself. He did real well in the twenties. At his peak he had over five hundred men working for him all over the state. Even the depression didn't cramp his style. He was a wheeler and dealer as well as a builder. The only things going up in those days were public works, so he went out in a big way for the federal and state contracts. He married Senator Osborne's daughter, and that didn't do him any harm, either.'

'I hear Mrs Deloney's still alive.'

'Sure she is. She lives in the house the Senator built in nineteen-oh-one on Glenview Avenue on the north side. Number one-oh-three, I think.' He was straining to live up to his encyclopædic reputation.

I made a mental note of the address. Preceded by clinking Bert Haggerty came into the room with ice and water and glasses on a tin tray. I cleared a space on the desk and he set the tray down. It had originally belonged to the Bridgeton Inn.

'You took long enough,' Hoffman said offhandedly.

Haggerty stiffened. His eyes seemed to regroup themselves more closely at the sides of his nose.

'Don't talk to me like that, Earl. I'm not a servant.'

'If you don't like it you know what you can do.'

'I realize you're tight, but there's a limit –'

'Who's tight? I'm not tight.'

'You've been drinking for twenty-four hours.'

'So what? A man has a right to drown his sorrows. But my brain is as clear as a bell. Ask Mr Arthur here. Mr Archer.'

Haggerty laughed, mirthlessly, falsetto. It was a very queer sound, and I tried to cover it over with a broad flourish:

'The Lieutenant's been filling me in on some ancient history. He has a memory like an elephant.'

But Hoffman wasn't feeling good any more. He rose cumbrously and advanced on Haggerty and me. One of his eyes looked at each of us. I felt like a man in a cage with a sick bear and his keeper.

'What's funny, Bert? You think my sorrow is funny, is that it? She wouldn't be dead if you were man enough to keep her at home. Why didn't you bring her home from Reno with you?'

'You can't blame me for everything,' Haggerty said a little wildly. 'I got along with her better than you did. If she hadn't had a father-fixation—'

'Don't give me that, you lousy intellectual. Ineffectual. Ineffectual intellectual. You're not the only one that can use four-bit words. And stop calling me Earl. We're not related. We never would have been if I had any say in the matter. We're not even related and you come into my house prying on my personal habits. What are you, an old woman?'

Haggerty was speechless. He looked at me helplessly.

'I'll break your neck,' his father-in-law said.

I stepped between them. 'Let's have no violence, Lieutenant. It wouldn't look good on the blotter.'

'The little pipsqueak accused me. He said I'm drunk. You tell him he's mistaken. Make him apologise.'

I turned to Haggerty, closing one eye. 'Lieutenant Hoffman is sober, Bert. He can carry his liquor. Now you better get out of here before something happens.'

He was glad to. I followed him out into the hall.

'This is the third or fourth time,' he said in a low voice. 'I didn't mean to set him off again.'

'Let him cool for a bit. I'll sit with him. I'd like to talk to you afterward.'

'I'll wait outside in my car.'

I went back into the bear cage. Hoffman was sitting on the edge of the couch with his head supported by his hands.

'Everything's gone to hell in a hand-car,' he said. 'That sissy willow of a Bert Haggerty gets under my skin. I dunno what he thinks he's sucking around for.' His mood changed. 'You haven't deserted me, anyway. Go ahead, make yourself a drink.'

I manufactured a light highball and brought it back to the couch. I didn't offer Hoffman any. In wine was truth, perhaps, but in whisky, the way Hoffman sluiced it down, was an army of imaginary rats climbing your legs.

'You were telling me about Luke Deloney and how h
grew.'

He squinted at me. 'I don't know why you're so intereste
in Deloney. He's been dead for twenty-two years. Twenty
two years and three months. He shot himself, but I guess yo
know that, eh?' A hard intelligence glinted momentarily i
his eyes and drew them into focus on my face.

I spoke to the hard intelligence: 'Was there anythin,
between Helen and Deloney?'

'No, she wasn't interested in *him*. She had a crush on th
elevator boy. George. I ought to know, she made me get hin
the job. I was sort of managing the Deloney Apartments a
the time. Luke Deloney and me, we were like that.'

He tried to cross his second finger over his forefinger. I
kept slipping. He finally completed the manœuvre with th
help of his other hand. His fingers were thick and mottled lik
uncooked breakfast sausages.

'Luke Deloney was a bit of a womanizer,' he said indul
gently, 'but he didn't mess around with the daughters of hi
friends. He never cared for the young stuff, anyway. His wif
must of been ten years older than he was. Anyway, h
wouldn't touch my daughter. He knew I'd kill him.'

'Did you?'

'That's a lousy question, mister. If I didn't happen to lik
you I'd knock your block off.'

'No offence.'

'I had nothing against Luke Deloney. He treated me fai
and square. Anyway, I told you he shot himself.'

'Suicide?'

'Naw. Why would he commit suicide? He had everythin,
money and women and a hunting lodge in Wisconsin. H
took me up there personally more than once. The shootin
was an accident. That's the way it went into the books an
that's the way it stays.'

'How did it happen, Lieutenant?'

'He was cleaning his .32 automatic. He had a permit t
tote it on his person – I helped him get it myself – because h
used to carry large sums of money. He took the clip out a
right but he must of forgot the shell that was in the chambe
It went off and shot him in the face.'

'Where?'

'Through the right eye.'

'I mean where did the accident occur?'

'In one of the bedrooms in his apartment. He kept the ro
apartment in the Deloney building for his private use. Mo

than once I drank with him up there. Prewar Green River, boy.' He slapped my knee, and noticed the full glass in my hand. 'Drink up your drink.'

I knocked back about half of it. It wasn't prewar Green River. 'Was Deloney drinking at the time of the shooting?'

'Yeah, I think so. He knew guns. He wouldn't of made that mistake if he was sober.'

'Was anybody with him in the apartment?'

'No.'

'Can you be sure?'

'I can be sure. I was in charge of the investigation.'

'Did anybody share the apartment with him?'

'Not on a permanent basis, you might say. Luke Deloney had various women on the string. I checked them out, but none of them was within a mile of the place at the time it happened.'

'What kind of women?'

'All the way from floozies to one respectable married woman here in town. Their names didn't go into the record then and they're not going to now.'

There was a growl in his voice. I didn't pursue the subject. Not that I was afraid of Hoffman exactly. I had at least fifteen years on him, and a low alcohol content. But if he went for me I might have to hurt him badly.

'What about Mrs Deloney?' I said.

'What about her?'

'Where was she when all this was going on?'

'At home, out on Glenview. They were sort of separated. She didn't believe in divorce.'

'People who don't believe in divorce sometimes believe in murder.'

Hoffman moved his shoulders belligerently. 'You trying to say that I hushed up a murder?'

'I'm not accusing you of anything, Lieutenant.'

'You better not. I'm a cop, remember, first last and always.' He raised his fist and rotated it before his eyes like a hypnotic device. 'I been a good cop all my life. In my prime I was the best damn' cop this burg ever saw. I'll have a drink on that.' He picked up his tumbler. 'Join me?'

I said I would. We were moving obscurely on a collision course. Alcohol might soften the collision, or sink him. I finished my drink and handed him my glass. He filled it to the brim with neat whisky. Then he filled his own. He sat down and stared into the brown liquid as if it was a well where his life had drowned.

'Bottoms up,' he said.

'Take it easy, Lieutenant. You don't want to kill yourself.' It occurred to me as I said it that maybe he did.

'What are you, another pussy willow? Bottoms up.'

He drained his glass and shuddered. I held mine in my hand. After a while he noticed this.

'You didn't drink your drink. What you trying to do, pull a fast one on me? Insult my hosh – my hoshpit – ?' His lips were too numb to frame the word.

'No insult intended. I didn't come here for a drinking party, Lieutenant. I'm seriously interested in who killed your daughter. Assuming Deloney was murdered –'

'He wasn't.'

'Assuming he was, the same person may have killed Helen. In view of everything I've heard, from her and other people, I think it's likely. Don't you?'

I was trying to get his mind under my control: the sloppy drunken sentimental part, and the drunken violent part, and the hard intelligent part hidden at the core.

'Deloney was an accident,' he said clearly and stubbornly.

'Helen didn't think so. She claimed it was murder, and that she knew a witness to the murder.'

'She was lying, trying to make me look bad. All she ever wanted to do was make her old man look bad.'

His voice had risen. We sat and listened to its echoes. He dropped his empty glass, which bounced on the rug, and clenched the fist which seemed to be his main instrument of expression. I got ready to block it, but he didn't throw it at me.

Heavily and repeatedly, he struck himself in the face, on the eyes and cheeks, on the mouth, under the jaw. The blows left dull red welts in his clay-coloured flesh. His lower lip split.

Hoffman said through the blood: 'I clobbered my poor little daughter. I chased her out of the house. She never came back.'

Large tears the colour of pure distilled alcohol or grief rolled from his puffing eyes and down his damaged face. He fell sideways on the couch. He wasn't dead. His heart was beating strongly. I straightened him out – his legs were as heavy as sandbags – and put a bolster under his head. With blind eyes staring straight up into the light, he began to snore.

I closed the roll-top desk. The key was in it, and I turned it on the liquor and switched off the light and took the key outside with me.

ert Haggerty was sitting in the Chevrolet coupé, wearing a
talled expression. I got in beside him and handed him the
key.

'What's this?'

'The key to the liquor. You better keep it. Hoffman's had
s much as he can take.'

'Did he throw you out?'

'No. He passed out, while hitting himself on the face.
lard.'

Haggerty thrust his long sensitive nose toward me. 'Why
vould Earl do a thing like that?'

'He seemed to be punishing himself for hitting his daughter
long time ago.'

'Helen told me about that. Earl treated her brutally before
he left home. It's one thing I can't forgive him for.'

'He can't forgive himself. Did Helen tell you what they
quarrelled about?'

'Vaguely. It was something to do with a murder here in
ridgeton. Helen believed, or pretended to believe, that her
ather deliberately let the murderer go free.'

'Why do you say she pretended to believe it?'

'My dear dead wife,' he said, wincing at the phrase, 'had
uite a flair for the dramatic, especially in her younger days.'

'Did you know her before she left Bridgeton?'

'For a few months. I met her in Chicago at a party in
lyde Park. After she left home I helped her to get a job as a
ub reporter. I was working for the City News Bureau then.
ut as I was saying, Helen always had this dramatic flair and
vhen nothing happened in her life for it to feed on she'd
nake something happen or pretend that it had happened. Her
avourite character was Mata Hari,' he said with a chuckle
nat was half a sob.

'So you think she invented this murder?'

'I suppose I thought so at the time, because I certainly
idn't take it seriously. I have no opinion now. Does it
natter?'

'It could matter very much. Did Helen ever talk to you
bout Luke Deloney?'

'Who?'

'Luke Deloney, the man who was killed. He owned th apartment building they lived in, and occupied the penthous himself.'

Haggerty lit a cigarette before he answered. His first fe words came out as visible puffs of smoke: 'I don't recall th name. If she talked about him, it couldn't have made much c an impression on me.'

'Her mother seems to think Helen had a crush on D loney.'

'Mrs Hoffman's a pretty good woman, and I love her lik a mother, but she gets some wild ideas.'

'How do you know that this one is so wild? Was Helen i love with *you* then?'

He took a deep drag on his cigarette, like an unweane child sucking on a dry bottle. It burned down to his yellov fingers. He tossed it into the street with a sudden angr gesture.

'She never was in love with me. I was useful to her, for while. Later, in some sense, I was the last chance. The faitl ful follower. The last chance for gas before the desert.'

'The desert?'

'The desert of love. The desert of *un*love. But I don think I'll go into the long and dreary chronicle of my ma riage. It wasn't a lucky one, for either of us. I loved her, a far as I'm able to love, but she didn't love me. Proust say it's always that way. I'm teaching Proust to my sophomor class this fall, if I can summon up the élan to go on teaching

'Who did Helen love?'

'It depends on which year you're talking about. Whic month of which year.' He didn't move, but he was hurtin himself, hitting himself in the face with bitter words.

'Right at the beginning, before she left Bridgeton.'

'I don't know if you'd call it love, but she was deepl involved with a fellow-student at the City College. It was Platonic affair, the kind bright young people have, or used t have. It consisted largely of reading aloud to each other fror their own works and others'. According to Helen, she neve went to bed with him. I'm pretty sure she was a virgin whe I met her.'

'What was his name?'

'I'm afraid I don't remember. It's a clear case of Freudia repression.'

'Can you describe him?'

'I never met him. He's a purely legendary figure in m life. But obviously he isn't the elusive murderer you're searcl ing for. Helen would have been happy to see *him* go free.' He had withdrawn from the pain of memory and was using an almost flippant tone, as if he was talking about people in a play, or watching ceiling movies at the dentist's. 'Speaking of murder, as we seem to be doing, you were going to tell me about my ex-wife's death. She's completely ex now, isn't she, exed out?'

I cut in on his sad nonsense and gave him the story in some detail, including the man from Reno who ran away in the fog, and my attempts to get him identified. 'Earl tells me you went to Reno last summer to see your wife. Did you run into any of her acquaintances there?'

'Did I not. Helen played a trick on me involving a couple of them. Her purpose was to stall off any chance for an intimate talk with me. Anyway, the one evening we spent together she insisted on making it a foursome with this woman named Sally something and her alleged brother.'

'Sally Burke?'

'I believed that *was* her name. The hell of it was, Helen arranged it so that I was the Burke woman's escort. She wasn't a bad-looking woman, but we had nothing in common, and in any case it was Helen I wanted to talk to. But she spent the entire evening dancing with the brother. I'm always suspicious of men who dance too well.'

'Tell me more about this brother. He may be our man.'

'Well, he struck me as a rather sleazy customer. That may be projected envy. He was younger than I am, and healthier, and better looking. Also, Helen seemed to be fascinated by his line of chatter, which I thought was pointless – all about cars and horses and gambling odds. How a highly educated woman like Helen could be interested in such a man –' He tired of the sentence, and dropped it.

'Were they lovers?'

'How would I know? She wasn't confiding in me.'

'But you know your own wife, surely.'

He lit another cigarette and smoked half of it. 'I'd say they weren't lovers. They were simply playmates. Of course she was using him to hit at me.'

'For what?'

'For being her husband. For having been her husband. Helen and I parted on bad terms. I tried to put the marriage together again in Reno, but she wasn't even remotely inter-ested.'

'What broke up your marriage?'

'It had a major fracture in it from the beginning.' He

looked past me at the house where Earl Hoffman was lying senseless under the past. 'And it got worse. It was both our faults. I couldn't stop nagging her and she couldn't stop – doing what she was doing.'

I waited and listened. The church-bells were ringing, in different parts of the city.

'She was a tramp,' Haggerty said. 'A campus tramp. I started her on it when she was a nineteen-year-old babe in the woods in Hyde Park. Then she went on without me. Toward the end she was even taking money.'

'Who from?'

'Men with money, naturally. My wife was a corrupt woman, Mr Archer. I played a part in making her what she was, so I have no right to judge her.' His eyes were brilliant with the pain that came and went like truth in him.

I felt sorry for the man. It didn't prevent me from saying: 'Where were you Friday night?'

'At home in Maple Park in our – in my apartment, grading themes.'

'Can you prove it?'

'I have the marked papers to prove it. They were turned in to me Friday, and I marked them Friday night. I hope you're not imagining I did something fantastic like flying to California and back?'

'When a woman is murdered, you ask her estranged husband where he was at the time. It's the corollary of *cherchez la femme*.'

'Well, you have my answer. Check it out if you like. But you'll save yourself time and trouble simply by believing me. I've been completely frank with you – inordinately frank.'

'I appreciate that.'

'But then you turn around and accuse me –'

'A question isn't an accusation, Mr Haggerty.'

'It carried that implication,' he said in an aggrieved and slightly nagging tone. 'I thought the man in Reno was your suspect.'

'He's one of them.'

'And I'm another?'

'Let's drop it, shall we?'

'You brought it up.'

'Now I'm dropping it. Getting back to the man in Reno, can you remember his name?'

'I was introduced to him, of course, but I don't recall his surname. The woman called him Jud. I'm not sure whether it was a given name or a nickname.'

'Why did you refer to him as Mrs Burke's alleged brother?'

'They didn't strike me as brother and sister. They acted toward each other more like – oh – intimate friends who were simply going along with Helen's gag. I intercepted a couple of knowing glances, for example.'

'Will you describe the man in detail for me?'

'I'll try. My visual memory isn't too good. I'm strictly the verbal type.'

But under repeated questions, he built up an image of the man : age about thirty-two or -three, height just under six feet, weight about 175; muscular and active, good-looking in an undistinguished way; thinning black hair, brown eyes, no scars. He had worn a light grey silk or imitation silk suit and pointed low black shoes in the Italian style. Haggerty had gathered that the man Jud worked in some undetermined capacity for one of the gambling clubs in the Reno-Tahoe area.

It was time I went to Reno. I looked at my watch : nearly eleven : and remembered that I would gain time on the flight west. I could still have a talk with Luke Deloney's widow, if she was available, and get to Reno at a reasonable hour.

I went into the house with Haggerty, called O'Hare Airport, and made a reservation on a late afternoon flight. Then I called Mrs Deloney. She was at home, and would see me.

Bert Haggerty offered to drive me out to her house. I told him he'd better stay with his father-in-law. Hoffman's snores were sounding through the house like muffled lamentations, but he could wake up at any time and go on the rampage.

CHAPTER TWENTY-ONE

Glenview Avenue wound through the north side of the north side, in a region of estates so large that it almost qualified as country. Trees lined the road and sometimes met above it. The light that filtered through their turning leaves on to the great lawns was the colour of sublimated money.

I turned in between the brick gate-posts of 103 and shortly came in sight of an imposing old red brick mansion. The driveway led to a brick-columned *porte-cochère* on the right. I was hardly out of my car when a Negro maid in uniform opened the door.

'Mr Archer?'

'Yes.'

'Mrs Deloney is expecting you, in the downstairs sitting room.'

She was sitting by a window looking out on a countryside where red sumac blazed among less brilliant colours. Her hair was white, and bobbed short. Her blue silk suit looked like Lily Daché. Her face was a mass of wrinkles but its fine bones remained in all their delicacy. She was handsome in the way an antique object can be handsome without regard to the condition of the materials. Her mind must have been very deep in the past, because she didn't notice us until the maid spoke.

'Mr Archer is here, Mrs Deloney.'

She rose with the ease of a younger woman, putting down a book she was holding. She gave me her hand and a long look. Her eyes were the same colour as her blue silk suit, unfaded and intelligent.

'So you've come all the way from California to see me. You must be disappointed.'

'On the contrary.'

'You don't need to flatter me. When I was twenty I looked like everybody else. Now I'm past seventy, I look like myself. It's a liberating fact. But do sit down. This chair is the most comfortable. My father Senator Osborne preferred it to any other.'

She indicated a red leather armchair polished and dark with use. The chair she sat in opposite me was a ladder-backed rocker with worn cushions attached to it. The rest of the furnishings in the room were equally old and unpretentious, and I wondered if she used it as a place to keep the past.

'You've had a journey,' she reminded herself. 'Can I give you something to eat or drink?'

'No thanks.'

She dismissed the maid. 'I'm afraid you're going to be doubly disappointed. I can add very little to the official account of my husband's suicide. Luke and I hadn't been in close touch for some time before it occurred.'

'You already have added something,' I said. 'According to the official account it was an accident.'

'So it was. I'd almost forgotten. It was thought best to omit the fact of suicide from the public reports.'

'Who thought it best?'

'I did, among others. Given my late husband's position in the state, his suicide was bound to have business and political repercussions. Not to mention the personal ugliness.'

'Some people might think it was uglier to alter the fact

of a man's death.'

'Some people might think it,' she said with a *grande dame* expression. 'Not many of them would say it in my presence. In any case the fact was not altered, only the report of it. I've had to live with the fact of my husband's suicide.'

'Are you perfectly certain that it is a fact?'

'Perfectly.'

'I've just been talking to the man who handled the case, Lieutenant Hoffman. He says your husband shot himself by accident while he was cleaning an automatic pistol.'

'That was the story we agreed upon. Lieutenant Hoffman naturally sticks to it. I see no point in your trying to change it at this late date.'

'Unless Mr Deloney was murdered. Then there would be some point.'

'No doubt, but he was *not* murdered.' Her eyes came up to mine, and they hadn't changed, except that they may have become a little harder.

'I've heard rumours that he was, as far away as California.'

'Who's been spreading such nonsense?'

'Lieutenant Hoffman's daughter Helen. She claimed she knew a witness to the killing. The witness may have been herself.'

The insecurity that had touched her face changed into cold anger. 'She has no right to tell such lies. I'll have her stopped!'

'She's been stopped,' I said. 'Somebody stopped her Friday night, with a gun. Which is why I'm here.'

'I see. Where in California was she killed?'

'Pacific Point. It's on the coast south of Los Angeles.'

Her eyes flinched, ever so slightly. 'I'm afraid I never heard of it. I'm naturally sorry that the girl is dead, though I never knew her. But I can assure you that her death had nothing to do with Luke. You're barking up the wrong tree, Mr Archer.'

'I wonder.'

'There's no need to. My husband wrote me a note before he shot himself which made the whole thing very clear. Detective Hoffman brought it to me himself. No one knew it existed except him and his superiors. I hadn't intended to tell you.'

'Why?'

'Because it was ugly. In effect he blamed me and my family for what he intended to do. He was in financial hot water, he'd been gambling in stocks and other things, his business was overextended. We refused to help him, for reasons both personal and practical. His suicide was an attempt to strike back at us. It succeeded, even though we altered the facts, as you put it.' She touched her flat chest. 'I was hurt, as I was meant to be.'

'Was Senator Osborne alive at the time?'

'I'm afraid you don't know your history,' she chided me. 'My father died on December 14, 1936, three-and-a-half years before my husband killed himself. At least my father was spared that humiliation.'

'You referred to family.'

'I meant my sister Tish and my late Uncle Scott, the guardian of our trust. He and I were responsible for refusing further assistance to Luke. The decision was essentially mine. Our marriage had ended.'

'Why?'

'The usual reason, I believe. I don't care to discuss it.' She rose and went to the window and stood there straight as a soldier looking out. 'A number of things ended for me in 1940. My marriage, and then my husband's life, and then my sister's. Tish died in the summer of that same year, and I cried for her all that fall. And now it's fall again,' she said with a sigh. 'We used to ride together in the fall. I taught her to ride when she was five years old and I was ten. That was before the turn of the century.'

Her mind was wandering off into remoter and less painful times. I said:

'Forgive me for labouring the point, Mrs Deloney, but I have to ask you if that suicide note still exists.'

She turned, trying to smooth the marks of grief from her face. They persisted. 'Of course not. I burned it. You can take my word as to its contents.'

'It isn't your word that concerns me so much. Are you absolutely certain your husband wrote it?'

'Yes. I couldn't be mistaken about his handwriting.'

'A clever forgery can fool almost anybody.'

'That's absurd. You're talking the language of a melodrama.'

'We live it every day, Mrs Deloney.'

'But who would forge a suicide note?'

'It's been done, by other murderers.'

She flung back her white head and looked at me down her delicate curved nose. She resembled a bird, even in the sound of her voice:

'My husband was not murdered.'

'It seems to me you're resting a great deal of weight on a

single handwritten note which might have been forged.'

'It was not forged. I know that by internal evidence. It referred to matters that only Luke and I were privy to.'

'Such as?'

'I have no intention of telling you, or anyone. Besides, Luke had been talking for months about killing himself, especially when he was in his cups.'

'You said you hadn't been close to him for months.'

'No, but I got reports, from mutual friends.'

'Was Hoffman one of them?'

'Hardly. I didn't consider him a friend.'

'Yet he hushed up your husband's suicide for you. Your husband's alleged suicide.'

'He was ordered to. He had no choice.'

'Who gave the order?'

'Presumably the Commissioner of Police. He *was* a friend of mine, and a friend of Luke's.'

'And that made it all right for him to order the falsification of records?'

'It's done every day,' she said, 'in every city in the land. Spare me your moralizing, Mr Archer. Commissioner Robertson is long since dead. The case itself is a dead issue.'

'Maybe it is to you. It's very much on Hoffman's mind. His daughter's murder revived it.'

'I'm sorry for both of them. But I can't very well alter the past to accommodate some theory you may have. What are you trying to prove, Mr Archer?'

'Nothing specific. I'm trying to find out what the dead woman meant when she said that Bridgeton had caught up with her.'

'No doubt she meant something quite private and personal. Women usually do. But as I said, I never knew Helen Hoffman.'

'Was she involved with your husband?'

'No. She was not. And please don't ask me how I can be sure. We've scratched enough at Luke's grave, don't you think? There's nothing hidden there but a poor suicide. I helped to put him there, in a way.'

'By cutting off his funds?'

'Precisely. You didn't think I was confessing to shooting him?'

Her face crinkled up in a rather savage smile. 'Very well. I shot him. What do you propose to do about it?'

'Nothing. I don't believe you.'

'Why would I say it if it wasn't true?' She was playing the

kind of fantastic girlish game old women sometimes revert to.

'Maybe you wanted to shoot your husband. I have no doubt you did want to. But if you actually had, you wouldn't be talking about it.'

'Why not? There's nothing you could possibly do. I have too many good friends in this city, official and otherwise. Who incidentally would be greatly disturbed if you persisted in stirring up that old mess.'

'Am I to take that as a threat?'

'No, Mr Archer,' she said with her tight smile, 'I have nothing against you except that you're a zealot in your trade, or do you call it a profession? Does it really matter so much how people died? They're dead, as we all shall be, sooner or later. Some of us sooner. And I feel I've given you enough of my remaining time on earth.'

She rang for the maid.

CHAPTER TWENTY-TWO

I still had time for another try at Earl Hoffman. I drove back toward his house, through downtown streets depopulated by the Sabbath. The questions Mrs Deloney had raised, or failed to answer, stuck in my mind like fishhooks which trailed their broken lines into the past.

I was almost certain Deloney hadn't killed himself, by accident or intent. I was almost certain somebody else had, and that Mrs Deloney knew it. As for the suicide note, it could have been forged, it could have been invented, it could have been misread or misremembered. Hoffman would probably know which.

As I turned into Cherry Street, I saw a man in the next block walking away from me. He had on a blue suit and he moved with the heavy forcefulness of an old cop, except that every now and then he staggered and caught himself. I saw when I got closer that it was Hoffman. The orange cuffs of his pyjama legs hung below his blue trousers.

I let him stay ahead of me, through slums that became more blighted as we went south. We entered a Negro district. The adult men and women on the sidewalk gave Hoffman a wide berth. He was walking trouble.

He wasn't walking too well. He stumbled and fell on his hands and knees by a gap-toothed picket fence. Some chilren came out from behind the fence and followed him, prancing and hooting, until he turned on them with upraised arms. He turned again and went on.

We left the Negro district and came to a district of very old three-storeyed frame houses converted into rooming houses and business buildings. A few newer apartment buildings stood among them, and Hoffman's destination was one of these.

It was a six-storey concrete structure with a slightly run-down aspect: cracked and yellowing blinds in the rows of windows, brown watermarks below them. Hoffman went in the front entrance. I could see the inscription in the concrete arch above it: Deloney Apartments, 1928. I parked my car and followed Hoffman into the building.

He had evidently taken the elevator up. The tarnished brass arrow above the elevator door slowly turned clockwise to seven and stuck there. I gave up pushing the button after a while – Hoffman had probably left the door ajar – and found the fire stairs. I was breathing hard by the time I reached the metal door that let out on to the roof.

I opened the door a crack. Except for some pigeons coo-ooing on a neighbouring rooftop, everything outside seemed very quiet. A few potted shrubs and a green Plexiglass wind-screen jutting out at right angles from the wall of the pent-house had converted a corner of the roof into a terrace.

A man and a woman were sunning themselves there. She was lying face down on an air mattress with the brassière of her bikini unfastened. She was blonde and nicely made. He sat in a deck chair, with a half-empty Cola bottle on the table beside him. He was broad and dark, with coarse black hair matting his chest and shoulders. He wore a diamond ring on the little finger of his left hand, and had a faint Greek accent.

'So you think the restaurant business is low class? When you say that you're biting the hand that feeds you. The res-aurant business put mink on your back.'

'I didn't say it. What I said, the insurance business is a nice clean business for a man.'

'And restaurants are dirty? Not my restaurants. I even got violet rays in the toilets – '

'Don't talk filthy,' she said.

'Toilet is not a filthy word.'

'It is in my family.'

'I'm sick of hearing about your family. I'm sick of hearing about your good-for-nothing brother Theo.'

'Good-for-nothing?' She sat up, exposing a pearly flash of

breast before she fastened its moorings. 'Theo made the
Million Dollar Magic Circle last year.'

'Who bought the policy that put him over the top? I did.
Who set him up in the insurance agency in the first place? I
did.'

'Mr God.' Her face was a beautiful mask. It didn't change
when she said: 'Who's that moving around in the house? I
I sent Rosie home after breakfast.'

'She came back maybe.'

'It doesn't sound like Rosie. It sounds like a man.'

'Could be Theo coming to sell me this year's Magic Circle
policy.'

'That isn't funny.'

'I think it's very funny.'

He laughed to prove it. He stopped laughing when Earl
Hoffman came out from behind the Plexiglass windscreen.
Every mark on his face was distinct in the sunlight. His
orange pyjamas were down over his shoes.

The dark man got out of his deck chair and pushed air
toward Hoffman with his hands. 'Beat it. This is a private
roof.'

'I can't do that,' Hoffman said reasonably. 'We got a
report of a dead body. Where is it?'

'Down in the basement. You'll find it there.' The man
winked at the woman.

'The basement? They said the penthouse.' Hoffman's damaged mouth opened and shut mechanically, like a dummy's,
as if the past was ventriloquising through him. 'You moved it,
eh? It's against the law to move it.'

'You move yourself out of here.' The man turned to the
woman, who had covered herself with a yellow terrycloth
robe: 'Go in and phone the you-know-who.'

'I am the you-know-who,' Hoffman said. 'And the woman
stays. I have some questions to ask her. What's your name?'

'None of your business,' she said.

'Everything's my business.' Hoffman flung one arm out
and almost lost his balance. 'I'm detective inves'gating
murder.'

'Let's see your badge, detective.'

The man held out his hand, but he didn't move toward
Hoffman. Neither of them had moved. The woman was on
her knees, with her beautiful scared face slanting up at
Hoffman.

He fumbled in his clothes, produced a fifty-cent piece,
looked at it in a frustrated way, and flung it spinning over

he parapet. Faintly, I heard it ring on the pavement six storeys down.

'Must of left it home,' he said mildly.

The woman gathered herself together and made a dash for the penthouse. Moving clumsily and swiftly, Hoffman caught her around the waist. She didn't struggle, but stood stiff and white-faced in the circle of his arm.

'Not so fast now, baby. Got some questions to ask you. You the broad that's been sleeping with Deloney?'

She said to the man: 'Are you going to let him talk to me this way? Tell him to take his hands off me.'

'Take your hands off my wife,' the man said without force.

'Then tell her to sit down and co-operate.'

'Sit down and co-operate,' the man said.

'Are you crazy? He smells like a still. He's crazy drunk.'

'I know that.'

'Then *do* something.'

'I am doing something. You got to humour them.'

Hoffman smiled at him like a public servant who was used to weathering unjust criticism. His hurt mouth and mind made the smile grotesque. The woman tried to pull away from him. He only held her closer, his belly nudging her flank.

'You look a little bit like my dau'er Helen. You know my dau'er Helen?'

The woman shook her head frantically. Her hair fluffed out.

'She says there was a witness to the killing. Were you there when it happened, baby?'

'I don't even know what you're talking about.'

'Sure you do. Luke Deloney, Somebody drilled him in the eye and tried to make it look like suicide.'

'I remember Deloney,' the man said. 'I waited on him in my father's hamburg joint once or twice. He died before the war.'

'Before the war?'

'That's what I mean. Where you been the last twenty years, detective?'

Hoffman didn't know. He looked around at the rooftops of his city as if it was a strange place. The woman cried out: 'Let me go, fatso.'

He seemed to hear her from a long way off. 'You speak with some respect to your old man.'

'If you were my old man I'd kill myself.'

'Don't give me no more of your lip. I've had as much of your lip as I'm going to take. You hear me?'

'Yes I hear you. You're a crazy old man and take your filthy paws off me.'

Her hooked fingers raked at his face, leaving three bright parallel tracks. He slapped her. She sat down on the gravel roof. The man picked up the half-empty Cola bottle. Its brown contents gushed down his arm as he raised it, advancing on Hoffman.

Hoffman reached under the back of his coat and took a revolver out of his belt. He fired it over the man's head. The pigeons flew up from the neighbouring rooftop, whirling in great spirals. The man dropped the bottle and stood still with his hands raised. The woman, who had been whimpering, fell silent.

Hoffman glared at the glaring sky. The pigeons diminished into it. He looked at the revolver in his hand. With my eyes focused on the same object, I stepped out into the sun light.

'You need any help with these witnesses, Earl?'

'Naw, I can handle 'em. Everythin's under control.' He squinted at me. 'What was the name again? Arthur?'

'Archer.' I walked toward him, pushing my squat shadow ahead of me across the uneven surface of the gravel. 'You'll get some nice publicity out of this, Earl. Solving the Deloney killing single-handed.'

'Yeah. Sure.' His eyes were deeply puzzled. He knew I was talking nonsense, as he knew he had been acting nonsense out, but he couldn't admit it, even to himself. 'They hid the body in the basement.'

'That means we'll probably have to dig.'

'Is everybody crazy?' the man said between his upraised arms.

'Keep quiet, you,' I said. 'You better call for reinforcements, Earl. I'll hold the gun on these characters.'

He hesitated for a stretching moment. Then he handed me the revolver and went into the penthouse, bumping the door frame heavily with his shoulder.

'Who are you?' the man said.

'I'm his keeper. Relax.'

'Did he escape from the insane asylum?'

'Not yet.'

The man's eyes were like raisins thumbed deep into dough. He helped his wife to her feet, awkwardly brushing off the seat of her robe. Suddenly she was crying in his arms and he was patting her back with his diamonded hand and saying something emotional in Greek.

Through the open door I could hear Hoffman talking on the phone: 'Six men with shovels an' a drill for concrete. Her body's under the basement floor. Want 'em here in ten minutes or somebody gets reamed!'

The receiver crashed down, but he went on talking. His voice rose and fell like a wind, taking up scattered fragments of the past and blowing them together in a whirl. 'He never touched her. Wouldn't do that to the daughter of a friend. She was a good girl, too, a clean little daddy's girl. 'Member when she was a little baby, I used to give her her bath. She was soft as a rabbit. I held her in my arms, she called me da.' His voice broke. 'What happened?'

He was silent. Then he screamed. I heard him fall to the floor with a thud that shook the penthouse. I went inside. He was sitting with his back against the kitchen stove, trying to remove his trousers. He waved me back.

'Keep away from me. There's spiders on me.'

'I don't see any spiders.'

'They're under my clothes. Black widows. The killer's trying to poison me with spiders.'

'Who is the killer, Earl?'

His face worked. 'Never found out who put the chill on Deloney. Word came down from the top, close off the case. What can a man – ?' Another scream issued from his throat. 'My God, there's hundreds of 'em crawling on me.'

He tore at his clothes. They were in blue and orange rags when the police arrived, and his old wrestler's body was naked and writhing on the linoleum.

The two patrolmen knew Earl Hoffman. I didn't even have to explain.

CHAPTER TWENTY-THREE

The red sun sank abruptly when the plane came down into the shadow of the mountains. I had wired my ETA to the Walters agency, and Phyllis was waiting for me at the airport.

She took my hand and offered me her cheek. She had a peaches-and-cream complexion, a little the worse for sun, and opaque smiling eyes the colour of Indian enamel.

'You look tired, Lew. But you do exist.'

'Don't tell me. It makes me feel tireder. You look wonderful.'

'It gets more difficult as I get older. But then some other things get easier.' She didn't say what things. We walked toward her car in the sudden evening. 'What were you doing in Illinois, anyway? I thought you were working on a case in Pacific Point.'

'It's in both places. I found an old pre-war murder in Illinois which seems to be closely tied in with the current ones. Don't ask me how. It would take all night to explain, and we have more important things to do.'

'You do, anyway. You have a dinner date at eight-thirty with Mrs Sally Burke. You're an old friend of mine from Los Angeles, business unspecified. You take it from there.'

'How did you fix it?'

'It wasn't hard. Sally dotes on free dinners and unattached men. She wants to get married again.'

'But how did you get to know her?'

'I sort of happened into her at the bar where she hangs out and we got drunk together last night. One of us got drunk, anyway. She did some talking about her brother Judson, who may be the man you want.'

'He is. Where does he live?'

'Somewhere on the South Shore. It's a hard place to find people, as you know. Arnie's out there looking for him now.'

'Lead me to the sister.'

'You sound like a lamb asking to be led to the slaughter. Actually she's a pretty nice gal,' she said with female solidarity. 'Not bright, but she has her heart in the right place. She's very fond of her brother.'

'So was Lucrezia Borgia.'

Phyllis slammed the car door. We drove toward Reno, a city where nothing good had ever happened to me, but I kept hoping.

Mrs Sally Burke lived close in on Riley Street, in the upper flat of an old two-storey house. Phyllis dropped me off in front of it at eight-twenty-nine, having extracted my promise to come back and spend the night with Arnie and her. Mrs Burke was waiting in full panoply on the upper landing; tight black sheath with foxes, pearls and ear-rings, four-inch heels. Her hair was mingled brown and blonde, as if to express the complexity of her personality. Her brown eyes appraised me, as I came up to her level, the way an ante-bellum plantation owner might look over an able-bodied slave on the auction block.

She smelled nice, anyway, and she had a pleasant friendly anxious smile. We exchanged greetings and names. I was to call her Sally right away.

'I'm afraid I can't ask you in, the place is a mess. I never seem to get anything done on Sunday. You know the old song, "Gloomy Sunday"? That is, since my divorce. Phyllis says you're divorced.'

'Phyllis is right.'

'It's different for a man,' she said with some faint resentment. 'But I can see you could use a woman to look after you.'

She was one of the fastest and least efficient workers I'd ever met. My heart went down toward my boots. She was looking at my boots, and at the clothes I had slept in on the plane. On the other hand I was able-bodied. I had climbed the stairs unaided.

'Where shall we eat?' she said. 'The Riverside is nice.'

It was nice and expensive. After a couple of drinks I ceased to care about spending Alex's money. I began to be fascinated, in a way, by Sally Burke's conversation. Her ex-husband, if I could believe her, was a combination of Dracula, Hitler, and Uriah Heep. He made at least twenty-five thousand a year as a salesman in the Northwest, but more than once she had to attach his salary to collect her measly six hundred a month alimony. She was having a rough time making ends meet, especially now that her little brother had lost his job at the club.

I ordered her another drink and indicated mild sympathy.

'Jud's a good boy,' she said, as if somebody had just denied it. 'He played football at Washington State and led the team in rushing. A lot of people in Spokane thought he would have made All-American if he'd played for a better-known school. But he never got due recognition, he never has. He lost his coaching job out of sheer politics pure and simple. The charges they made were a lot of poppycock, he told me so himself.'

'What charges?'

'Nothing. They were a lot of poppycock, I mean it.' She finished her fourth Martini and regarded me with simple cunning over the empty glass. 'I don't believe you told me what kind of business that you're in, Lew?'

'I don't believe I did. I run a small agency in Hollywood.'

'Isn't that interesting? Jud has always been interested in acting. He hasn't done any, actually, but he's said to be a very handsome boy. Jud was down in Hollywood last week.'

'Looking for an acting job?'

'Anything,' she said. 'He's a willing worker, but the trouble is he isn't trained for anything, I mean after he lost his teaching credentials, and then the dance studio folded. Do you think you could get him something to do in Hollywood?'

'I'd certainly like to talk to him,' I said truthfully.

She was tipsy and hopeful, and she wasn't surprised by my interest in her brother.

'*That* can be arranged,' she said. 'As a matter of fact he's at my apartment right now. I could call him and tell him to come over here.'

'Let's have dinner first.'

'I don't mind paying for Jud's dinner.' She realized she had made a tactical error, and quickly back-tracked: 'But I guess three's company, eh? I mean two.'

She talked so much about her brother at dinner that it was almost like having him there. She recited his old football statistics. She told me, with a kind of vicarious enthusiasm, all about his prowess with the ladies. She explained about the brilliant ideas Jud was always hatching. The one I liked best was a plan for a condensed version of the Bible, with all the offensive passages removed, for family reading.

Sally couldn't drink. She was coming apart by the time we finished eating. She wanted to pick up her brother and go and hell around in the clubs, but my heart wasn't in it. I took her home. In the cab she went to sleep on my shoulder. This I didn't mind.

I woke her up on Riley Street and got her into the house and up the stairs. She seemed very large and loosely put together, and the foxes kept slipping. I felt as if I'd been nursing drunks all week-end.

A man in shirtsleeves and form-fitting trousers opened the door of her flat. With Sally leaning on me, I got a quick impression of him: a man of half-qualities who lived in a half-world: he was half-handsome, half-lost, half-spoiled, half-smart, half-dangerous. His pointed Italian shoes were scuffed at the toes.

'Need any help?' he said to me.

'Don't be ridic,' Sally said. 'I'm in perfect control. Mr Archer, meet brother Jud, Judson Foley.'

'Hello,' he said. 'You shouldn't have let her drink. She's got a weak head for liquor. Here, I'll take her.'

With weary skill he looped her arm over his shoulders, clasped her around the waist, walked her through the front room into a lighted bedroom, laid her out on the Hollywood bed, and turned off the light.

He seemed unpleasantly surprised to find me still in the front room. 'Good night, Mr Archer, or whatever your name is. We're closing up for the night now.'

'You're not very hospitable.'

'No. My sister is the hospitable one.' He cast a sour glance around the little room, at overflowing ashtrays, clouded glasses, scattered newspapers. 'I never saw you before, I'll never see you again. Why should I be hospitable?'

'You're sure you never saw me before? Think hard.'

His brown eyes studied my face, and then my body. He scratched nervously at the front of his thinning hair. He shook his head.

'If I ever saw you before I must have been drunk at the time. Did Sally bring you here when I was drunk?'

'No. Were you drinking last Friday night?'

'Let's see, what night was that? I think I was out of town. Yeah. I didn't get back here until Saturday morning.' He was trying to sound casual and look unconcerned. 'It must have been two other guys.'

'I don't think so, Jud. I ran into you, or you ran into me, about nine last Friday night in Pacific Point.'

Panic brightened his face like a flash of lightning. 'Who are you?'

'I chased you down Helen Haggerty's driveway, remember? You were too fast for me. It took me two days to catch up.'

He was breathing as if he'd just finished the run. 'Are you from the police?'

'I'm a private detective.'

He sat down in a Danish chair, gripping the fragile arms so hard I thought they might break. He snickered. It was very close to a sob.

'This is Bradshaw's idea, isn't it?'

I didn't answer him. I cleared a chair and sat in it.

'Bradshaw said he was satisfied with my story. Now he sends you up against me.' His eyes narrowed. 'I suppose you were pumping my sister about me.'

'She doesn't need much priming.'

Twisting in the chair, he threw a wicked look in the direction of her bedroom. 'I wish she'd keep her mouth shut about my business.'

'Don't blame her for what you did yourself.'

'But the hell of it is I didn't *do* anything. I *told* Bradshaw that, and he believed me, at least he said he did.'

'Are you talking about Roy Bradshaw?'

'Who else? He recognized me the other night, or thought he did. I didn't know who it was I bumped in the dark. I just wanted out of there.'

'Why?'

He lifted his heavy shoulders and sat with them lifted, head down between them. 'I didn't want trouble with the law.'

'What were you doing at Helen's?'

'She *asked* me to come. Hell, I went there as a good Samaritan. She called me at the motel in Santa Monica and practically begged me to come and spend the night. It wasn't my beautiful blue eyes. She was frightened, she wanted company.'

'What time did she call you?'

'Around seven or seven-thirty. I was just coming in from getting something to eat.' He dropped his shoulders. 'Listen, you know all this, you got it from Bradshaw, didn't you? What are you trying to do, trap me into a mistake?'

'It's an idea. What sort of a mistake did you have in mind?'

He shook his head, and went on shaking it as he spoke. 'I didn't have anything particular in mind. I mean, I can't afford to make any mistakes.'

'You already made the big one, when you ran.'

'I know. I panicked.' He shook his head some more. 'There she was with a bullet hole in her skull and there I was a natural set-up for a patsy. I heard you fellows coming, and I panicked. You've got to believe me.'

They always said that. 'Why do I have to believe you?'

'Because I'm telling the truth. I'm innocent as a little child.'

'That's pretty innocent.'

'I didn't mean in general, I meant in this particular situation. I went a long way out of my way to give Helen a helping hand. It doesn't make sense I'd go there to knock her off. I *liked* the girl. She and I had a lot in common.'

I didn't know if this was a compliment to either of them. Bert Haggerty had described his ex-wife as corrupt. The man in front of me was a dubious character. Behind the mask of his good looks he seemed dilapidated, as if he'd painfully bumped down several steps in the social scale. In spite of this, I half-believed his story. I would never more than half-believe anything he said.

'What did you and Helen have in common?'

He gave me a quick sharp up-from-under look. This wasn't the usual line of questioning. He thought about his answer.

'Sports. Dancing. Fun and games. We had some real fun times, I mean it. I almost died when I found her the other night.'

'How did you happen to meet her?'

'You *know* all this,' he said impatiently. 'You're working for Bradshaw, aren't you?'

'Put it this way: Bradshaw and I are on the same side.'

I wanted to know why Roy Bradshaw loomed so large in Foley's mind, but other questions had priority. 'Now why don't you humour me and tell me how you knew Helen?'

'It's simple enough.' He jabbed his thumb downward like a decadent emperor decreeing death. 'She rented the downstairs apartment when she was putting in her six weeks this summer. She and my sister hit it off, and eventually I got into the act. The three of us used to go places together.'

'In Sally's car?'

'I had my own car then – sixty-two Galaxie five hundred,' he said earnestly. 'This was back in August before I lost my job and couldn't keep up with the payments.'

'How did you happen to lose your job?'

'That wouldn't interest you. It had nothing to do with Helen Haggerty, nothing whatever.'

His overinsistence on the point made me suspicious. 'What were you working at?'

'I said you wouldn't be interested.'

'I can easily find out where you were working. You might as well tell me.'

He said with his eyes down: 'I was in the cashier's cage at the Solitaire in Stateline. I guess I made one mistake too many.' He looked at his strong square fumbling hands.

'So you were looking for work in Los Angeles?'

'Correcto.' He seemed relieved to get away from the subject of his job and why he lost it. 'I didn't make a connection, but I've got to get out of this place.'

'Why?'

He scratched his hair. 'I can't go on living on my sister. It *cuts* me, being on the ding. I'm going down to LA again and have another look around.'

'Let's get back to the first time. You say Helen called you at your motel Friday night. How did she know you were here?'

'I already called her earlier in the week.'

'What for?'

'The usual. I mean, I thought we could get together, have some fun.' He kept talking about having fun but he looked

157

as if he hadn't had any for years. 'Helen already had a date that night, Wednesday night. As a matter of fact she had a date with Bradshaw. They were going to some concert. She said she'd call me back another time. Which she did, Friday night.'

'What did she say on the telephone?'

'That somebody threatened to kill her, and she was scared. I never heard her talk like that before. She said that she had nobody to turn to but me. And I got there too late.' There seemed to be grief in him, but even this was ambiguous, as if he felt defrauded by Helen's death.

'Were Helen and Bradshaw close?'

He answered cautiously: 'I wouldn't say that. I guess they lucked into each other last summer the same way Helen and I did. Anyway, he was busy Friday night. He had to give a speech at some big dinner. At least that's what he told me this morning.'

'He wasn't lying. Did Bradshaw and Helen meet here in Reno?'

'Where else?'

'I thought Bradshaw spent the summer in Europe.'

'You thought wrong. He was here all through August, anyway.'

'What was he doing here?'

'He told me once he was doing some kind of research at the University of Nevada. He didn't say what kind. I hardly knew him, actually. I ran into him a couple of times with Helen, and that was it. I didn't see him again until today.'

'And you say he recognized you Friday night and came here to question you?'

'That's the truth. He came here this morning, gave me quite a grilling. *He* believed I didn't do that murder. I don't see why you can't believe me.'

'I'll want to talk to Bradshaw before I make up my mind. Where is he now, do you know?'

'He said he was staying at the Lakeview Inn, on the North Shore. I don't know if he's still there or not.'

I stood up and opened the door. 'I think I'll go and see.'

I suggested to Jud that he stay where he was, because a second run-out would make him look very bad. He nodded. He was still nodding when a counter-impulse took hold of him and he rushed me. His heavy shoulder caught me under the ribs and slammed me back against the doorframe wheezing for air.

He threw a punch at my face. I shifted my head. His fist

crunched into the plaster wall. He yipped with pain. He hit me low in the belly with his other hand. I slid down the door-frame. He kneed me, a glancing blow on the side of the jaw.

This impelled me to get up. He rushed me again, head down. I stepped to one side and chopped the back of his neck as he went by. He staggered rapidly through the door and across the landing, and plunged down. At the foot of the stairs he lay still.

But he was conscious when the police arrived. I rode along to the station to make sure they nailed him down. We hadn't been there five minutes when Arnie came in. He had an understanding with the officers. They booked Foley for assault and related charges, and promised to hold him.

CHAPTER TWENTY-FOUR

Arnie drove me out to the Lakeview Inn, a rambling California Gothic pile which must have dated from the early years of the century. Generations of summer visitors had marched through the lobby and trampled out any old-world charm it might once have had. It seemed an unlikely place for Roy Bradshaw to be staying.

But Bradshaw was there, the elderly night clerk said. He took a railroad watch out of his vest pocket and consulted it. 'It's getting pretty late, though. They may be asleep.'

'They?'

'Him and his wife. I can go up and call him, if you want me to. We never did put telephones in the rooms.'

'I'll go up. I'm a friend of Dr Bradshaw's.'

'I didn't know he was a doctor.'

'A doctor of philosophy,' I said. 'What's his room number?'

'Thirty-one, on the top floor.' The old man seemed relieved at not having to make the climb.

I left Arnie with him and went up to the third floor. Light shone through the transom of 31, and I could hear the indistinct murmur of voices. I knocked. There was a silence, followed by the noise of slippered feet.

Roy Bradshaw spoke through the door. 'Who is it?'

'Archer.'

He hesitated. A sleeper in the room across the hall, perhaps disturbed by our voices, began to snore. Bradshaw said:

'What are you doing here?'

'I have to see you.'

'Can't it wait till morning?' His voice was impatient, and he had temporarily mislaid his Harvard accent.

'No. It can't. I need your advice on what to do about Judson Foley.'

'Very well. I'll get dressed.'

I waited in the narrow ill-lit hallway. It had the faintly acrid smell which old buildings seem to absorb from the people who pass through them night by night, the smell of transient life. The snoring man was uttering terrible moans between his snores. A woman told him to turn over, and he subsided.

I could hear a quick interchange of voices in Bradshaw's room. The woman's voice seemed to want something, which Bradshaw's voice denied. I thought I recognized the woman's voice, but I couldn't be sure.

I was sure when Bradshaw finally opened the door. He tried to slip out without letting me see in, but I caught a glimpse of Laura Sutherland. She was sitting upright on the edge of the unmade bed in a severely cut Paisley robe. Her hair was down around her shoulders, and she was rosy and beautiful.

Bradshaw jerked the door shut. 'So now you know.'

He had pulled on slacks and a black turtleneck sweater which made him look more undergraduate than ever. In spite of the tension in him, he seemed quite happy.

'I don't know what I know,' I said.

'This is not an illicit liaison, believe me. Laura and I were married some time ago. We're keeping our marriage secret, for the present. I'm going to ask you to go along with that.'

I didn't say whether I would or not. 'Why all the secrecy?'

'We have our reasons. For one thing, under college regulations, Laura would have to give up her post. She intends to, of course, but not immediately. And then there's Mother. I don't know how I'm going to break it to her.'

'You could just tell her. She'll survive.'

'It's easy enough to say. It isn't possible.'

The thing that made it impossible, I thought, was Mother's money. Having money and looking forward to inheriting more were difficult habits for a man to break in early middle age. But I felt a sneaking admiration for Bradshaw. He had more life in him than I'd suspected.

We went downstairs and through the lobby, where Arnie was playing gin rummy with the night clerk. The bar was a gloomy cavern with antlers on the walls instead of stalactites and customers instead of stalagmites. One of the customers, a local man wearing a cap and windbreaker and carrying a load, wanted to buy Bradshaw and me a drink. The bartender told him it was time to go home. Surprisingly, he went, and most of the others drifted out after him.

We sat at the bar. Bradshaw ordered a double bourbon and insisted on one for me, though I didn't need it. There was some aggression in his insistence. He hadn't forgiven me for stumbling on his secret, or for dragging him away from his wife's bed.

'Well,' he said, 'what about Judson Foley?'

'He tells me you recognized him Friday night.'

'I had an intuition that it was he.' Bradshaw had recovered his accent, and was using it as a kind of vocal mask.

'Why didn't you say so? You could have saved a lot of leg-work and expense.'

He looked at me solemnly over his drink. 'I had to be certain and I was very far from being that. I couldn't accuse a man, and set the police on his trail, unless I were certain.'

'So you came here to make certain?'

'It happened to work out that way. There are times in a man's life when everything seems to fall together into place, have you noticed?' A momentary flash of glee broke through his eagerness. 'Laura and I had been planning to steal a week-end here for some time, and the conference gave us the opportunity. Foley was a side issue, but of course a very important one. I looked him up this morning and questioned him thoroughly. He seems completely innocent to me.'

'Innocent of what?'

'Of Helen's murder. Foley went to her house to give her what protection he could, but she was already beyond protection when he got there. He lost his nerve and ran.'

'What was he afraid of?'

'A false accusation, what he calls a frame-up. He's had some trouble with the law in the past. It had to do with shaving points, as they call it, in football games.'

'How do you know?'

'He told me. I have,' he said with a chuckle of vanity, 'a certain capacity to inspire confidence in these – ah – disaffiliates. The man was utterly forthright with me, and in my considered opinion he had nothing to do with Helen's murder.'

'You're probably right. I'd still like to find out more about him.'

'I know very little about him. He was a friend of Helen's. I saw him once or twice in her company.'

'In Reno.'

'Yes. I spent a part of the summer in Nevada. It's another fact about myself that I'm not publicising.' He added rather vaguely: 'A man has a right to some private life, surely.'

'You mean you were here with Laura?'

He dropped his eyes. 'She was with me a part of the time. We hadn't quite made up our minds to get married. It was quite a decision. It meant the end of her career and the end of my – life with Mother,' he concluded lamely.

'I can understand your reason for keeping it quiet. Still I wish you'd told me that you met Foley and Helen last month in Reno.'

'I should have. I apologise. One acquires the habit of secrecy.' He added in a different, passionate voice: 'I'm deeply in love with Laura. I'm jealous of anything that threatens to disturb our idyll.' His words were formal and old-fashioned, but the feeling behind them seemed real.

'What was the relationship between Foley and Helen?'

'They were friends, nothing more, I'd say. Frankly I was a little surprised at her choice of companion. But he was younger than she, and I suppose that was the attraction. Presentable escorts are at a premium in Reno, you know. I had quite a time myself fending off the onslaughts of various predatory females.'

'Does that include Helen?'

'I suppose it does.' Through the gloom I thought I could discern a faint blush on his cheek. 'Of course she didn't know about my – my *thing* with Laura. I've kept it a secret from everyone.'

'Is that why you don't want Foley taken back for questioning?'

'I didn't say that.'

'I'm asking you.'

'I suppose that's partly it.' There was a long silence. 'But if you think it's necessary, I won't argue. Laura and I have nothing really to hide.'

The bartender said: 'Drink up, gentlemen. It's closing time.'

We drank up. In the lobby Bradshaw gave me a quick nervous handshake, muttering something about getting back to his wife. He went up the stairs two at a time, on his toes.

I waited for Arnie to finish his game of gin. One of the things that made him a first-rate detective was his ability to merge with almost any group, nest into almost any situation, and start a conversation rolling. He and the night man shook hands where we left the hotel.

'The woman your friend registered with,' he said in the car, 'is a good-looking brownette type, well stacked, who talks like a book.'

'She's his wife.'

'You didn't tell me Bradshaw was married,' he said rather irritably.

'I just found out. The marriage is *sub rosa*. The poor beggar has a dominating mother in the background. In the foreground. The old lady has money, and I think he's afraid of being disinherited.'

'He better come clean with her, and take his chances.'

'That's what I told him.'

Arnie put the car in gear and as we drove west and south along the lakeshore, recounted a long story about a client he had handled for Pinkerton in San Francisco before the war. She was a well-heeled widow of sixty or so who lived in Hillsborough with her son, a man in his thirties. The son was always home by midnight, but seldom before, and the mother wanted to know what he was doing with his evenings. It turned out he had been married for five years to an ex-waitress whom he maintained, with their three small children, in a row house in South San Francisco.

Arnie seemed to think that this was the end of the story.

'What happened to the people?' I asked him.

'The old lady fell in love with her grandchildren and put up with the daughter-in-law for their sake. They all lived happily ever after, on her money.'

'Too bad Bradshaw hasn't been married long enough to have any children.'

We drove in silence for a while. The road left the shore and tunnelled among trees which enclosed it like sweet green coagulated night. I kept thinking about Bradshaw and his unsuspected masculinity.

'I'd like you to do some checking on Bradshaw, Arnie.'

'Has this marriage business escalated him into a suspect?'

'Not in my book. Not yet, anyway. But he did suppress the fact that he met Helen Haggerty in Reno last summer. I want to know exactly what he was doing here in the month of August. He told Judson Foley he was doing research at the University of Nevada, but that doesn't seem likely.'

'Why not?'

'He's got a doctorate from Harvard, and he'd normally do his research there or at Berkeley or Stanford. I want you to do some checking on Foley, too. Find out if you can why

Foley was fired by the Solitaire Club.'

'That shouldn't be too hard. Their top security man is an old friend of mine.' He looked at his watch in the light from the dash. 'We could go by there now but he probably won't be on duty this late on a Sunday night.'

'Tomorrow will do.'

Phyllis was waiting for us with food and drink. We sat up in her kitchen foolishly late, getting mildly drunk on beer and shared memories and exhaustion. Eventually the conversation came full circle, back to Helen Haggerty and her death. At three o'clock in the morning I was reading aloud her translated poem in the *Bridgeton Blazer* about the violins of the autumn winds.

'It's terribly sad,' Phyllis said. 'She must have been a remarkable young girl, even if it is only a translation.'

'That was her father's word for her. Remarkable. He's remarkable, too, in his own way.'

I tried to tell them about the tough old drunken heartbroken cop who had sired Helen. Suddenly it was half-past three and Phyllis was asleep with her head resting like a tousled dahlia among the bottles on the kitchen table. Arnie began gathering up the bottles, carefully, so as not to wake her unnecessarily soon.

Alone in their guest-room I had one of those intuitions that come sometimes when you're very tired and emotionally stirred up. I became convinced that Hoffman had given me the *Blazer* for a reason. There was something in it he wanted me to see.

I sat in my underwear on the edge of the open fresh-smelling bed and read the little magazine until my eyes crossed. I learned a good deal about student activities at Bridgeton City College twenty-two years ago, but nothing of any apparent consequences to my case.

I found another poem I liked, though. It was signed with the initials G.R.B., and it went:

> If light were dark
> And dark were light,
> And dark were light,
> In the blaze of night,
>
> A raven's wing
> As bright as tin,
> Then you, my love,
> Would be darker than sin.

I read it aloud at breakfast. Phyllis said she envied the woman it had been written to. Arnie complained that his scrambled eggs weren't moist. He was older than Phyllis, and it made him touchy.

We decided after breakfast to leave Judson Foley sitting for the present. If Dolly Kincaid were arrested and arraigned, Foley would make a fairly good surprise witness for the defence. Arnie drove me to the airport, where I caught a Pacific flight to Los Angeles.

I picked up an LA paper at International Airport, and found a brief account of the Haggerty killing in the Southland News on an inside page. It informed me that the wife-slayer Thomas McGee, released from San Quentin earlier in the year, was being sought for questioning. Dolly Kincaid wasn't mentioned.

CHAPTER TWENTY-FIVE

Around noon I walked into Jerry Marks's store-front office. His secretary told me that Monday was the day for the weekly criminal docket and Jerry had spent the morning in court. He was probably having lunch somewhere near the courthouse. Yes, Mr Kincaid had got in touch with Mr Marks on Sunday, and retained him.

I found them together in the restaurant where Alex and I lunched the day it began. Alex made room for me on his side of the booth, facing the front. Business was roaring, and there was a short line-up inside the front door.

'I'm glad the two of you got together,' I said.

Alex produced one of his rare smiles. 'So am I. Mr Marks has been wonderful.'

Jerry flapped his hand in a deprecating way. 'Actually I haven't been able to do anything yet. I had another case to dispose of this morning. I did make an attempt to pick Gil Stevens's brains, but he told me I'd better go to the transcript of the trial, which I plan to do this afternoon. Mrs Kincaid,' he said, with a sidelong glance at Alex, 'was just as uncommunicative as Stevens.'

'You've talked to Dolly then?'

He lowered his voice. 'I tried, yesterday. We've got to know where we stand before the police get to her.'

'Is that going to happen?'

Jerry glanced around him at the courthouse crowd, and lowered his voice still further. 'According to the grapevine, they were planning to make their move today, when they completed their ballistics tests. But something's holding them up. The Sheriff and the experts he brought in are still down in the shooting gallery under the courthouse.'

'The bullet may be fragmented. It often is in head wounds. Or they may have shifted their main attention to another suspect. I see in the paper they've put out an APB for Thomas McGee.'

'Yes, it was done yesterday. He's probably over the Mexican border by now.'

'Do you consider him a major suspect, Jerry?'

'I'll want to read that transcript before I form an opinion. Do you?'

It was a hard question. I was spared having to answer it by a diversion. Two elderly ladies, one in serviceable black and one in fashionable green, looked in through the glass front door. They saw the waiting queue and turned away. The one in black was Mrs Hoffman, Helen's mother. The other was Luke Deloney's widow.

I excused myself and went out after them. They had crossed the street in the middle of the block and were headed downtown, moving through light and shadow under the giant yuccas that hedged the courthouse grounds. Though they seemed to keep up an incessant conversation, they walked together like strangers, out of step and out of sympathy. Mrs Deloney was much the older, but she had a horsewoman's stride. Mrs Hoffman stubbed along on tired feet.

I stayed on the other side of the street and followed them at a distance. My heart was thudding. Mrs Deloney's arrival in California confirmed my belief that her husband's murder and Helen's were connected, and that she knew it.

They walked two blocks to the main street and went into the first restaurant they came to, a tourist trap with empty tables visible through its plate glass windows. There was an open-fronted cigar store diagonally across the street. I looked over its display of paperbacks, bought a pack of cigarettes, and smoked three or four which I lit at the old-fashioned gas flame, and eventually bought a book about ancient Greek philosophy. It had a chapter on Zeno which I read standing. The old ladies were a long time over lunch.

'Archer will never catch the old ladies,' I said.

The man behind the counter cupped his ear. 'What was that?'

166

'I was thinking aloud.'

'It's a free country. I like to talk to myself when I'm off work. In the store here it wouldn't be appropriate.' He smiled over the word, and his gold teeth flashed like jewellery.

The old ladies came out of the restaurant and separated. Mrs Hoffman limped south, toward her hotel. Mrs Deloney strode in the opposite direction, moving rapidly now that she was unencumbered by her companion. From the distance you could have taken her for a young woman who had unaccountably bleached her hair white.

She turned off the main street in the direction of the courthouse, and half-way down the block disappeared into a modern concrete and glass building. 'Law Offices of Stevens and Ogilvy,' said the brass sign beside the entrance. I walked on to the next corner, sat on a bench at a bus stop, and read in my new book about Heraclitus. All things flow like a river, he said; nothing abides. Parmenides, on the other hand, believed that nothing ever changed, it only seemed to. Both views appealed to me.

A cab pulled up in front of the Stevens and Ogilvy office. Mrs Deloney came out, and the cab took her away. I made a note of its licence number before I went into the building.

It was a large office, and a working one. Typewriters were clacking in a row of cubicles behind the waiting-room. A very junior attorney in a flannel suit was telling the middle-aged woman at the front desk how he wanted a brief set up on her typewriter.

He went away. Her steel-grey glance met mine, and we happened to smile at each other. She said:

'I was typing briefs when he was just a gleam in his daddy's eye. Can I help you?'

'I'm very eager to see Mr Gil Stevens. My name is Archer.'

She looked in her appointment book, and then at her watch. 'Mr Stevens is due for lunch in ten minutes. He won't be coming back to the office today. I'm sorry.'

'It has to do with a murder case.'

'I see. I may be able to slip you in for five minutes if that will do any good.'

'It might.'

She talked to Stevens on the phone and waved me past the cubicles to an office at the end of the hall. It was large and sumptuous. Stevens sat on leather behind mahogany, flanked by a glass-faced cabinet of yachting trophies. He was lion-faced, with a big soft masterful mouth, a high brow overhung by broken wings of yellowish white hair, pale blue eyes that had seen everything at least once and were watching the second time around. He wore tweeds and a florid bow tie.

'Close the door behind you, Mr Archer, and sit down.'

I parked myself on a leather settee and started to tell him what I was doing there. His heavy voice interrupted me:

'I have only a very few minutes. I know who you are, sir, and I believe I know what you have in mind. You want to discuss the McGee case with me.'

I threw him a curve: 'And the Deloney case.'

His eyebrows went up, forcing the flesh above them into multiple corrugations. Sometimes you have to give away information on the chance of gaining other information. I told him what had happened to Luke Deloney.

He leaned forward in his chair. 'You say this is connected in some way with the Haggerty murder?'

'It has to be. Helen Haggerty lived in Deloney's apartment bulding. She said she knew a witness to Deloney's murder.'

'Strange she didn't mention it.' He wasn't talking to me. He was talking to himself about Mrs Deloney. Then he remembered that I was there. 'Why do you come to me with this?'

'I thought you'd be interested, since Mrs Deloney is your client.'

'Is she?'

'I assumed she was.'

'You're welcome to your assumptions. I suppose you followed her here.'

'I happened to see her come in. But I've wanted to get in touch with you for a couple of days.'

'Why?'

'You defended Tom McGee. His wife's death was the second in a series of three related murders which started with Deloney and ended with Helen Haggerty. Now they're trying to pin the Haggerty death on McGee or his daughter, or both of them. I believe McGee is innocent, and has been all along.'

'Twelve of his peers thought otherwise.'

'Why did they, Mr Stevens?'

'I get no pleasure from discussing past mistakes.'

'This could be very relevant to the present. McGee's daughter admits she lied on the witness stand. She says she lied her father into prison.'

'Does she now? The admission comes a little belatedly. I should have borne down on her in cross, but McGee didn't vant me to. I made the mistake of respecting his wishes.'

'What was the motive behind them?'

'Who can say? Paternal love, perhaps, or his feeling that
the child had been made to suffer enough. Ten years in prison
is a big price to pay for such delicacies of feeling.'

'You're convinced that McGee was innocent?'

'Oh, yes. The daughter's admission that she was lying
removes any possible doubt.' Stevens took a blotched green
cigar out of a glass tube, clipped it and lit it. 'I take it that is
highly confidential advice.'

'On the contrary, I'd like to see it publicized. It might help
to bring McGee in. He's on the run, as you probably know.'

Stevens neither affirmed nor denied this. He sat like a
mountain behind a blue haze of smoke.

'I'd like to ask him some questions,' I said.

'What about?'

'The other man, for one thing – the man Constance McGee
was in love with. I understand he played some part in your
case.'

'He was my hypothetical alternative.' Stevens's face crumpled
in a rueful smile. 'But the judge wouldn't let him in, except
in my summing-up, unless I put McGee on the stand. Which
didn't seem advisable. That other man was a two-edged
weapon. He was a motive for McGee, as well as an alternative
suspect. I made the mistake of going for an outright acquittal.'

'I don't quite follow.'

'It doesn't matter. It's only history.' He waved his hand,
and the smoke shifted around him like strata of time in an
old man's memory.

'Who was the other man?'

'Come now, Mr Archer, you can't expect to walk in off
the street and pump me dry. I've been practising law for forty
years.'

'Why did you take McGee's case?'

'Tom used to do some work on my boats. I rather liked
him.'

'Aren't you interested in clearing him?'

'Not at the expense of another innocent man.'

'You know who the other man is?'

'I know who he is, if Tom can be believed.' While he still
sat solidly in his chair, he was withdrawing from me like a
magician through dissolving mirrors. 'I don't divulge the
secrets that came to me. I bury 'em, sir. That's why they
come to me.'

'It would be a hell of a thing if they put Tom back in San

Quentin for the rest of his life, or gassed him.'

'It certainly would. But I suspect you're trying to enlist me in your cause, rather than Tom's.'

'We could certainly use you.'

'Who are "we"?'

'McGee's daughter Dolly and her husband Alex Kincaid, Jerry Marks and me.'

'And what *is* your case?'

'The solution of those three murders.'

'You make it sound very simple and neat,' he said. 'Life never is. Life always has loose ends, and it's sometimes best to let them ravel out.'

'Is that what Mrs Deloney wants?'

'I wasn't speaking on behalf of Mrs Deloney. I don't expect to.' He worked a speck of tobacco on to the tip of his tongue and spat it out.

'Did she come to you for information about the McGee case?'

'No comment.'

'That probably means yes. It's a further indication that the McGee case and the Deloney killing are connected.'

'We won't discuss it,' he said shortly. 'As for your suggestion that I join forces with you, Jerry Marks had the same idea this morning. As I told him, I'll think about it. In the mean time I want you and Jerry to think about something. Tom McGee and his daughter may be on opposite sides of the issue. They certainly were ten years ago.'

'She was a child then, manipulated by adults.'

'I know that.' He rose, bulking huge in his light tweed suit. 'It's been interesting talking to you but I'm overdue for a luncheon meeting.' He moved past me to the door, gesturing with his cigar. 'Come along.'

CHAPTER TWENTY-SIX

I walked down the main street to the Pacific Hotel and asked for Mrs Hoffman. She had just checked out, leaving no forwarding address. The bellhop who handled her bag said she had ridden away in a taxi with another old lady wearing a green coat. I gave him five dollars and my motel address, and told him it would be worth another five to find out where they'd gone.

It was past two o'clock, and my instinct told me this was the crucial day. I felt cut off from what was happening in the private offices of the courthouse, in the shooting gallery and laboratory where the ballistics tests were being conducted, behind the locked door of the nursing home. Time was slipping away, flowing past me like Heraclitus's river, while I was checking up on the vagaries of old ladies.

I went back to the telephone booths behind the hotel lobby and called Godwin's office. The doctor was with a patient, and wouldn't be available until ten minutes to three. I tried Jerry Marks. His secretary told me he was still out.

I made a collect call to the Walters agency in Reno. Arnie answered the phone:

'Nice timing, Lew. I just got the word on your boy.'

'Which one? Bradshaw or Foley?'

'Both of them in a way. You wanted to know why Foley lost his job at the Solitaire Club. The answer is he used his position in the cashier's cage to find out how much Bradshaw was worth.'

'How did he do that?'

'You know how the clubs check up on their customers when they open an account. They put in a query to the customer's bank, get an approximate figure on his bank balance, and set a limit to his credit accordingly. "Low three" means a three-figure bank balance on the low side, and maybe a limit of a couple of hundred. A "high four" might be seven or eight thousand, and a 'low five' maybe twenty or thirty thousand. Which incidentally is Bradshaw's bracket.'

'Is he a gambler?'

'He isn't. That's the point. He never opened an account at the Solitaire, or anywhere else that I know of, but Foley put in a query on him anyway. The club caught it, did a double check on Foley, and got him out of there fast.'

'It smells like possible blackmail, Arnie.'

'More than possible,' he said. 'Foley admits to a bit of a record in that line.'

'What else does he admit?'

'Nothing else yet. He claims he got the information for a friend.'

'Helen Haggerty?'

'Foley isn't saying. He's holding back in the hope of making a deal.'

'Go ahead and deal with him. He got hurt worse than I did. I'm willing to drop charges.'

'It may not be necessary, Lew.'

'Deal with him. Assuming blackmail, which I do, the question is what makes Bradshaw blackmailable.'

'Could be his divorce,' Arnie said smoothly. 'You were interested in what Bradshaw was doing in Reno between the middle of July and the end of August. The answer is on the court record. He was establishing residence for a divorce from a woman named Letitia O. Macready.'

'Letitia who?'

'Macready.' He spelled it out. 'I haven't been able to get any further information on the woman. According to the lawyer who handled the divorce, Bradshaw didn't know where she lived. Her last known address was in Boston. The official notice of the proceedings came back from there with a "Gone – No Order" stamp.'

'Is Bradshaw still at Tahoe?'

'He and his new wife checked out this morning. They were on their way back to Pacific Point. That makes him your baby.'

'Baby isn't quite the word for Bradshaw. I wonder if his mother knows about the first marriage.'

'You could always ask her.'

I decided to try and talk to Bradshaw first. I got my car out of the courthouse lot and drove out to the college. The students on the mall and in the corridors, particularly the girls, wore subdued expressions. The threat of death and judgment had invaded the campus. I felt a little like its representative.

The blonde secretary in the Dean's outer office looked tense, as if only her will was holding her, and the whole institution, together.

'Dean Bradshaw isn't in.'

'Not back from the week-end yet?'

'Of course he's back.' She added in a defensive tone: 'Dean Bradshaw was here this morning for over an hour.'

'Where is he now?'

'I don't know. I guess he went home.'

'You sound kind of worried about him.'

She answered me with a machine-gun burst from her typewriter. I retreated, across the hall to Laura Sutherland's office. Her secretary told me she hadn't come in today. She'd phoned in the middle of the morning that she was afraid she was coming down with something. I hoped it wasn't something serious, like death and judgment.

I drove back to Foothill and along it to the Bradshaw house. Wind rustled in the trees. The fog had been completely dissipated, and the afternoon sky was a brilliant aching blue. The mountains rising into it were distinct in every scarred and wrinkled detail.

I was more aware than usual of these things, but I felt cut off from them. I must have had some empathy for Roy Bradshaw and his new wife and was afraid of being hurt in my empathy. I drove past his gate without seeing it and had to turn in the next driveway and come back to the Bradshaw house. I was somewhat relieved to be told by the Spanish woman, Maria, that Bradshaw wasn't there and hadn't been all day.

Mrs Bradshaw called from the stairs in a cracked penetrating voice: 'Is that you, Mr Archer? I want to talk to you.'

She came down the steps in a quilted dressing robe and cloth slippers. The week-end had aged her. She looked very old and haggard.

'My son hasn't been home for three days,' she complained, 'and he hasn't telephoned once. What do you suppose has happened to him?'

'I'd like to discuss that question with you, in private.'

Maria, who had been listening with her entire body, went off in a hip-swinging dudgeon. Mrs Bradshaw took me to a room I hadn't been in before, a small sitting-room opening on a patio at the side of the house. Its furnishings were informal and old-fashioned, and they reminded me slightly of the room where I had interviewed Mrs Deloney.

This room was dominated by an oil painting over the fireplace. It was a full-length portrait, almost life-size, of a handsome gentleman wearing sweeping white moustaches and a cutaway. His black eyes followed me across the room to the armchair which Mrs Bradshaw indicated. She sat in an upholstered platform rocker with her slippered feet on a small petit-point hassock.

'I've been a selfish old woman,' she said unexpectedly. 'I've been thinking it over, and I've decided to pay your expenses after all. I don't like what they're doing to that girl.'

'You probably know more about it than I do.'

'Probably. I have some good friends in this city.' She didn't elaborate.

'I appreciate the offer,' I said, 'but my expenses are being taken care of. Dolly's husband came back.'

'Really? I'm so glad.' She tried to warm herself at the thought, and failed. 'I'm deeply concerned about Roy.'

'So am I, Mrs Bradshaw.' I decided to tell her what I

knew, or part of it. She was bound to find out soon about his marriage, his marriages. 'You don't have to worry about his physical safety. I saw him last night in Reno, and he was in good shape. He checked in at the college today.'

'His secretary lied to me then. I don't know what they're trying to do to me out there, or what my son is up to. What was he really doing in Reno?'

'Attending a conference, as he said. He also went there to look into a suspect in Helen Haggerty's murder.'

'He must have been very fond of her, after all, to go to such lengths.'

'He was involved with Miss Haggerty. I don't think the involvement was romantic.'

'What was it then?'

'Financial. I think he was paying her money, and incidentally he got her a job at the college, through Laura Sutherland. To put it bluntly, the Haggerty woman was blackmailing your son. She may have called it something different herself. But she used a crooked friend in Reno to check on his bank balance before she ever came here. This was the same man Roy went to Reno to talk to.'

Mrs Bradshaw didn't throw a fit, as I was afraid she might. She said in a grave tone: 'Are these facts, Mr Archer, or are you exercising your imagination?'

'I wish I were. I'm not.'

'But how could Roy be blackmailed? He's led a blameless life, a dedicated life. I'm his mother. I ought to know.'

'That may be. But the standard varies for different people. A rising college administrator has to be lily-white. An unfortunate marriage, for instance, would queer his chances for that university presidency you were telling me about.'

'An unfortunate marriage? But Roy has never been married.'

'I'm afraid he has,' I said. 'Does the name Letitia Macready mean anything to you?'

'It does not.'

She was lying. The name drew a net of lines across her face, reduced her eyes to bright black points and her mouth to a purse with a drawstring. She knew the name and hated it, I thought; perhaps she was even afraid of Letitia Macready.

'The name ought to mean something to you, Mrs Bradshaw. The Macready woman was your daughter-in-law.'

'You must be insane. My son has never married.'

She spoke with such force and assurance that I had a moment of doubt. It wasn't likely that Arnie had made a mis take – he seldom did – but it was possible that there were two Roy Bradshaws. No, Arnie had talked to Bradshaw's lawyer in Reno, and must have made a positive identification.

'You have to get married,' I said, 'before you can get a divorce. Roy got a Reno divorce a few weeks ago. He was in Nevada establishing residence for it from the middle of July till the end of August.'

'Now I know you're insane. He was in Europe all that time, and I can prove it.' She got up, on creaking reluctant limbs, and went to the eighteenth-century secretary against one wall. She came back toward me with a sheaf of letters and postcards in her shaking hands. 'He sent me these. You can see for yourself that he was in Europe.'

I looked over the postcards. There were about fifteen of them, arranged in order: the Tower of London (postmarked London, July 18), the Bodleian Library (Oxford, July 21), York Cathedral (York, July 25), Edinburgh Castle (Edinburgh, July 29), The Giant's Causeway (Londonderry, August 3), The Abbey Theatre (Dublin, August 6), Land's End (St Ives, August 8), The Arc de Triomphe (Paris, August 12), and so on through Switzerland and Italy and Germany. I read the card from Munich (a view of the English Gardens, postmarked August 25):

Dear Moms:
    Yesterday I visited Hitler's eyrie at Berchtesgaden – a beautiful setting made grim by its association – and today, by way of contrast, I took a bus to Oberammergau, where the Passion Play is performed. I was struck by the almost Biblical simplicity of the villagers. This whole Bavarian countryside is studded with the most stunning little churches. How I wish you could enjoy them with me! I'm sorry to hear that your summer companion is presenting certain prickly aspects. Well, the summer will soon be over and I for one will be happy to turn my back on the splendours of Europe and come home. All my love.

                                                                Roy

turned to Mrs Bradshaw. 'Is this your son's handwriting?'
'Yes. It's unmistakable. I know he wrote those cards, and these letters, too.'
She brandished several letters under my nose. I looked at the postmarks: London, July 19; Dublin, August 7; Geneva, August 15; Rome, August 20; Berlin, August 27; Amsterdam, August 30. I started to read the last one ('Dear Moms: Just

a hasty note, which may arrive after I do, to tell you how I loved your letter about the blackbirds . . .') but Mrs Bradshaw snatched it out of my hand.

'Please don't *read* the letters. My son and I are very close and he wouldn't like me to show our correspondence to a stranger.' She gathered all the letters and cards and locked them up in the secretary. 'I believe I've proved my point that Roy couldn't have been in Nevada when you say he was.'

For all her assurance, her voice was questioning. I said: 'Did you write letters to him while he was away?'

'I did. That is to say, I dictated them to Miss What's-her name, except for once or twice when my arthritis allowed me to write. I had a nurse-companion during the summer. Miss Wadley, her name was. She was one of these completely self centred young women—'

I cut in: 'Did you write a letter about the blackbirds?'

'Yes. We had an invasion of them last month. It was more of a fanciful little tale than a letter, having to do with blackbirds baked in a pie.'

'Where did you send the blackbird letter?'

'Where? I think to Rome, to American Express in Rome. Roy gave me an itinerary before he left here.'

'He was supposed to be in Rome on August 20. The black bird letter was answered from Amsterdam on August 30.'

'You have an impressive memory, Mr Archer, but I fail to see what you're getting at.'

'Just this. There was a lapse of at least ten days between the receiving and the answering of that letter—time enough for an accomplice to pick it up in Rome, airmail it to Roy in Reno, get his airmail reply in Amsterdam, and remail it to you here.'

'I don't believe it.' But she half-believed it. 'Why would he go to such lengths to deceive his mother?'

'Because he was ashamed of what he was actually doing—divorcing the Macready woman in Reno—and he didn't want you, or anyone else, to know about it. Has he been to Europe before?'

'Of course. I took him there soon after the war, when he was in graduate school at Harvard.'

'And did you visit many of these same places?'

'Yes. We did. Not Germany, but most of the others.'

'Then it wouldn't have been hard for him to fake th letters. As for the postcards, his accomplice must have bough them in Europe and mailed them to him.'

'I dislike your use of the word "accomplice" in connection with my son. There is, after all, nothing criminal about this – this deception. It's a purely personal matter.'

'I hope so, Mrs Bradshaw.'

She must have known what I meant. Her face went through the motions of swallowing pain. She turned her back on me and went to the window. Several white-eyed blackbirds were walking around on the tiles of the patio. I don't suppose she saw them. One of her hands combed roughly at her hair, over and over, until it stuck up like moulting thistles. When she turned around at last, her eyes were half-closed, and her face seemed tormented by the light.

'I'm going to ask you to keep all this in confidence, Mr Archer.'

Roy Bradshaw had used very similar language last night, about his marriage to Laura.

'I can try,' I said.

'Please do. It would be tragic if Roy's career were to be ruined by a youthful indiscretion. That's all it was, you know – a youthful indiscretion. It would never have happened if his father had lived to give him a father's guidance.' She gestured toward the portrait over the fireplace.

'By "it" you mean the Macready woman?'

'Yes.'

'You know her then?'

'I know her.'

As if the admission had exhausted her, she collapsed in the platform rocker, leaning her head on the high cushioned back. Her loose throat seemed very vulnerable.

'Miss Macready came to see me once,' she said. 'It was before we left Boston, during the war. She wanted money.'

'Blackmail money?'

'That's what it amounted to. She asked me to finance a Nevada divorce for her. She'd picked Roy up on Scollay Square and tricked the boy into marrying her. She was in a position to wreck his future. I gave her two thousand dollars. Apparently she spent it on herself and never bothered getting a divorce.' She sighed. 'Poor Roy.'

'Did he know that you knew about her?'

'I never told him. I thought I had ended the threat by paying her money. I wanted it over with and forgotten, with no recriminations between my son and me. But apparently she's been haunting him all these years.'

'Haunting him in the flesh?'

'Who knows? I thought I understood my son, and all the

details of his life. It turns out that I don't.'

'What sort of a woman is she?'

'I saw her only once, when she came to my house in Belmont. I formed a most unfavourable impression. She claimed to be an actress, unemployed, but she dressed and talked like a member of an older profession than that.' Her voice rasped with irony. 'I suppose I had to admit that the redheaded hussy was handsome, in a crude way. But she was utterly unsuitable for Roy, and of course she knew it. He was an innocent lad, hardly out of his teens. She was obviously an experienced woman.'

'How old was she?'

'Much older than Roy, thirty at least.'

'So she'd be pushing fifty now.'

'At least,' she said.

'Have you ever seen her in California?'

She shook her head so hard that her face went loose and wobbly.

'Has Roy?'

'He's never mentioned her to me. We've lived together on the assumption that the Macready woman never existed. And I beg you not to tell him what I've told you. It would destroy all confidence between us.'

'There may be more important considerations, Mrs Bradshaw.'

'What could be more important?'

'His neck.'

She sat with her thick ankles crossed, more stunned than impassive. Her broad sexless body made her resemble a dilapidated Buddha. She said in a hushed voice:

'Surely you can't suspect my son of murder?'

I said something vague and soothing. The eyes of the man in the portrait followed me out. I was glad the father wasn't alive, in view of what I might have to do to Roy.

CHAPTER TWENTY-SEVEN

I hadn't eaten since breakfast, and on my way into town I stopped at a drive-in. While I was waiting for my sandwich I made another call to Arnie Walters from an outside booth

Arnie had made his deal with Judson Foley. It was Helen Haggerty who had wanted the word on Bradshaw's financia status. Foley couldn't or wouldn't swear that she had black-mail in mind. But shortly after he sold her the information she came into sudden wealth, by Foley's standards.

'How much did she pay Foley?'

'Fifty dollars, he says. Now he feels cheated.'

'He always will,' I said. 'Did she tell Foley what she had on Bradshaw?'

'No. She was very careful not to, apparently. But there's a piece of negative evidence: She didn't mention to Foley that Bradshaw had been married, or was getting a divorce. Which probably means that that information was worth money to her.'

'It probably does.'

'One other fact came out, Lew. The Haggerty woman knew Bradshaw long before they met in Reno.'

'Where and how?'

'Foley says he doesn't know, and I believe him. I offered to pay him for any information that checked out. It broke his heart when he couldn't do business with me.'

I found Jerry Marks in the law library on the second floor of the courthouse. Several bound volumes of typescript were piled on the table in front of him. There was dust on his hands, and a smudge on the side of his nose.

'Have you turned up anything, Jerry?'

'I've come to one conclusion. The case against McGee was weak. It consisted of two things, mainly: prior abuse of his wife, and the little girl's testimony, which some judges would have thrown out of court. I've been concentrating on her testimony, because I'm going to have a chance to question her under Pentothal.'

'When?'

'Tonight at eight, at the nursing home. Dr Godwin isn't free till then.'

'I want to be there.'

'That suits me, if Godwin can be persuaded. It was all I could do to get myself invited, and I'm her lawyer.'

'I think Godwin is sitting on something. There's a job that needs doing between now and eight. It's properly my job but this is your town and you can do it faster. Find out if Roy Bradshaw's alibi for Helen Haggerty's murder is waterproof and dustproof and antimagnetic.'

Jerry sat up straight and used his forefinger to smudge his nose some more. 'How should I go about it?'

'Bradshaw addressed an alumni banquet Friday evening. I want to know if he could have slipped out during one of the other speeches, or left in time to kill her. You have a right to any facts the sheriff's men and the pathologist can provide about time of death.'

'I'll do my best,' he said, pushing his chair back.

'One other thing, Jerry. Is there any word on the ballistics tests?'

'The rumour says they're still going on. The rumour doesn't say why. Do you suppose they're trying to fake something?'

'No, I don't. Ballistics experts don't go in for fakery.'

I left him gathering up his transcripts and walked downtown to the Pacific Hotel. My bellhop had contacted Mrs Deloney's cab-driver, and told me in return for a second five that the two elderly ladies had checked in at the Surf House. I bought a drip-dry shirt and some underwear and socks and went back to my motel to shower and change. I needed that before I tackled Mrs Deloney again.

Someone was knocking as I stepped out of the shower, tapping ever so gently as if the door was fragile.

'Who's there?'

'Madge Gerhardi. Let me in.'

'As soon as I'm dressed.'

It was a little time. I had to pick the pins out of my new shirt, and my hands were jerking.

'*Please* let me in,' the woman said at the door. 'I don't want to be seen.'

I pulled on my trousers and went to the door in my bare feet. She pressed in past me as if there was a storm at her back. Her garish blonde hair was windblown. She took hold of my hands with both of her clammy ones.

'The police are watching my house. I don't know if they followed me here or not. I came along the beach.'

'Sit down,' I said, and placed a chair for her. 'I'm sure the police aren't after you. They're looking for your friend Begley-McGee.'

'Don't call him that. It sounds as though you're making fun of him.' It was an avowal of love.

'What do you want me to call him?'

'I still call him Chuck. A man has a right to change his name, after what they did to him, and what they're doing. Anyway, he's a writer, and writers use pen names.'

'Okay, I'll call him Chuck. But you didn't come here to argue about a name.'

She fingered her mouth, pushing her full lower lip from side to side. She wasn't wearing lipstick or any other make-up.

Without it she looked younger and more innocent.

'Have you heard from Chuck?' I said.

She nodded almost imperceptibly, as if too great a movement would endanger him.

'Where is he, Madge?'

'In a safe place. I'm not to tell you where unless you promise not to tell the police.'

'I promise.'

Her pale eyes brightened. 'He wants to talk to you.'

'Did he say what about?'

'I didn't talk to him personally. A friend of his down at the harbour telephoned the message.'

'I take it he's somewhere around the harbour then.'

She gave me another of her barely visible nods.

'You've told me this much,' I said. 'You might as well tell me the rest. I'd give a lot for an interview with Chuck.'

'And you won't lead the police to him?'

'Not if I can help it. Where is he, Madge?'

She screwed up her face and made the plunge: 'He's on Mr Stevens's yacht, the *Revenant*.'

'How did he get aboard her?'

'I'm not sure. He knew that Mr Stevens was racing her at Balboa over the week-end. I think he went there and surrendered to Mr Stevens.'

I left Madge in my room. She didn't want to go out again by herself, or ride along with me. I took the waterfront boulevard to the harbour. While a few tugboats and tuna-fishers used its outer reaches, most of the boats moored at the slips or anchored within the long arm of the jetty were the private yachts and cruisers of week-end sailors.

On a Monday, not many of them were at sea, but I noticed a few white sails on the horizon. They were headed shoreward, like homing dreams.

A man in the harbourmaster's glass-enclosed look-out pointed out Stevens's yacht to me. Though she rode at the far end of the outer slip, she was easy to spot because of her towering mast. I walked out along the floating dock to her.

Revenant was long and sleek, with a low streamlined cabin and a racing cockpit. Her varnish was smooth and clear, her brass was bright. She rocked ever so slightly on the enclosed water, like an animal trembling to run.

I stepped aboard and knocked on the hatch. No answer, but it opened when I pushed. I climbed down the short ladder and made my way past some short-wave radio equipment, and a tiny galley smelling of burned coffee, into the sleeping quarters. An oval of sunlight from one of the ports, moving reciprocally with the motion of the yacht, fluttered against the bulkhead like a bright and living soul. I said to it:

'McGee?'

Something stirred in an upper bunk. A face appeared at eye level. It was a suitable face for the crew of a boat named *Revenant*. McGee had shaved off his beard, and the lower part of his face had a beard-shaped pallor. He looked older and thinner and much less sure of himself.

'Did you come here by yourself?' he whispered.

'Naturally I did.'

'That means you don't think I'm guilty, either.' He was reduced to such small momentary hopefulnesses.

'Who else doesn't think you're guilty?'

'Mr Stevens.'

'Was this his idea?' I said, with a gesture that included McGee and myself.

'He didn't say I *shouldn't* talk to you.'

'Okay, McGee, what's on your mind?'

He lay still watching me. His mouth was twitching, and his eyes held a kind of beseeching brightness. 'I don't know where to start. I've been living in my thoughts for ten years – so long it hardly seems real. I know what happened to me but I don't know why. Ten years in the pen, with no chance of parole because I wouldn't admit that I was guilty. How could I? I was bum-rapped. And now they're getting ready to do it again.'

He gripped the polished mahogany edge of the bunk. 'I can't go back to "Q", brother. I did ten years and it was *hard* time. There's no time as hard as the time you do for somebody else's mistake. God, but the days crawled. There weren't enough jobs to go round and half the time I had nothing to do but sit and think.

'I'll kill myself,' he said, 'before I let them send me back again.'

He meant it, and I meant what I said in reply: 'It won't happen, McGee. That's a promise.'

'I only wish I could believe you. You get out of the habit of believing people. They don't believe you, you don't believe them.'

'Who killed your wife?'

'I don't know.'

'Who do you think killed her?'

'I'm not saying.'

'You've gone to a lot of trouble, and taken quite a risk, to get me out here and tell me you're not saying. Let's go back to where it started, McGee. Why did your wife leave you?'

'I left her. We had been separated for months when she was killed. I wasn't even in Indian Springs that night, I was here in the Point.'

'Why did you leave her?'

'Because she asked me to. We weren't getting along. We never did get along after I came back from the services. Constance and the kid spent the war years living with her sister, and she couldn't adjust to me after that. I admit I was a wild man for a while then. But her sister Alice promoted the trouble between us.'

'Why?'

'She thought the marriage was a mistake. I guess she wanted Constance all to herself. I just got in the way.'

'Did anybody else get in the way?'

'Not if Alice could help it.'

I phrased my question more explicitly: 'Was there another man in Constance's life?'

'Yeah. There was.' He seemed ashamed, as if the infidelity had been his. 'I've given it a lot of thought over the years, and I don't see much point in opening it up now. The guy had nothing to do with her death, I'm sure of that. He was crazy about her. He wouldn't hurt her.'

'How do you know?'

'I talked to him about her, not long before she was killed. The kid told me what was going on between him and her.'

'You mean your daughter Dolly?'

'That's right. Constance used to meet the guy every Saturday, when she brought Dolly in to see the doctor. On one of my visiting days with the kid – the last one we ever had together, in fact – she told me about those meetings. She was only eleven or twelve and she didn't grasp the full significance, but she knew something fishy was going on.

'Every Saturday afternoon Constance and the guy used to park her in a double-feature movie and go off by themselves some place, probably some motel. Constance asked the kid to cover for her, and she did. The guy even gave her money to tell Alice that Constance went to those movies with her. I thought that was a lousy trick.' McGee tried to warm over his old anger but he had suffered too much, and thought too much, to be able to. His face hung like a cold moon over the edge of the bunk.

'We might as well use his name,' I said. 'Was it Godwin?'

'Hell no. It was Roy Bradshaw. He used to be a professor

183

at the college.' He added with a kind of mournful pride: 'Now he's the Dean out there.'

He wouldn't be for long. I thought: his sky was black with chickens coming home to roost.

'Bradshaw was one of Dr Godwin's patients,' McGee was saying. 'That's where he and Connie met, in Godwin's waiting-room. I think the doctor kind of encouraged the thing between them.'

'What makes you think that?'

'Bradshaw told me himself the doctor said it was good for them, for their emotional health. It's a funny thing, I went to Bradshaw's house to get him to lay off Connie, even if I had to beat him up. But by the time he was finished talking he had me half-convinced that he and Connie were right, and I was wrong. I still don't know who was right and who was wrong. I know I never gave her any real happiness, after the first year. Maybe Bradshaw did.'

'Is that why you didn't inject him into your trial?'

'That was one reason. Anyway, what was the use of fouling it up? It would only make me look worse.' He paused. A deeper tone rose from a deeper level of his nature: 'Besides, I loved her. I loved Connie. It was the one way I had to prove I loved her.'

'Did you know that Bradshaw was married to another woman?'

'When?'

'For the last twenty years. He divorced her a few weeks ago.'

McGee looked shocked. He'd been living on illusions for a long time, and I was threatening his sustenance. He pulled himself back into the bunk, almost out of sight.

'Her name was Letitia Macready – Letitia Macready Bradshaw. Have you ever heard of her?'

'No. How could he be married? He was living at home with his mother.'

'There are all kinds of marriages,' I said. 'He may not have seen his wife in years, and then again he may have. He may have had her living here in town, unknown to his mother or any of his friends. I suspect that was the case, judging from the lengths he went to to cover up his divorce.'

McGee said in a confused and shaken voice: 'I don't see what it has to do with me.'

'It may have a very great deal. If the Macready woman was in town ten years ago, she had a motive for killing your wife – a motive as strong as your own.'

He didn't want to think about the woman. He was too used to thinking about himself. 'I *had* no motive. I wouldn't hurt a hair of her head.'

'You did, though, once or twice.'

He was silent. All I could see of him was his wavy grey hair, like a dusty wig, and his large dishonest eyes trying to be honest:

'I hit her a couple of times, I admit it. I suffered the tortures of the damned afterward. You've got to understand, I used to get mean when I got plastered. That's why Connie sent me away. I don't blame her. I don't blame her for anything. I blame myself.' He drew in a long breath and let it out slowly.

I offered him a cigarette, which he refused. I lit one for myself. The bright trembling patch of sunlight was climbing the bulkhead – It would soon be evening.

'So Bradshaw had a wife,' McGee said. He had had time to absorb the information. 'And he told me he intended to marry Connie.'

'Maybe he did intend to. It would strengthen the woman's motive.'

'You honestly think she did it?'

'She's a prime suspect. Bradshaw is another. He must have been a suspect to your daughter, too. She enrolled in his college and took a job in his household to check on him. Was that your idea, McGee?'

He shook his head.

'I don't understand her part in all this. She hasn't been much help in explaining it, either.'

'I know,' he said. 'Dolly's done a lot of lying, starting away back when. But when a little kid lies you don't put the same construction on it as you would an adult.'

'You're a forgiving man.'

'Oh no I'm not. I went to her with anger in my heart that Sunday I saw her picture in the paper, with her husband. What right did she have to a happy marriage after what she did to me? That's what was on my mind.'

'Did you tell her what was on your mind?'

'Yessir, I did. But my anger didn't last. She reminded me so of her mother in appearance. It was like going back twenty years to happier times, when we were first married. We had a real good year when I was in the Navy and Connie was pregnant, with her.'

His mind kept veering away from his current troubles. I could hardly blame him, but I urged him back to them:

'You gave your daughter a hard time the other Sunday, didn't you?'

'I did at first. I admit that. I asked her why she lied about me in court. That was a legitimate question, wasn't it?'

'I should say so. What was her reaction?'

'She went into hysterics and said she wasn't lying, that she saw me with the gun and everything and heard me arguing with her mother. Which was false, and I told her so. I wasn't even in Indian Springs that night. That stopped her cold.'

'Then what?'

'I asked her why she lied about me.' He licked his lips and said in a hushed voice: 'I asked her if she shot her mother herself, maybe by accident, the way Alice kept that revolver lying around loose. It was a terrible question, but it had to come out. It'd been on my mind for a long time.'

'As long ago as your trial?'

'Yeah. Before that.'

'And that's why you wouldn't let Stevens cross-examine her?'

'Yeah. I should have let him go ahead. I ended up cross-questioning her myself ten years later.'

'What was the result?'

'More hysterics. She was laughing and crying at the same time. I never felt so sorry for anybody. She was as white as a sheet and the tears popped out of her eyes and ran down her face. Her tears looked so *pure*.'

'What did she say?'

'She said she didn't do it, naturally.'

'Could she have? Did she know how to handle a gun?'

'A little. I gave her a little training, and so did Alice. It doesn't take much gun-handling to pull a trigger, especially by accident.'

'You still think it could have happened that way?'

'I don't know. It's mainly what I wanted to talk to you about.'

These words seemed to release him from an obscure bondage. He climbed down out of the upper bunk and stood facing me in the narrow aisle. He had on a seaman's black turtleneck, levis, and rubber-soled deck shoes.

'You're in a position to go and talk to her,' he said. 'I'm not. Mr Stevens won't. But you can go and ask her what really happened.'

'She may not know.'

'I realize that. She got pretty mixed up the other Sunday. God knows I wasn't trying to mix her up. I only asked her

ome questions. But she didn't seem to know the difference
between what happened and what she said in court.'

'That story she told in court – did she definitely admit she
made it up?'

'She made it up with a lot of help from Alice. I can
imagine how it went. "This is the way it happened, isn't it?"
Alice would say. "You saw your old man with the gun, didn't
you?" And after a while the kid had her story laid out for
her.'

'Would Alice deliberately try to frame you?'

'She wouldn't put it that way to herself. She'd know for a
fact I was guilty. All she was doing was making sure I got
punished for my crime. She probably fed the kid her lines
without knowing she was faking evidence. My dear sister-in-
law was always out to get me, anyway.'

'Was she out to get Connie, too?'

'Connie? She doted on Connie. Alice was more like her
mother than her sister. There was fourteen-fifteen years' difference in their ages.'

'You said she wanted Connie to herself. Her feelings for
Connie could have changed if she found out about Bradshaw.'

'Not *that* much. Anyway, who would tell her?'

'Your daughter might have. If she told you, she'd tell Alice.'
McGee shook his head. 'You're really reaching.'

'I have to. This is a deep case, and I can't see the bottom
of it yet. Did Alice ever live in Boston, do you know?'

'I think she always lived here. She's a Native Daughter.
I'm a native son, but nobody ever gave me a medal for it.'

'Even Native Daughters have been known to go to Boston.
Did Alice ever go on the stage, or marry a man named Mac-
eady, or dye her hair red?'

'None of those things sound like Alice.'
I thought of her pink fantastic bedroom, and wondered.

'They sound more,' McGee was saying, and then he
stopped. He was silent for a moment watching. 'I'll take
that cigarette you offered me.'

I gave him a cigarette and lighted it. 'What were you
going to say?'

'Nothing. I must have been thinking aloud.'

'Who were you thinking about?'

'Nobody you know. Forget it, eh?'

'Come on, McGee. You're supposed to be levelling with
me.'

'I still have a right to my private thoughts. It kept me
alive in prison.'

'You're out of prison now. Don't you want to stay out?'
'Not if somebody else has to go in.'
'Sucker,' I said. 'Who are you covering for now?'
'Nobody.'
'Madge Gerhardi?'
'You must be off your rocker.'
I couldn't get anything more out of him. The long slow
weight of prison forces men into unusual shapes. McGee had
become a sort of twisted saint.

CHAPTER TWENTY-EIGHT

He was about to be given another turn of the screw. When
climbed out into the cockpit I saw three men approaching
along the floating dock. Their bodies, their hatted heads
were dark as iron against the exploding sunset.

One of them showed me a deputy's badge and a gun, which
he held on me while the others went below. I heard McGee
cry out once. He scrambled up through the hatch with blue
handcuffs on his wrists and a blue gun at his back. The single
look he gave me was full of fear and loathing.

They didn't handcuff me, but they made me ride to the
courthouse with McGee in the screened rear compartment of
the Sheriff's car. I tried to talk to him. He wouldn't speak to
me or look in my direction. He believed I had turned him in,
and perhaps I had without intending to.

I sat under guard outside the interrogation-room while they
questioned him in tones that rose and fell and growled and
palavered and yelled and threatened and promised and refused and wheedled. Sheriff Crane arrived, looking tired but
important. He stood over me smiling, with his belly thrust
out.

'Your friend's in real trouble now.'

'He's been in real trouble for the last ten years. You ought
to know, you helped to cook it for him.'

The veins in his cheeks lit up like intricate little networks
of infra-red tubing. He leaned toward me spewing Martini-
scented words:

'I could put you in jail for loose talk like that. You know
where your friend is going? He's going all the way to the
green room this time.'

'He wouldn't be the first innocent man who was gassed.'

'Innocent? McGee's a mass murderer, and we've got the
evidence to prove it. It took my experts all day to nail it
down: The bullet in the Haggerty corpse came from the same
gun as the bullet we found in McGee's wife – the same gun he
stole from Alice Jenks in Indian Springs.'

I'd succeeded in provoking the Sheriff into an indiscretion.
I tried for another. 'You have no proof he stole it. You have
no proof he fired it either time. Where's he been keeping the
gun for the last ten years?'

'He cached it some place, maybe on Stevens's boat. Or
maybe an accomplice kept it for him.'

'Then he hid it in his daughter's bed to frame her?'

'That's the kind of man he is.'

'Nuts!'

'Don't talk to me like that!' He menaced me with the
cannon ball of his belly.

'Don't talk like that to the Sheriff,' the guard said.

'I don't know of any law against the use of the word
"nuts." And incidentally I wasn't violating anything in the
California Code when I went out to the yacht to talk to
McGee. I'm co-operating with a local attorney in this investigation and I have a right to get my information where I can
and keep it confidential.'

'How did you know he was there?'

'I got a tip.'

'From Stevens?'

'Not from Stevens. You and I could trade information,
Sheriff. How did you know he was there?'

'I don't make deals with suspects.'

'What do you suspect me of? Illegal use of the word
"nuts"?'

'It isn't so funny. You were taken with McGee. I have a
right to hold you.'

'I have a right to call an attorney. Try kicking my rights
around and see where it gets you. I have friends in Sacramento.'

They didn't include the Attorney General or anybody close
to him, but I liked the sound of the phrase. Sheriff Crane did
not. He was half a politician, and like most of his kind he was
an insecure man. He said after a moment's thought:

'You can make your call.'

The Sheriff went into the interrogation-room – I caught a
glimpse of McGee hunched grey-faced under a light – and
added his voice to the difficult harmony there. My guard took
me into a small adjoining room and left me by myself with a

189

telephone. I used it to call Jerry Marks. He was about to leave for his appointment with Dr Goodwin and Dolly, but he said he'd come right over to the courthouse and bring Gil Stevens with him if Stevens was available.

They arrived together in less than fifteen minutes. Stevens shot me a glance from under the broken white wings of his hair. It was a covert and complex glance which seemed to mean that for the record we were strangers. I suspected the old lawyer had advised McGee to talk to me, and probably set up the interview. I was in a position to use McGee's facts in ways that he couldn't.

With soft threats of *habeas corpus* proceedings, Jerry Marks sprung me out. Stevens remained behind with the Sheriff and a Deputy DA. It was going to take longer to spring his client.

A moon like a fallen fruit reversing gravity was hoisting itself above the rooftops. It was huge and slightly squashed.

'Pretty,' Jerry said in the parking lot.

'It looks like a rotten orange to me.'

'Ugliness is in the eye of the beholder. I learned that at my mother's knee and other low joints, as a well-known statesman said.' Jerry always felt good when he tried something he learned in law school, and it worked. He walked to his car swiftly, on the balls of his feet, and made the engine roar. 'We're late for our appointment with Godwin.'

'Did you have time to check on Bradshaw's alibi?'

'I did. It seems to be impregnable.' He gave me the details as we drove across town. 'Judging by temperature loss, rate of blood coagulation, and so on, the Deputy Coroner places the time of Miss Haggerty's death was no later than eight thirty. From about seven until about nine-thirty Dean Bradshaw was sitting, or standing up talking, in front of over a hundred witnesses. I talked to three of them, three alumni picked more or less at random, and they all agreed he didn't leave the speakers' table during that period. Which lets him out.'

'Apparently it does.'

'You sound disappointed, Lew.'

'I'm partly that, and partly relieved. I rather like Bradshaw. But I was pretty certain he was our man.'

In the remaining minutes before we reached the nursing home, I told him briefly what I'd learned from McGee, and from the Sheriff. Jerry whistled, but made no other comment.

Dr Godwin opened the door for us. He wore a clean white smock and an aggrieved expression.

'You're late, Mr Marks. I was just about ready to call the

whole thing off.'

'We had a little emergency. Thomas McGee was arrested about seven o'clock tonight. Mr Archer happened to be with him, and he was arrested, also.'

Godwin turned to me. 'You were with McGee?'

'He sent for me, and he talked. I'm looking forward to comparing his story with his daughter's.'

'I'm afraid you aren't – ah – co-opted to this session,' Godwin said with some embarrassment. 'As I pointed out to you before, you don't have professional immunity.'

'I do if I'm acting on Mr Marks's instructions. Which I am.'

'Mr Archer is correct, on both counts,' Jerry said.

Godwin let us in reluctantly. We were outsiders, interlopers in his shadowy kingdom. I had lost some of my confidence in his benevolent despotism, but I kept it to myself for the present.

He took us to the examination-room where Dolly was waiting. She was sitting on the end of a padded table, wearing a sleeveless white hospital gown. Alex stood in front of her, holding both her hands. His eyes stayed on her face, hungry and worshipping, as if she was the priestess or the goddess of a strange one-member cult.

Her hair was shining and smooth. Her face was composed. Only her eyes had a sullen restlessness and inwardness. They moved across me and failed to give any sign of recognition.

Godwin touched her shoulder. 'Are you ready, Dolly?'

'I suppose I am.'

She lay back on the padded table. Alex held on to one of her hands.

'You can stay if you like, Mr Kincaid. It might be easier you didn't.'

'Not for me,' the girl said. 'I feel safer when he's with me. I want Alex to know all about – everything.'

'Yes. I want to stay.'

Godwin filled a hypodermic needle, inserted it in her arm, and taped it to the white skin. He told her to count backward from one hundred. At ninety-six the tension left her body and an inner light left her face. It flowed back in a diffused form when the doctor spoke to her:

'Do you hear me, Dolly?'

'I hear you,' she murmured.

'Speak louder. I can't hear you.'

'I hear you,' she repeated. Her voice was faintly slurred.

'Who am I?'

'Dr Godwin.'

'Do you remember when you were a little girl you used to come and visit me in my office?'

'I remember.'

'Who used to bring you to see me?'

'Mommy did. She used to bring me in in Aunt Alice' car.'

'Where were you living then?'

'In Indian Springs, in Aunt Alice's house.'

'And Mommy was living there, too?'

'Mommy was living there, too. She lived there, too.'

She was flushed, and talking like a drunken child. The doctor turned to Jerry Marks with a handing-over gesture. Jerry's dark eyes were mournful.

'Do you remember a certain night,' he said, 'when your Mommy was killed?'

'I remember. Who are you?'

'I'm Jerry Marks, your lawyer. It's all right to talk to me.'

'It's all right,' Alex said.

The girl looked up at Jerry sleepily. 'What do you want me to tell you?'

'Just the truth. It doesn't matter what I want, or anybody else. Just tell me what you remember.'

'I'll try.'

'Did you hear the gun go off?'

'I heard it.' She screwed up her face as if she was hearing it now. 'I am – it frightened me.'

'Did you see anyone?'

'I didn't go downstairs right away. I was scared.'

'Did you see anyone out the window?'

'No. I heard a car drive away. Before that I heard her running.'

'You heard *who* running?' Jerry said.

'I thought it was Aunt Alice at first, when she was talking to Mommy at the door. But it couldn't have been Aunt Alice. She wouldn't shoot Mommy. Besides, her gun was missing.'

'How do you know?'

'She said I took it from her room. She spanked me with a hairbrush for stealing it.'

'When did she spank you?'

'Sunday night, when she came home from church. Mommy said she had no right to spank me. Aunt Alice asked Mommy if *she* took the gun.'

'Did she?'

'She didn't say – not while I was there. They sent me to bed.'

'*Did* you take the gun?'

'No. I never touched it. I was afraid of it.'

"Why?"

'I was afraid of Aunt Alice.'

She was rosy and sweating. She tried to struggle up on to her elbows. The doctor eased her back into her supine position, and made an adjustment to the needle. The girl relaxed again, and Jerry said:

'Was it Aunt Alice talking to your Mommy at the door?'

'I thought it was at first. It sounded like her. She had a big scary voice. But it couldn't have been Aunt Alice.'

'Why couldn't it?'

'It just couldn't.'

She turned her head in a listening attitude. A lock of hair fell over her half-closed eyes. Alex pushed it back with a gentle hand. She said:

'The lady at the door said it had to be true, about Mommy and Mr Bradshaw. She said she got it from Daddy's own lips, and Daddy got it from me. And then she shot my Mommy and ran away.'

There was silence in the room, except for the girl's heavy breathing. A tear as slow as honey was exuded from the corner of one eye. It fell down her temple. Alex wiped the blue-veined hollow with his handkerchief. Jerry leaned across her from the other side of the table:

'Why did you say your Daddy shot your Mommy?'

'Aunt Alice wanted me to. She didn't say so, but I could tell. And I was afraid she'd think that I did it. She spanked me for taking the gun, and I *didn't* take it. I said it was Daddy. She made me say it over and over and over.'

There were more tears than one now. Tears for the child she had been, frightened and lying, and tears for the woman she was painfully becoming. Alex wiped her eyes. He looked close to tears himself.

'Why,' I said, 'did you try to tell us that you killed your mother?'

'Who are you?'

'I am Alex's friend Lew Archer.'

'That's right,' Alex said.

She lifted her head and let it fall back. 'I forget what you asked me.'

'Why did you say you killed your mother?'

'Because it was all my fault. I told my Daddy about her and Mr Bradshaw, and that's what started everything.'

'How do you know?'

'The lady at the door said so. She came to shoot Mommy because of what Daddy told her.'

'Do you know who she was?'

'No.'

'Was it your Aunt Alice?'

'No.'

'Was it anyone you know?'

'No.'

'Did your mother know her?'

'I don't know. Maybe she did.'

'Did she talk as if she knew her?'

'She called her by name.'

'What name?'

'Tish. She called her Tish. I could tell Mommy didn't like her, though. She was afraid of her, too.'

'Why haven't you ever told anyone this before?'

'Because it was all my fault.'

'It wasn't,' Alex said. 'You were only a child. You weren't responsible for what the adults did.'

Godwin shushed him with his finger to his lips. Dolly rolled her head from side to side:

'It was all my fault.'

'This has gone on long enough,' Godwin whispered to Jerry. 'She's made some gains. I want to have a chance to consolidate them.'

'But we haven't even got to the Haggerty case.'

'Make it short then.' Godwin said to the girl: 'Dolly, are you willing to talk about last Friday night?'

'Not about finding her.' She screwed up her face until her eyes were hidden.

'You needn't go into the details of finding the body,' Jerry said. 'But what were you doing there?'

'I wanted to talk to Helen. I often walked up the hill to talk to her. We were friends.'

'How did that happen to be?'

'I ingratiated myself with Helen,' she said with queer blank candour. 'I thought at first she might be the lady – the woman who shot my mother. The rumour was going around the campus that she was close to Dean Bradshaw.'

'And you were on the campus to find that woman?'

'Yes. But it wasn't Helen. I found out she was new in town, and she told me herself there was nothing between her and Bradshaw. I had no right to drag her into this.'

'How did you drag her in?'

'I told her everything, about my mother and Bradshaw and the murder and the woman at the door. Helen was killed because she knew too much.'

'That may be,' I said, 'but she didn't learn it from you.'

'She did! I told her everything.'

Godwin pulled at my sleeve. 'Don't argue with her. She's coming out of it fast, but her mind is still operating below the conscious level.'

'Did Helen ask you questions?' I said to the girl.

'Yes. She asked me questions.'

'Then you didn't force the information on her.'

'No. She wanted to know.'

'What did she want to know?'

'All about Dean Bradshaw and my mother.'

'Did she say why?'

'She wanted to help me in my crusade. I went on a sort of crusade after I talked to Daddy in the hotel. A children's crusade.' Her giggled turned into a sob before it left her throat. 'The only thing it accomplished was the death of my good friend Helen. And when I found her body—'

Her eyes opened wide. Then her mouth opened wide. Her body went rigid, as if it was imitating the rigour of the dead. She stayed like that for fifteen or twenty seconds.

'It was like finding Mommy again,' she said in a small voice, and came fully awake. 'Is it all right?'

'It's all right,' Alex said.

He helped her up to a sitting position. She leaned on him, her hair mantling his shoulder. A few minutes later, still leaning on him, she walked across the hallway to her room. They walked like husband and wife.

Godwin closed the door of the examination-room. 'I hope you gentlemen got what you wanted,' he said with some distaste.

'She talked very freely,' Jerry said. The experience had left him drained.

'It was no accident. I've been preparing her for the last three days. Pentothal, as I've told you before, is no guarantee of truth. If a patient is determined to lie, the drug can't stop him.'

'Are you implying she wasn't telling the truth?'

'No. I believe she was, so far as she knows the truth. My problem now is to enlarge her awareness and make it fully conscious. If you gentlemen will excuse me?'

'Wait a minute,' I said. 'You can spare me a minute, doctor. I've spent three days and a lot of Kincaid's money developing facts that you already had in your possession.'

'Have you indeed?' he said coldly.

'I have indeed. You could have saved me a good deal of work by filling me in on Bradshaw's affair with Constance McGee.'

'I'm afraid I don't exist for the purpose of saving detectives work. There's a question of ethics involved here which you probably wouldn't understand. Mr Marks probably would.'

'I don't understand the issue,' Jerry said, but he edged between us as if he expected trouble. He touched my shoulder. 'Let's get out of here, Lew, and let the doctor get about his business. He's co-operated beautifully and you know it.'

'Who with? Bradshaw?'

Godwin's face turned pale. 'My first duty is to my patients.'

'Even when they murder people?'

'Even then. But I know Roy Bradshaw intimately and I can assure you he's incapable of killing anyone. Certainly he didn't kill Constance McGee. He was passionately in love with her.'

'Passion can cut two ways.'

'He didn't kill her.'

'A couple of days ago you were telling me McGee did. You can be mistaken, doctor.'

'I know that, but not about Roy Bradshaw. The man has lived a tragic life.'

'Tell me about it.'

'He'll have to tell you himself. I'm not a junior G-man, Mr Archer. I'm a doctor.'

'What about the woman he recently divorced, Tish or Letitia? Do you know her?'

He looked at me without speaking. There was sad knowledge in his eyes. 'You'll have to ask Roy about her,' he said finally.

CHAPTER TWENTY-NINE

On his way to the courthouse to question McGee, Jerry dropped me at the harbour, where my car had been left sitting. The moon was higher now, and had regained its proper shape and colour. Its light converted the yachts in the slips into a ghostly fleet of Flying Dutchmen.

I went back to my motel to talk to Madge Gerhardi. She had evaporated, along with the rest of the whisky in my pint bottle. I sat on the edge of the bed and tried her number and got no answer.

I called the Bradshaw house. Old Mrs Bradshaw seemed to have taken up a permanent position beside the telephone. She picked up the receiver on the first ring and quavered into it:

'Who is that, please?'

'It's only Archer. Roy hasn't come home, has he?'

'No, and I'm worried about him, deeply worried. I haven't seen him or heard from him since early Saturday morning. I've been calling his friends—'

'I wouldn't do that, Mrs Bradshaw.'

'I have to do something.'

'There are times when it's better to do nothing. Keep still and wait.'

'I can't. You're telling me there's something terribly wrong, aren't you?'

'I think you know it.'

'Does it have to do with that dreadful woman – that Macready woman?'

'Yes. We have to find out where she is. I'm pretty sure your son could tell me, but he's made himself unavailable. Are you sure you haven't seen the woman since Boston?'

'I'm quite certain. I saw her only once, when she came to me for money.'

'Can you describe her for me?'

'I thought I had.'

'In more detail, please. It's very important.'

She paused to think. I could hear her breathing over the line, a faint rhythmic huskiness. 'Well, she was quite a large woman, taller than I, red-haired. She wore her hair bobbed. She had quite a good figure, rather lush, and quite good features, too – a kind of brassy good looks. And she had green eyes, murky green eyes which I didn't like at all. She wore very heavy make-up, more appropriate for the stage than the street, and she was hideously overdressed.'

'What was she wearing?'

'It hardly seems relevant, after twenty years. But she had on a leopardskin – an imitation leopardskin coat, as I recall, and under it something striped. Sheer hose, with runs in them. Ridiculously high heels. A good deal of costume jewellery.'

'How did she talk?'

'Like a woman of the streets. A greedy, pushing, lustful woman.' The moral indignation in her voice hardly surprised me. She had almost lost Roy to the woman, and might yet.

'Would you know her if you saw her again, in different clothes, with her hair perhaps a different colour?'

'I think so, if I had a chance to study her.'

'You'll have that chance when we find her. '

I was thinking that the colour of a woman's eyes was harder to change than her hair. The only green-eyed woman connected with the case was Laura Sutherland. She had a conspicuously good figure and good features, but nothing else that seemed to jibe with the description of the Macready woman. Still, she might have changed. I'd seen other women change unrecognizably in half the time.

'You know Laura Sutherland, Mrs Bradshaw?'

'I know her slightly.'

'Does she resemble the Macready woman?'

'Why do you ask that?' she said on a rising note. 'Do you suspect Laura?'

'I wouldn't go that far. But you haven't answered my question.'

'She couldn't possibly be the same woman. She's a wholly different type.'

'What about her basic physical characteristics?'

'I suppose there is some resemblance,' she said dubiously. 'Roy has always been attracted to women who are obviously mammals.'

And obviously mother figures, I thought. 'I have to ask you one other question, a more personal question.'

'Yes?' She seemed to be bracing herself for a blow.

'I suppose you're aware that Roy was Dr Godwin's patient.'

'Dr Godwin's patient? I don't believe it. He wouldn't go behind my back.' For all her half-cynical insight into his nature, she seemed to know very little about him.

'Dr Godwin says he did, apparently for some years.'

'There must be a mistake. Roy has nothing the matter with his mind.' There was a vibrating silence. 'Has he?'

'I was going to ask you, but I'm sorry I brought it up. Take it easy, Mrs Bradshaw.'

'How can I, with my boy in jeopardy.'

She wanted to hold me on the line, siphoning comfort into her frightened old ears, but I said good night and hung up. One suspect had been eliminated: Madge Gerhardi: the description didn't fit her and never could have. Laura was still in the running.

It wouldn't make sense, of course, for Bradshaw to divorce her and remarry her immediately. But I had only Bradshaw's word for his recent marriage to Laura. I was gradually realising that his word stretched like an elastic band, and was as easily broken. I looked up Laura's address – she lived in College Heights – and was copying it into my notebook when the phone rang.

It was Jerry Marks. McGee denied having told the woman Tish or anyone else about the affair between Bradshaw and his wife. The only one he had discussed the subject with was Bradshaw.

'Bradshaw may have told the woman himself,' I said. 'Or possibly the woman overheard McGee.'

'Possibly, but hardly likely. McGee says his conversation with Bradshaw took place in Bradshaw's house.'

'He could have had the woman there while his mother was away.'

'You think she lives around here?'

'Somewhere in Southern California, anyway. I believe Bradshaw's been leading a split-level life with her, and that she's responsible for both the McGee and the Haggerty killings. I just got an improved description of her from Bradshaw's mother. Better pass it along to the police. Do you have something to write on?'

'Yes. I'm sitting at the Sheriff's desk.'

I recited Letitia Macready's description, but I didn't say anything about Laura Sutherland. I wanted to talk to her myself.

College Heights was a detached suburb on the far side of the campus from the city. It was a hodgepodge of tract houses and fraternity houses, duplexes and apartment buildings, interspersed with vacant lots sprouting for-sale signs. A boy with a guitar in one of the lighted fraternity houses was singing that this land belongs to you and me.

Laura lived in one of the better apartments, a garden apartment built around an open court with a swimming-pool. A shirt-sleeved man slapping mosquitoes in a deck chair by the pool pointed out her door to me and mentioned with some complacency that he owned the place.

'Is anybody with her?'

'I don't think so. She did have a visitor, but he went home.'

'Who was he?'

The man peered up at my face. 'That's her private business, mister.'

'I expect it was Dean Bradshaw, from the college.'

'If you know, why ask?'

I walked to the back of the court and knocked on her door. She opened it on a chain. Her face had lost a good deal of its rose beauty. She had on a dark suit, as if she was in mourning.

'What do you want? It's late.'

'Too late for us to have a talk, Mrs Bradshaw?'

'I'm not Mrs Bradshaw,' she said without much conviction. 'I'm not married.'

'Roy said you were last night. Which one of you is lying?'

'Please, my landlord's out there.' She unchained the door and stepped back out of the widening light. 'Come inside if you must.'

She closed the door and chained it behind me. I was looking at her instead of the room, but I had the impression of a tastefully decorated place where shaded lights gleamed peacefully on wooden and ceramic surfaces. I was searching her face for traces of a past wholly different from her present. There were no visible traces, no cruel lines or pouches of dissipation. But she hadn't much peace in her. She was watching me as though I was a burglar.

'What are you afraid of?'

'I'm not afraid,' she said in a frightened voice. She tried to control it with her hand at her throat. 'I resent your barging into my home and making personal remarks.'

'You invited me in, more or less.'

'Only because you were talking indiscreetly.'

'I called you by your married name. What's your objection to it?'

'I *have* no objection,' she said with a wan smile. 'I'm very proud of it. But my husband and I are keeping it a secret.'

'A secret from Letitia Macready?'

She showed no particular reaction to the name. I'd already

200

given up on the idea that it would be hers. No matter how well preserved her body or her skin might be, she was clearly too young. When Bradshaw married Letitia, Laura couldn't have been more than a girl in her teens.

'Letitia who?' she said.

'Letitia Macready. She's also known as Tish.'

'I have no idea who you're talking about.'

'I'll tell you if you really want to know. May I sit down?'

'Please do,' she said without much warmth. I was the messenger who brought bad tidings, the kind they used to kill in the old days.

I sat on a soft leather hassock with my back against the wall. She remained standing.

'You're in love with Roy Bradshaw, aren't you?'

'I wouldn't have married him if I weren't.'

'Just when did you marry him?'

'Two weeks ago last Saturday, September the tenth.' A little colour returned to her cheeks with the memory of the day. 'He'd just got back from his European tour. We decided to go to Reno on the spur of the moment.'

'Had you spent some time with him there earlier in the summer?'

She frowned in a puzzled way, and shook her head.

'Whose idea was it to go to Reno?'

'Roy's of course, but I was willing. I've been willing for some time,' she added in a spurt of candour.

'What held up the marriage?'

'It wasn't held *up*, exactly. We postponed it, for various reasons. Mrs Bradshaw is a very possessive mother, and Roy has nothing of his own except his salary. It may sound mercenary –' She paused in some embarrassment, and tried to think of a better way to phrase it.

'How old is his mother?'

'Somewhere in her sixties. Why?'

'She's a vigorous woman, in spite of her infirmities. She may be around for a long time yet.'

Her eyes flashed with some of their fine old iceberg fire. 'We're not waiting for her to die, if that's what you think. We're simply waiting for the psychological moment. Roy hopes to persuade her to take a more reasonable view of – of me. In the meantime –' She broke off, and looked at me distrustfully. 'But none of this is any concern of yours. You promised to tell me about the Macready person, whoever she is. Tish Macready? The name sounds fictitious.'

'I assure you the woman isn't. Your husband divorced her

in Reno shortly before he married you.'

She moved to a chair and sat down very suddenly, as if her legs had lost their strength. 'I don't believe it. Roy has never been married before.'

'He has, though. Even his mother admitted it, after a struggle. It was an unfortunate marriage, contracted when he was a student at Harvard. But he waited until this summer to end it. He spent part of July and all of August establishing residence in Nevada.'

'Now I know you're mistaken. Roy was in Europe all that time.'

'I suppose you have letters and postcards to prove it?'

'Yes, I do,' she said with a relieved smile.

She went into another room and came back with a handful of mail tied with a red ribbon. I riffled through the postcards and put them in chronological order: Tower of London (postmarked London, July 18), Bodleian Library (Oxford, July 21), and so on down to the view of the English Gardens (Munich, August 25). Bradshaw had written on the back of this last card:

Dear Laura:

Yesterday I visited Hitler's eyrie at Berchtesgaden – a beautiful setting made grim by its association – and today, by way of contrast, I took a bus to Oberammergau, where the Passion Play is performed. I was struck by the almost Biblical simplicity of the villagers. This whole Bavarian countryside is studded with the most stunning little churches. How I wish you could enjoy them with me! I'm sorry to hear that your summer has turned out to be a lonely one. Well, the summer will soon be over and I for one will be happy to turn my back on the splendour of Europe and come home. All my love.

Roy

I sat and re-read the incredible message. It was almost word by word the same as the one Mrs Bradshaw had shown me. I tried to put myself in Bradshaw's place, to understand his motive. But I couldn't imagine what helpless division in a man's nature, what weary self-mockery or self-use, would make him send identical lying postcards to his mother and his fiancée.

'What's the matter?'

'Merely everything.'

I gave her back her documents. She handled them lovingly.

'Don't try to tell me Roy didn't write these. They're in his writing and his style.'

'He wrote them in Reno,' I said, 'and shipped them for remailing to a friend or accomplice who was travelling in Europe.'

'Do you *know* this?'

'I'm afraid I do. Can you think of any friend of his who might have helped him?'

She bit her lower lip. 'Dr Godwin spent the late summer travelling in Europe. He and Roy are very close. In fact Roy was his patient for a long time.'

'What was Godwin treating him for?'

'We haven't discussed it, really, but I expect it had something to do with his excessive – his excessive dependence on his mother.' A slow angry flush mounted from her neck to her cheekbones. She turned away from the subject. 'But why would two grown men collaborate in such a silly letter-writing game?'

'It isn't clear. Your husband's professional ambitions probably enter into it. He obviously didn't want anyone to know about his previous, bad marriage, or his divorce, and he went to great lengths to keep everything quiet. He got off a similar set of European postcards and letters to his mother. He may have sent a third set to Letitia.'

'Who *is* she? *Where* is she?'

'I think she's here in town, or was as recently as last Friday night. She's very likely been here for the last ten years. I'm surprised your husband never gave it away, even to someone as close as you.'

She was still standing over me, and I looked up into her face. Her eyes were heavy. She shook her head.

'Or maybe it isn't so surprising. He's very good at deceiving people, living on several levels, maybe deceiving himself to a certain extent. Mother's boys get that way sometimes. They need their little escape hatches from the hothouse.'

Her bosom rose. 'He isn't a mother's boy. He may have had a problem when he was younger, but now he's a virile man, and I *know* he loves me. There must be a reason for all this.' She looked down at the cards and letters in her hand.

'I'm sure there is. I suspect the reason has to do with our two murders. Tish Macready is the leading suspect for both of them.'

'*Two* murders?'

'Actually there have been three, spaced over a period of

twenty-two years: Helen Haggerty on Friday night, Constance McGee ten years ago, Luke Deloney in Illinois before the war.'

'Deloney?'

'Luke Deloney. You wouldn't know about him, but I think Tish Macready does.'

'Is he connected with the Mrs Deloney at the Surf House?'

'She's his widow. You know her?'

'Not personally. But Roy was talking to her on the telephone shortly before he left here.'

'What did he say?'

'Simply that he was coming over to see her. I asked him who she was, but he was in too great a hurry to explain.'

I got up. 'If you'll excuse me, I'll see if I can catch him at the hotel. I've been trying to catch him all day.'

'He was here, with me.' She smiled slightly, involuntarily, but her eyes were confused. 'Please don't tell him I told you. Don't tell him I told you anything.'

'I'll try, but it may come out.'

I moved to the door and tried to open it. The chain delayed my exit.

'Wait,' she said behind me. 'I've remembered something – something he wrote in a book of poems he lent me.'

'What did he write?'

'Her name.'

She started into the other room. Her hip bumped the door-frame, and Bradshaw's cards and letters fell from her hands. She didn't pause to pick them up.

She returned with an open book and thrust it at me a little blindly. It was a well-worn copy of Yeats's *Collected Poems*, open to the poem 'Among School Children.' The first four lines of the fourth stanza were underlined in pencil, and Bradshaw had written in the margin beside them the single word, 'Tish.'

I read the four lines to myself:

> Her present image floats into the mind –
> Did Quattrocento finger fashion it
> Hollow of cheek as though it drank the wind
> And took a mess of shadows for its meat?

I wasn't certain what they meant, and said so.

Laura answered bitterly: 'It means that Roy still loves her Yeats was writing about Maud Gonne – the woman he loved all his life. Roy may even have lent me the Yeats to let me know about Tish. He's very subtle.'

'He probably wrote her name there long ago, and forgot about it. If he still loved her, he wouldn't have divorced her and married you. I have to warn you, though, that your marriage may not be legal.'

'Not legal?' She was a conventional woman, and the possibility jarred her. 'But we were married in Reno by a judge.'

'His divorce from Tish,' I said, 'is probably voidable. I gather she wasn't properly informed of Bradshaw's action. Which means that under California law he's still married to her if she wants it that way.'

Shaking her head, she took the book of poems from my hands and tossed it with some violence into a chair. A piece of paper fluttered from between the leaves. I picked it up from the floor.

It was another poem, in Bradshaw's handwriting:

To Laura

If light were dark
And dark were light,
Moon a black hole
In the blaze of night,

A raven's wing
As bright as tin,
Then you, my love,
Would be darker than sin.

At breakfast I had read the same poem aloud to Arnie and Phyllis. It had been printed twenty-odd years ago in the Bridgeton *Blazer*, over the initials G.R.B. I had a gestalt, and Bridgeton and Pacific Point came together in a roaring traffic of time. G.R.B. George Roy Bradshaw.

'When did he write this poem to you, Laura?'

'Last spring, when he lent me the Yeats.'

I left her reading it over to herself, trying to recapture the spring.

CHAPTER THIRTY

Passing through the lobby of the Surf House, I noticed Helen's mother sitting by herself in a far corner. She was deep in thought and she didn't look up until I spoke:

'You're sitting up late, Mrs Hoffman.'

'I don't have much choice,' she said resentfully. 'I'm supposed to be sharing a cottage with Mrs Deloney, and it was entirely her idea. But she put me out so she can entertain her friend in private.'

'You mean Roy Bradshaw?'

'That's what he calls himself now. I knew George Bradshaw when he was glad to be given a good hot meal, and I served him more than once in my own kitchen.'

I pulled up a chair beside hers. 'All this adds up to an interesting coincidence.'

'I think it does, too. But I'm not supposed to talk about it.'

'Who says so?'

'Mrs Deloney.'

'Does she tell you what to do?'

'No, but it was nice of her to take me out of that crummy room in the Pacific Hotel and –' She paused, considering.

'And stash you in the lobby here?'

'It's only temporary.'

'So is life. Are you and your husband going to take orders from people like the Deloneys until the day you die? You get nothing out of it, you know, except the privilege of being pushed around.'

'Nobody pushes Earl around,' she defensively. 'You leave Earl out of this.'

'Have you heard from him?'

'I haven't, and I'm worried about Earl. I tried to phone home two nights in a row, and nobody answered. I'm afraid he's drinking.'

'He's in the hospital,' I said.

'Is he sick?'

'He made himself sick with too much whisky.'

'How do you know that?'

'I helped to get him to the hospital. I was in Bridgeton yesterday morning. Your husband talked to me, quite freely toward the end. He admitted Luke Deloney had been murdered but he had orders from the top to let it go as an accident.'

Her eyes darted around the lobby, shyly and shamefully. There was no one in sight but the night clerk and a couple who didn't look married renting a room from him. But Mrs Hoffman was as nervous as a cricket on a crowded floor.

'You might as well tell me what you know,' I said. 'Let me buy you a cup of coffee.'

'I'd be up all night.'

'A cup of cocoa then.'

'Cocoa sounds good.'

We went into the coffee shop. Several orchestra members in mauve jackets were drinking coffee at the counter and complaining in the language of their tribe about the pay. I sat in a booth facing Mrs Hoffman and the plate glass door, so that I could see Bradshaw if he came out through the lobby.

'How did you come to know Bradshaw, Mrs Hoffman?'

'Helen brought him home from City College. I think she was stuck on him for a while, but I could see that he wasn't stuck on her. They were more friends. They had interests in common.'

'Like poetry?'

'Like poetry and play-acting. Helen said he was very talented for a boy his age, but he was having a hard time staying in college. We wangled him a part-time job running the elevator in the apartments. All it paid was five a week, but he was glad to have it. He was as thin as a rake and as poor as Job's turkey when we knew him. He claimed to come from a wealthy family in Boston, that he ran away from his freshman year at Harvard to be on his own. I never really believed him at the time – I thought he was maybe ashamed of his folks and putting on the dog – but I guess it was true after all. They tell me his mother is loaded.' She gave me a questioning look.

'Yes. I know her.'

'Why would a young fellow run away from all that money? I spent most of my own life trying to get a little to stick to my fingers.'

'Money usually has strings attached to it.'

I didn't go into a fuller explanation. The waitress brought Mrs Hoffman's cocoa and my coffee. I said when she had retreated behind the counter:

'Have you ever known a woman named Macready? Letitia O. Macready?'

Mrs Hoffman's hand fumbled with her cup and spilled some brown liquid in the saucer. I was fleetingly conscious that her hair was dyed an unlikely shade of red and that she might once have been a handsome woman with a good figure and a gaudy taste in clothes. But she couldn't be Tish Macready. She'd been married to Earl Hoffman for over forty years.

She put a folded paper napkin under her cup to absorb the spillage. 'I knew her to say hello to.'

'In Bridgeton? '

'I'm not supposed to talk about Letitia. Mrs Deloney —'

'Your daughter's in a refrigerated drawer and all you give me is Mrs Deloney.'

She bowed her head over the shiny formica table. 'I'm afraid of her,' she said, 'of what she can do to Earl.'

'Be afraid of what she's already done to him. She and her political pals made him seal up the Deloney case, and it's been festering inside of him ever since.'

'I know. It's the first time Earl ever laid down on the job deliberately.'

'You admit that?'

'I guess I have to. Earl never said it out in so many words, but I knew, and Helen knew. It's why she left us.'

And why, perhaps, in the long run Helen couldn't stay honest.

'Earl had a great respect for Luke Deloney,' the woman was saying, 'even if Luke did have his human failings. He was the one who made good for all of us in a manner of speaking. His death hit Earl real hard, and he started drinking right after, seriously I mean. I'm worried about Earl.' She reached across the table and touched the back of my hand with her dry fingertips. 'Do you think he'll be all right?'

'Not if he keeps on drinking. He ought to survive this bout. I'm sure he's being well taken care of. But Helen isn't.'

'Helen? What can anybody do for Helen?'

'You can do something for her by telling the truth. Her death deserves an explanation at least.'

'But I don't know who killed her. If I did I'd shout it from the housetops. I thought the police were after that man McGee who killed his wife.'

'McGee has been cleared. Tish Macready killed his wife, and probably your daughter as well.'

She shook her head solemnly. 'You're mistaken, mister. What you say isn't possible. Tish Macready — Tish Osborne that was — she died long ago before either of those tragedies happened. I admit there were rumours about her at the time

208

of Luke Deloney's death, but then she had her own tragedy, poor thing.'

'You said "Tish Osborne that was."'

'That's right. She was one of Senator Osborne's girls – Mrs Deloney's sister. I told you about them the other night when we were driving down here from the airport, how they used to ride to hounds.' She smiled faintly, nostalgically, as if she had caught a flash of red coats from her childhood.

'What were the rumours about her, Mrs Hoffman?'

'That she was carrying on with Luke Deloney before his death. Some people said she shot him herself, but I never believed that.'

'Was she having an affair with Luke Deloney?'

'She used to spend some time in his apartment, that was no secret. She was kind of his unofficial hostess when Luke and Mrs Deloney were separated. I didn't think too much about it. She was already divorced from Val Macready. And she was Luke's sister-in-law after all, I guess she had a right to be in his penthouse.'

'Did she have red hair?'

'More auburn, I'd say. She had beautiful auburn hair.' Mrs Hoffman absently stroked her own dyed curls. 'Tish Osborne had a lot of life in her. I was sorry to hear when she died.'

'What happened to her?'

'I don't know exactly. She died in Europe when the Nazis ran over France. Mrs Deloney still hasn't got over it. She was talking about her sister's death today.'

Something that felt like a spider with wet feet climbed up the back of my neck into the short hairs and made them bristle. The ghost of Tish or a woman (or a man?) using her name had come to the door of the house in Indian Springs ten years ago, more than ten years after the Germans overran France.

'Are you certain she's dead, Mrs Hoffman?'

She nodded. 'There was quite a write-up in the papers, even the Chicago papers. Tish Osborne was the belle of Bridgeton in her time. I can remember back in the early twenties her parties were famous. The man she married, Val Macready, had meat-packing money on his mother's side.'

'Is he still alive?'

'The last I heard of him, he married an Englishwoman during the war and was living in England. He wasn't a Bridgeton boy and I never really knew him. I just read the society pages, and the obituaries.'

She sipped her cocoa. Her look, her self-enclosed posture, seemed to be telling me that she had survived. Her daughter Helen had been brighter, Tish Osborne had been wealthier, but she was the one who had survived. She would survive Earl, too, and probably make a shrine of the study where he kept his liquor in the roll-top desk.

Well, I had caught one of the old ladies. The other one would be tougher.

'Why did Mrs Deloney fly out here?'

'I guess it was just a rich woman's whim. She said she wanted to help me out in my time of trouble.'

'Were you ever close to her?'

'I hardly knew her. Earl knows her better.'

'Was Helen close to her?'

'No. If they ever met each other, it's news to me.'

'Mrs Deloney came a long way to help out a comparative stranger. Has she given you any particular help, apart from changing hotels?'

'She bought me lunch and dinner. I didn't want her to pay, but she insisted.'

'What were you to do in return for the free room and board?'

'Nothing.'

'Didn't she ask you not to talk about her sister Tish?'

'That's true, she did. I wasn't to say anything about her carrying on with Luke Deloney, or the rumours that went around about his death. She's very sensitive about her sister's reputation.'

'Abnormally sensitive, if Tish has really been dead for over twenty years. Who weren't you supposed to mention these things to?'

'Anybody, especially you.'

She drowned her nervous little giggle in the remains of her cocoa.

CHAPTER THIRTY-ONE

I went out into the grounds of the hotel. The high moon floated steadily in the sky and in the ornamental pools of the Spanish garden. There was a yellower light behind the shutters of Mrs Deloney's cottage, and the sound of voices too low to be eavesdropped on.

I knocked on the door.

'What is it?' she said.

'Service.' Detective service.

'I didn't order anything.'

But she opened the door. I slipped in past her and stood against the wall. Bradshaw was sitting on an English sofa beside the fireplace in the opposite wall. A low fire burned in the grate, and gleamed on the brass fittings.

'Hello,' he said.

'Hello, George.'

He jumped visibly.

Mrs Deloney said: 'Get out of here.' She seemed to have perfectly round blue eyes in a perfectly square white face, all bone and will. 'I'll call the house detective.'

'Go ahead, if you want to spread the dirt around.'

She shut the door.

'We might as well tell him,' Bradshaw said. 'We have to tell someone.'

The negative jerk of her head was so violent it threw her off balance. She took a couple of backward steps and regrouped her forces, looking from me to Bradshaw as if we were both her enemies.

'I absolutely forbid it,' she said to him. 'Nothing is to be said.'

'It's going to come out anyway. It will be better if we bring it out ourselves.'

'It is not going to come out. Why should it?'

'Partly,' I said, 'because you made the mistake of coming here. This isn't your town, Mrs Deloney. You can't put a lid on events the way you could in Bridgeton.'

She turned her straight back on me. 'Pay no attention to him, George.'

'My name is Roy.'

'Roy,' she corrected herself. 'This man tried to bluff me yesterday in Bridgeton, but he doesn't know a thing. All we have to do is remain quiet.'

'What will that get us?'

'Peace.'

'I've had my fill of that sort of peace,' he said. 'I've been living close up to it all these years. You've been out of contact. You have no conception of what I've been through.' He rested his head on the back of the sofa and lifted his eyes to the ceiling.

'You'll go through worse,' she said roughly, 'if you let down your back hair now.'

'At least it will be different.'

'You're a spineless fool. But I'm not going to let you ruin what remains of my life. If you do, you'll get no financial help from me.'

'Even that I can do without.'

But he was being careful to say nothing I wanted to know. He'd been wearing a mask so long that it stuck to his face and controlled his speech and perhaps his habits of thought. Even the old woman with her back turned was playing to me as if I was an audience.

'This argument is academic, in more than one sense,' I said. 'The body isn't buried any longer. I know your sister Letitia shot your husband, Mrs Deloney. I know she later married Bradshaw in Boston. I have his mother's word for it – '

'His mother?'

Bradshaw sat up straight. 'I do have a mother after all.' He added in his earnest cultivated voice, with his eyes intent on the woman's: 'I'm still living with her, and she has to be considered in this matter, too.'

'You lead a very complicated life,' she said.

'I have a very complicated nature.'

'Very well, young Mr Complexity, the ball is yours. Carry it.' She went to a love-seat in a neutral corner of the room and sat down there.

'I thought the ball was mine,' I said, 'but you're welcome to it, Bradshaw. You can start where everything started, with the Deloney killing. You were Helen's witness, weren't you?'

He nodded once. 'I shouldn't have gone to Helen with that heavy knowledge. But I was deeply upset and she was the only friend I had in the world.'

'Except Letitia.'

'Yes. Except Letitia.'

'What was your part in the murder?'

'I was simply there. And it wasn't a murder, properly speaking. Deloney was killed in self-defence, virtually by accident.'

'This is where I came in.'

'It's true. He caught us in bed together in his penthouse.'

'Did you and Letitia make a habit of going to bed together?'

'It was the first time. I'd written a poem about her, which the college magazine printed, and I showed it to her in the elevator. I'd been watching her, admiring her, all through the spring. She was much older than I was, but she was fascinating. She was the first woman I ever had.' He spoke of her with a kind of awe still.

'What happened in the penthouse bedroom, Bradshaw?'

'He caught us, as I said. He got a gun out of the chest of drawers and hit me with the butt of it. Tish tried to stop him. He beat her face in with the gun. She got her hands on it somehow, and it went off and killed him.'

He touched the lid of his right eye, and nodded toward the old woman. She was watching us from the corner, from the distance of her years.

'Mrs Deloney hushed the matter up, or had it hushed up. You can hardly blame her, under the circumstances. Or blame us. We went to Boston, where Tish spent months in and out of hospital having her face rebuilt. Then we were married. I was in love with her, in spite of the discrepancy in our ages. I suppose my feeling for my own mother prepared me to love Tish.'

His hooded intelligence flared up in his eyes so bright it was half-insane. His mouth was wry.

'We went to Europe on our honeymoon. My mother put French detectives on our trail. I had to leave Tish in Paris and come home to make my peace with Mother and start my sophomore year at Harvard. The war broke out in Europe that same month. I never saw Tish again. She fell sick and died before I knew it.'

'I don't believe you. There wasn't time for all that.'

'It happened very rapidly, as tragedy does.'

'Not yours, it's been dragging on for twenty-two years.'

'No,' Mrs Deloney said. 'He's telling the truth, and I can prove it to you.'

She went into another room of the cottage and came back with a heavily creased document which she handed me. It was an *acte de déces* issued in Bordeaux and dated July 16, 1940. It stated in French that Letitia Osborne Macready, aged 45, had died of pneumonia.

I gave it back to Mrs Deloney. 'You carry this with you wherever you go?'

'I happened to bring it with me.'

'Why?'

She couldn't think of an answer.

'I'll tell you why. Because your sister is very much alive and you're afraid she'll be punished for her crimes.'

'My sister committed no crime. The death of my husband was either justifiable homicide or accident. The police commissioner realized that or he'd never have quashed the case.'

213

'That may be. But Constance McGee and Helen Haggerty weren't shot by accident.'

'My sister died long before either of those women.'

'Your own actions deny it, and they mean more than this phony death certificate. For instance, you visited Gil Stevens today and tried to pump him about the McGee case.'

'He broke my confidence, did he?'

'There was nothing there to be broken. You're not Stevens's client. He's still representing McGee.'

'He didn't tell me.'

'Why should he? This isn't your town.'

She turned in confusion to Bradshaw. He shook his head. I crossed the room and stood over him:

'If Tish is safely buried in France, why did you go to such elaborate trouble to divorce her?'

'So you know about the divorce. You're quite a digger for facts, aren't you, quite a Digger Indian? I begin to wonder if there's anything you don't know about my private life.'

He sat there, looking up at me brightly and warily. I was a little carried away by the collapse of his defences, and I said:

'Your private life, or your private lives, are something for the book. Have you been keeping up two establishments, dividing your time between your mother and your wife?'

'I suppose it's obvious that I have,' he said tonelessly.

'Does Tish live here in town?'

'She lived in the Los Angeles area. I have no intention of telling you where, and I can assure you you'll never find the place. There'd be no point in it, anyway, since she's no longer there.'

'Where and how did she die this time?'

'She isn't dead. That French death certificate is a fake, as you guessed. But she is beyond your reach. I put her on a plane to Rio de Janeiro on Saturday, and she'll be there by now.'

Mrs Deloney said: 'You didn't tell me that!'

'I hadn't intended to tell anyone. However, I have to make Mr Archer see that there's no point in pressing this thing any further. My wife – my ex-wife – is an old woman, and a sick one, and she's beyond extradition. I've arranged for her to have medical care, psychiatric care, in a South American city which I won't name.'

'You're admitting that she killed Helen Haggerty?'

'Yes. She confessed to me when I went to see her in Los Angeles early Saturday morning. She shot Helen and hid the gun in my gatehouse. I contacted Foley in Reno primarily to find out if he had witnessed anything. I didn't want him blackmailing me –'

'I thought he already was.'

'Helen was,' he said. 'She learned about my pending divorce in Reno, and she jumped to a number of conclusions, including the fact that Tish was still alive. I gave her a good deal of money, and got her a job here, in order to protect Tish.'

'And yourself.'

'And myself. I do have a reputation to protect, though I've done nothing illegal.'

'No. You're very good at arranging for other people to do your dirty work. You brought Helen here as a kind of decoy, didn't you?'

'I'm afraid I don't understand you.' But he shifted uneasily.

'You took Helen out a few times and passed the word that she was your intended. She wasn't, of course. You were already married to Laura and you hated Helen, with good reason.'

'That's not true. We were on quite a friendly basis, in spite of her demands. She was a very old friend, after all, and I couldn't help sympathizing with her feeling that she deserved something from the world.'

'I know what she got – a bullet in the head. The same thing Constance McGee got. The same thing Laura would have got if you hadn't set Helen up as a substitute victim for Tish.'

'I'm afraid you're getting much too complicated.'

'For a complicated nature like yours?'

He looked around the room as if he felt imprisoned in it, or in the maze of his own nature. 'You'll never prove any complicity on my part in Helen's death. It came as a fearful shock to me. Letitia's confession was another shock.'

'Why? You must have known she killed Constance McGee.'

'I didn't know it till Saturday. I admit I had my suspicions. Tish was always savagely jealous. I've lived with the dreadful possibility for ten years, hoping and praying that my suspicions were unfounded –'

'Why didn't you ask her?'

'I suppose I couldn't face it. Things were already so difficult between us. It would have meant admitting my love for Connie.' He heard his own words, and sat quiet for a moment, his eyes downcast, as if he was peering down into a chasm in himself. 'I really did love her, you know. Her death almost finished me.'

'But you survived to love again.'

'Men do,' he said. 'I'm not the sort of man who can live without love. I loved even Tish as long and as well as I could. But she got *old*, and sick.'

Mrs Deloney made a spitting sound. He said to her: 'I wanted a wife, one who could give me children.'

'God help any children of yours, you'd probably abandon them. You broke all your promises to my sister.'

'Everyone breaks promises. I didn't intend to fall in love with Connie. It simply happened. I met her in a doctor's waiting-room quite by accident. But I didn't turn my back on your sister. I never have. I've done more for her than she ever did for me.'

She sneered at him with the arrogance of a second-generation aristocrat. 'My sister lifted you out of the gutter. What were you – an elevator boy?'

'I was a college student, and an elevator boy by my own choice.'

'Very likely.'

He leaned toward her, fixing her with his bright eyes. 'I had family resources to draw on if I had wished.'

'Ah yes, your precious mother.'

'Be careful what you say about my mother.'

There was an edge on his words, the quality of a cold threat, and it silenced her. This was one of several moments when I sensed that the two of them were playing a game as complex as chess, a game of power on a hidden board. I should have tried to force it into the open. But I was clearing up my case, and as long as Bradshaw was willing to talk I didn't care about apparent side-issues.

'I don't understand the business of the gun,' I said. 'The police have established that Connie McGee and Helen were shot with the same gun – a revolver that belonged originally to Connie's sister Alice. How did Tish get hold of it?'

'I don't really know.'

'You must have some idea. Did Alice Jenks give it to her?'

'She very well may have.'

'That's nonsense, Bradshaw, and you know it. The revolver was stolen from Alice's house. Who stole it?'

He made a steeple of his fingers and admired its symmetry. 'I'm willing to tell you if Mrs Deloney will leave the room.'

'Why should I?' she said from her corner. 'Anything my sister could endure to live through I can endure to hear.'

'I'm not trying to spare your sensibilities,' Bradshaw said.

'I'm trying to spare myself.'

She nesitated. It became a test of wills. Bradshaw got up and opened the inner door. Through it I could see across a hall into a bedroom furnished in dull luxury. The bedside table held an ivory telephone and a leather-framed photograph of a white-moustached gentleman who looked vaguely familiar.

Mrs Deloney marched into the bedroom like a recalcitrant soldier under orders. Bradshaw closed the door sharply behind her.

'I'm beginning to hate old women,' he said.

'You were going to tell me about the gun.'

'I was, wasn't I?' He returned to the sofa. 'It's not a pretty story. None of it is. I'm telling you the whole thing in the hope that you'll be, completely satisfied.'

'And not bring in the authorities?'

'Don't you see there's nothing to be gained by bringing them in? The sole effect would be to turn the town on its ear, wreck the standing of the college which I've worked so hard to build up, and ruin more than one life.'

'Especially yours and Laura's?'

'Especially mine and Laura's. She's waited for me, God knows. And even I deserve something more than I've had. I've lived my entire adult life with the consequences of a neurotic involvement that I got into when I was just a boy.'

'Is that what Godwin was treating you for?'

'I needed *some* support. Tish hasn't been easy to deal with. She drove me half out of my mind sometimes with her animal violence and her demands. But now it's over.' His eyes changed the statement into a question and a plea.

'I can't make any promises,' I said. 'Let's have the entire story, then we'll think about the next step. How did Tish get hold of Alice's revolver?'

'Connie took it from her sister's room and gave it to me. We had some wild idea of using it to cut the Gordian knot.'

'Do you mean kill Tish with it?'

'It was sheer fantasy,' he said, '*folie à deux*. Connie and I would never have carried it out, desperate as we were. You'll never know the agony I went through dividing myself between two wives, two lovers – one old and rapacious, the other young and passionate. Jim Godwin warned me that I was in danger of spiritual death.'

'For which murder is known to be a sure cure.'

'I'd never have done it. I couldn't. Actually Jim made

217

me see that. I'm not a violent man.'

But there was violence in him now, pressing against the
conventional fears that corseted his nature and held him still
almost formal, under my eyes. I sensed his murderous hatred
for me. I was forcing all his secrets into the open, as I
thought.

'What happened to the gun Connie stole for you?'

'I put it away in what I thought was a safe place, but Tish
must have found it.'

'In your house?'

'In my mother's house. I sometimes took her there when
Mother was away.'

'Was she there the day McGee called on you?'

'Yes.' He met my eyes. 'I'm amazed that you should
know about that day. You're very thorough. It was the day
when everything came to a head. Tish must have found the
gun in the lockbox in my study where I'd hidden it. Before
that she must have heard McGee complaining to me about my
interest in his wife. She took the gun and turned it against
Constance. I suppose there was a certain poetic justice in
that.'

Bradshaw might have been talking about an event in someone else's past, the death of a character in history or fiction.
He no longer cared for the meaning of his own life. Perhaps
that was what Godwin meant by spiritual death.

'Do you still maintain you didn't know Tish killed her
until she confessed it last Saturday?'

'I suppose I didn't let myself realize. So far as I knew the
gun had simply disappeared. McGee might very well have
taken it from my study when he was in the house. The official
case against him seemed very strong.'

'It was put together with old pieces of string, and you know
it. McGee and his daughter are my main concern. I won't be
satisfied until they're completely cleared.'

'But surely that can be accomplished without dragging
Letitia back from Brazil.'

'I have only your word that she's in Brazil,' I said. 'Even
Mrs Deloney was surprised to hear it.'

'Good heavens, don't you believe me? I've literally exposed
my entrails to you.'

'You wouldn't do that unless you had a reason. I think
you're a liar, Bradshaw, one of those virtuosos who use real
facts and feelings to make their stories plausible. But there's
a basic implausibility in this one. If Tish was safe in Brazil, it's

be last thing you'd ever tell me. I think she's hiding out here
n California.'

'You're quite mistaken.'

His eyes came up to mine, candid and earnest as only an
ctor's can be. A telephone chirring behind the bedroom door
nterrupted our staring contest. Bradshaw moved toward the
ound. I was on my feet and I moved more rapidly, shoulder-
ng him against the doorframe, picking up the bedside phone
efore it rang a third time.

'Hello.'

'Is that you, darling?' It was Laura's voice. 'Roy, I'm
rightened. She *knows* about us. She called here just a minute
go and said she was coming over.'

'Keep the door locked and chained. And you better call
he police.'

'That isn't Roy. Is it?'

Roy was behind me. I turned in time to see the flash of
rass as the poker in his fist came down on my head.

CHAPTER THIRTY-TWO

Irs Deloney was slapping my face with a wet towel. I told
er to quit it. The first thing I saw when I got up was the
eather-framed photograph beside her telephone. It seemed
o my blurred vision to be a photograph of the handsome old
lack-eyed gentleman whose portrait hung over the fireplace
a Mrs Bradshaw's sitting-room.

'What are you doing with a picture of Bradshaw's father?'

'It happens to be my own father, Senator Osborne.'

I said: 'So Mrs Bradshaw's a virtuoso, too.'

Mrs Deloney looked at me as if my brains had been addled
y the poker. But the blow had been a glancing one, and I
ouldn't have been out for more than a few seconds. Brad-
haw was leaving the hotel parking lot when I got there.

His light car turned uphill away from the ocean. I fol-
wed him to Foothill Drive and caught him long before he
ached his house. He made it easy for me by braking sud-
enly. His car slewed sideways and came to a shuddering
alt broadside across the road.

It wasn't me he was trying to stop. Another car was coming
ownhill toward us. I could see its headlights approaching

under the trees like large calm insane eyes, and Bradshaw
silhouetted in their beam. He seemed to be fumbling with hi
seat-belt. I recognized Mrs Bradshaw's Rolls in the momen
before, with screeching brakes, it crashed into the smaller car

I pulled off the road, set out a red blinker, and ran uphil
towards the point of impact. My footsteps were loud in th
silence after the crash. The crumpled nose of the Rolls wa
nuzzled deep in the caved-in side of Bradshaw's car. He lolle
in the driver's seat. Blood ran down his face from his fore
head and nose and the corners of his mouth.

I went in through the undamaged door and got his seat-bel
unbuckled. He toppled limply into my arms. I laid him dow
in the road. The jagged lines of blood across his face re
sembled cracks in a mask through which live tissues showed
But he was dead. He lay pulseless and breathless under th
iron shadows of the tree branches.

Old Mrs Bradshaw had climbed down out of her high pro
tected seat. She seemed unhurt. I remember thinking at th
moment that she was an elemental power which nothing coul
ever kill.

'It's Roy, isn't it? Is he all right?'

'In a sense he is. He wanted out. He's out.'

'What do you mean?'

'I'm afraid you've killed him, too.'

'But I didn't mean to hurt him. I wouldn't hurt my ow
son, the child of my womb.'

Her voice cracked with maternal grief. I think she half
believed she was his mother, she had lived the role so long
Reality had grown dim as the moonlit countryside around her

She flung herself on the dead man, holding him close, as i
her old body could somehow warm him back to life and re
kindle his love for her. She wheedled and cooed in his ear
calling him a naughty malingering boy for trying to scare her

She shook him. 'Wake up! It's Moms.'

As she had told me, night wasn't her best season. But she
had a doubleness in her matching Roy's, and there was a
element of play-acting in her frenzy.

'Leave him alone,' I said. 'And let's drop the mother bi
The situation is ugly enough without that.'

She turned in queer slow furtiveness and looked up at me
'The mother bit?'

'Roy Bradshaw wasn't your son. The two of you put on
pretty good act – Godwin would probably say it fitted bot
your neurotic needs – but it's over.'

She got up in a surge of anger which brought her close t

ne. I could smell her lavender, and feel her force.

'I *am* his mother. I have his birth certificate to prove it.'

'I bet you do. Your sister showed me a death certificate which proves that you died in France in 1940. With your kind of money you can document anything. But you can't change the facts by changing them on paper. Roy married you in Boston after you killed Deloney. Eventually he fell in love with Constance McGee. You killed her. Roy lived with you for another ten years, if you can call it living, terrified that you'd kill again if he ever dared to love anyone again. But finally he dared, with Laura Sutherland. He managed to convince you that it was Helen Haggerty he was interested in. So you went up the bridle path on Friday night and shot her. Those are all facts you can't change.'

Silence set in between us, thin and bleak like a quality of the moonlight. The woman said:

'I was only protecting my rights. Roy owed me faithfulness at least. I gave him money and background, I sent him to Harvard, I made all his dreams come true.'

We both looked down at the dreamless man lying in the road.

'Are you ready to come downtown with me and make a formal statement about how you protected your rights over the years? Poor Tom McGee is back in jail, still sweating out your rap.'

She pulled herself erect. 'I won't permit you to use such language to me. I'm not a criminal.'

'You were on your way to Laura Sutherland's, weren't you? What were you planning to do to her, old woman?'

She covered the lower part of her face with her hand. I thought she was ill, or overcome with shame. But she said:

'You mustn't call me that. I'm not old. Don't look at my face, look into my eyes. You can see how young I am.'

It was true in a way. I couldn't see her eyes clearly, but I knew they were bright and black and vital. She was still greedy for life, like the imaginary Letitia, the weird projection of herself in imitation leopardskin she had used to hide behind.

She shifted her hand to her heavy chin and said: 'I'll give you money.'

'Roy took your money. Look what happened to him.'

She turned abruptly and started for her car. I guessed what was in her mind: another death, another shadow to feed on: and got to the open door of the Rolls before her. Her black leather bag was on the floor where it had fallen in the

collision. Inside the bag I found the new revolver which she
had intended to use on Roy's new wife.

'Give me that.'

She spoke with the authority of a Senator's daughter and
the more terrible authority of a woman who had killed two
other women and two men.

'No more guns for you,' I said.

No more anything, Letitia.

Ross Macdonald

'Classify him how you will, he is one of the best American novelists now operating . . . all he does is keep on getting better.' *New York Times Book Review*. 'Ross Macdonald must be ranked high among American thriller-writers. His evocations of scenes and people are as sharp as those of Raymond Chandler.' *Times Literary Supplement*. 'Lew Archer is, by a long chalk, the best private eye in the business.' *Sunday Times*

The Underground Man   *30p*

The Way Some People Die   *30p*

The Drowning Pool   *25p*

The Doomsters   *30p*

The Wycherly Woman   *30p*

The Ivory Grin   *30p*

The Barbarous Coast   *25p*

Find a Victim   *30p*

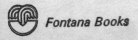 *Fontana Books*

Fontana Books

Fontana is best known as one of the leading paperback publishers of popular fiction and non-fiction. It also includes an outstanding, and expanding section of books on history, natural history, religion and social sciences.

Most of the fiction authors need no introduction. They include Agatha Christie, Hammond Innes, Alistair MacLean, Catherine Gaskin, Victoria Holt and Lucy Walker. Desmond Bagley and Maureen Peters are among the relative newcomers.

The non-fiction list features a superb collection of animal books by such favourites as Gerald Durrell and Joy Adamson.

All Fontana books are available at your bookshop or newsagent; or can be ordered direct. Just fill in the form below and list the titles you want.

FONTANA BOOKS, Cash Sales Department, P.O. Box 4, Godalming, Surrey, GU7, 1JY. Please send purchase price plus 7p postage per book by cheque, postal or money order. No currency.

NAME (Block letters)

ADDRESS